力得文化
Leader Culture

Lead your way. Be your own leader!

力得文化
Leader Culture

Lead your way. Be your own leader!

力得文化
Leader Culture

Smart English for Workplace

那些年你「會」，但「不會」用的英語
22堂全職業適用英文課

!
擺脫

辦公室卡卡英文

OFFICE

邱佳翔◎著

22堂職場**5大情境**必修課

從職場新鮮人不可不知的【**職前準備**】，到職後【**產品銷售**】的訣竅，
在職中【**面對客戶**】如何進對得宜，做【**會議簡報**】更簡明扼要，
【**職場應酬**】要留意的重點＋危險禁忌。

每堂課各有12個單元，中英對照

重點順序整理＋循序漸進學習→ 提升職場競爭力！

　　如果從國中開始算起，到大學畢業我們至少都學了十年的英文，照理來說，以這樣的學習時程，我們應該具備相當程度的英文基礎，但踏入職場後，很多人的共同心聲是：不知道如何或是不敢以英文與外國人溝通。

　　仔細探究這背後的原因，大致可以將其歸納成以下兩點，第一是受到媒體的影響，商務人士必須大量使用專業語彙，才符合其形象。第二則是學習環境所產生的盲點，我們一路學習大量的單字、片語與文法，但卻往往不知道該在怎樣的場合使用它們。

　　而事實上，英文講求的是邏輯，只要思路清晰，對方便可了解我們的想法。本書的撰寫便是要打破商用英語困難的迷思，透過複習我們過去所學過的英文，點出適用的場合，讓說英文不再是夢魘。

邱佳翔

　　還記得你的英文是從什麼時候就開始學的？大多數的人都是從國中開始的吧，而編者的那個年代，雖然英文還未編入小學課程，但兒童美語已算普遍，所以對於英文課的印象，應該是從兒童美語補習班開始建立的，然後才慢慢地累積英文實力。現在這個年代不同了，雙語幼兒園、雙語學校等的設立；英文納入小學課程之安排，接觸英文的時間點越來越早，在台灣，英文學習是必經過程，而具備一定的英文能力，則是升學、求職路上的基本門檻。

　　在英文聽、說、讀、寫能力中，四種能力都要不間斷地磨鍊、並累積實力，才能算真正具備英文能力。那麼如何磨練累積能力？除了下功夫，有時也需要技巧，勇氣和信心也是不能缺少的，遇到外籍人士時，其實也有不少人很想嘗試溝通，但總是怕說錯、怕丟臉；另外有些人則是或多或少懂得一些單字，只是不知如何組成完整的句子。發現了其中的問題嗎？那就是：其實這些單字、片語你以前都學過，都「會」，只是你可能沒有信心、可能不知道如何組織、而「不會」用。

　　來，快拿起這本書吧，看看你其實也「會」這些英文，信心增加了，就要學學「如何用」這些英文，進而學學「如何應用」這些英文在職場上，提升職場競爭力和自信心；看了你才知道，原來這些你都「會」，只是「不會」用，懂得「用」了、會「用」了，也才知道商用英文也沒那麼複雜、英文能力提升了，和外籍人士用英語溝通也不再卡卡啦。

力得文化編輯群

目次

Part 4 會議簡報

Part 5 職場應酬

商業英文 E-mail

　　在現今的網路時代，e-mail 儼然成為職場溝通最重要的方式之一。提到這樣商業書信寫作，許多人的第一印象常會是困難、需要專業。但事實上，商用書信撰寫並不像大家所想的這麼困難，只要熟悉商業書信常用的字彙句型與寫作要點，再透過足量的練習，你就會發現，要寫出一封完整商業書信其實並沒有你想像地那麼困難。

　　一般來說，不論其表達重點為何，一篇完整的商業 e-mail 會包含以下幾個部分：

1. 信頭（heading）
2. 稱謂（salutation）
3. 正文（body of letter）
4. 敬辭（terms of respect）
5. 簽署（signature）

　　以下針對上述的五個部分，會做更詳細的說明。

基礎 E-mail 寫作範例

信頭	Date: Sent: 13:07, Tue, 25, May 2013 From: James < James@abc.com> Subject: The Project To: Dennis <Dennis@abc.com> CC: Lynn <lynn@abc.com>
稱謂	Dear Dennis,
正文	First of all, thank you for your kindly help in this program. Customers do love our latest product.

正文	To copy this success mode, we have written a draft about the new campaign. We sincerely hope you can give us some suggestions Please find the document in the attachment. We look forward to your reply.
敬辭	Yours,
簽署	James Project Manager ABC Company Tel: +886-2-85466630 Fax: +886-2-85466631

　　首先是**信頭（heading）**。雖然不同的郵件軟體的版面配置可能會略有差異，但基本上 e-mail 的信頭幾乎都會包含以下幾個元素：

1. 寄件日期（Date sent）：

　　現今常用的郵件軟體，例如 hotmail、gmail 等，除了本日日期外，還會顯示寄出的詳細時間，讓使用者方便查詢。例：13:07, Mon, 4, Sep. 2014。

　　補充：雖然寫 e-mail 不用自己在標註日期，但英文標示日期的方式有以下兩種：

　　❶ mm/dd/yy（月／日／年）

　　❷ dd/mm/yy（日／月／年）

　　再加上中英語言習慣的差異，上述的兩種方式容易產生誤解，例如：06/07/14 到底指的是 6 月 7 日還是 7 月 6 日呢？因此在撰寫 e-mail 時，月份最好採用英文縮寫，以避免產生誤解。

　　關於日期的部分，雖然可以用數字表示，但像商業書信這類正式文

件，應以序號稱之，除以下之特例外，其餘數字轉序號只需要在數字後加 **th** 即可。

一日	First（1st）	九日	Ninth（9th）	二十一日- 二十九日	Twenty + 1-9（的序號）（21st~29th）
二日	Second（2nd）	十二日	Twelfth（12th）	三十日	Thirtieth（30th）
三日	Third（3rd）	十五日	Fifteenth（15th）	三十一日	Thirty-first（31st）
五日	Fifth（5th）	二十日	Twentieth（20th）		

2. 寄件者（from）：from 有從何處而來的意思，在 e-mail 指的就是寄信人的信箱。而根據重要性與需求的不同，在實務上會使用不同的信箱。舉例來說，個人信箱的格式通常會是姓名加郵件地址，例：jason@abc.com。

3. 主旨（subject）：此信件的主題。現在每人一天之內收到信件不計其數，許多人會根據主旨來篩選郵件，若信件有明確清楚的主旨，便可與垃圾信件有所區分，讓收信人願意開信。例：**Subject: Order no. 12345**。

4. 收件者（to）：此封信的收件人。為提升寄信的效率，可在通訊錄進行分類設定，輸入相關資訊，以利往後的搜尋。

5. 副本（cc）：寄件給除主收信人的第三者時使用。信件寄出後主收件人也會知道你有寄信給第三者。常見的使用時機有：寄送報告給主管，副本給共同參與的同事。

6. 附件（attachment）：可在附加檔案隨信件加入檔案。由於現今有心人士可能在附件中夾帶電腦病毒、木馬等，為免除收件人的疑慮，可於內文先行說明此信件包含怎樣的附件。

第二部分是**稱謂（salutation）**。稱謂代表對收信人的尊稱。因此要特別注意禮貌。若不知道對方姓名與性別，使用 Dear Sir/Madam（親愛的先生／小姐）最保險。而在稱呼女性時，若不知其婚姻狀況則用 Ms.，以免冒犯對方。

第三部分是**正文（body of letter）**。正文也是整份信件的核心，因此其內容要言之有物，忌諱廢話連篇。而一般來說，正文會包含以下三個部分：

1. 開場白（opening）：開場白的作用不外乎以下兩種：

❶向對方打招呼：

例 It has been a long time since the last time we met in Taipei.
自從上在台北碰面後，我們許久不見了。

❷說明寫信的緣由：

例 Thank you very much for your letter about the quotation
感謝您關於報價的來信。

2. 中間主文（middle context）：正文的內容是此信件是否達到預期效果的關鍵。因此撰寫時要能吸引對方注意，或是解決當前問題。如：

❶The quality of your product is good, but the price is not that competitive.
您的產品品質很好，但價格有點貴。

❷I have received you fax, and I will give you the reply in few days.
已收到您的來信，將於近日內回信。

3. 結束語（complimentary close）：為了要使文意能前後連貫，英文 e-mail 會於最末段使用客套的結束語。常見的結束語可分為以下幾類：

❶感謝對方：

例 Thank you for your help in this project.
感謝您在此專案所提供的協助。

❷有所期待：

例 We are looking forward to hearing from you.
我們期望能得到您的回覆。

❸做出要求：

例 Please inform us your decision in five days
請於五天內告知我方您的決定。

第四部分是**敬辭（terms of respect）**。敬辭的用法有點類似中文的敬啟、敬上，視為一個句子，因此開頭要大寫。根據與對方的熟識程度可分別採用以下兩類的敬辭：

1.初次接觸／長官：

例 Sincerely yours/Respectfully/Best regards

2.非常熟識／同事：

例 Take care/Cheers/All the best

第五部分是**簽署（signature）**。雖然電子郵件的寄件人欄位就已具備表明身分的作用，但簽署仍有其重要性，其原因可歸納以下幾點：

1.保持信件的正式與完整性。

2.對信件內容負責。

從與收信人的熟悉程度高低，簽署的方式可以再細分為以下幾類：

1.名字 例：Jason

2.姓氏＋名字 例：Jason Lin

3.姓名＋職稱

例 Jason Lin

Project Manager （專案經理）

4.姓名＋職稱＋公司名

例 Jason Lin

Project Manager

ABC Company

5. 姓名＋ 職稱 ＋ 公司名 ＋ 聯絡方式 （這樣的組合其實就是我們所常見的
簽名檔）

例 Jason Lin
Project Manager
ABC Company
Tel: +886-2-85466630
Fax: +886-2-85466631

Part 1

職前準備

自我介紹

挑戰難度 ★★☆☆☆

 真的你學過

　　很多人學習英文多年，但要用英文自我介紹時，才發現自己根本開不了口，總覺得需要有深厚英文底子才能以英文介紹自己。事實上，這樣的想法是錯誤的，只要懂得運用我們學過的一些基礎單字與文法，大家都能用英文做自我介紹。接下來我們來練習怎麼自我介紹讓人更印象深刻。

單元重點及學習方向

❶ 學會以人稱代名詞 I 與所有格 my 開頭的陳述句。
❷ 運用指示代名詞 this/that 來陳述概念。
❸ 運用 these/those are 進行敘述。
❹ 運用本單元基本字彙、句型、片語，練習求職、拜會廠商時的自我介紹。

必 check 句型 ||||||||||||||||||||||||||||||||

1. **This is** my resume.
   這是我的履歷。

2. **I am** the graduate of Vincent University.
   我畢業於文森大學。

3. **My** major is math.
   我主修數學。

4. **These** reports **are** sent to our customers.
   這些報告是要寄給客戶的。

5. **That is** the reason why I want to work in your company.
   這是為何我想到貴公司工作的原因。

 你有學過的單字 ||||||||||||||||||||||||||||||||

1. **take** [tek] *v.* 修課

2. **graduate** [`grædʒʊˌet] *v.* 畢業

3. **part-time** [`part`taɪm] *adj.* 兼職的

4. **personality** [ˌpɜ˞sn`æləti] *n.* 個性

5. **hobby** [`habɪ] *n.* 嗜好

6. **talk** [tɔk] *n.* 談話

7. **duty** [`djutɪ] *n.* 責任

8. **position** [pə`zɪʃən] *n.* 職位

9. **section** [`sɛkʃən] *n.* 部門

10. **job** [dʒab] *n.* 工作

Unit **01**
Unit **02**
Unit **03**
Unit **04**
Unit **05**
Unit **06**
Unit **07**
Unit **08**
Unit **09**
Unit **10**
Unit **11**

小試身手 ||||||||||||||||||||||||||||||||||||||||

1. _____, _____ Jason Lin

   早安，我是 Jason 林。

2. I _____ from Brown University, and I _____ in math.

   我大學就讀布朗大學，主修數學。

3. After I _____ those courses, my logical thinking ability is getting _____.

   修了這些課程後，我的邏輯思考能力變好了。

4. I am an _____ person, so I would always start the _____ when making new friends.

   我是外向的人，所以在認識新朋友時我會主動開啟話題。

5. My _____ job was the _____ in ABC Company.

   我的上一份工作是在 ABC 公司擔任工程師。

解答

1. Good morning; I am
2. graduated; majored
3. took; better
4. outgoing; conversation
5. previous; engineer

句型喚醒你的記憶

1. **This is** my resume.

   這是我的履歷。

   This is，為「這是…」的意思。可用來指稱離自己較近的物體。

   例 This is my book. 這是我的書。

2. **I am** the graduate of Vincent University.

   我畢業於文森大學。

   I am...為「我是…」的意思，用於敘述自身狀態或身分。

   例 I am the teacher of this school. 我是此校的教師。

3. **My major** is math.

   我主修數學。

   所有格 my + 名詞為「我的…」的意思，用於敘述自身擁有物或是狀態。

   例 My resume is the one with blue cover. 我的履歷是藍色封面。

4. I can use **those skills** in this position.

   我能將那些技巧應用在此職位上。

   These/those+名詞可指示方位，用 these 代表物體離說話者較近，用 those 則較遠。另外 those 也可表示過去的經驗或取得的事物。

   例 These data are used in our sales report. 銷售報告中使用了這些數據。

5. **That is** the reason why I want to work in your company.

   這是為何我想到貴公司工作的原因。

   That is，為「那是…」的意思。除指稱離自己較遠的物體，也有總結上述內容的意涵。

   例 That is why I quit. 這也是我為何辭職的原因。

Unit 01
Unit 02
Unit 03
Unit 04
Unit 05
Unit 06
Unit 07
Unit 08
Unit 09
Unit 10
Unit 11

知多少？多知道一點總是好

踏入職場後，除了簡述身家背景外，突顯自己與職位的連結性與專業能力的展現則是最大要點，因此除非面試官要求你進行簡短自我介紹，否則儘可能有系統且完整地表達自己，語氣上也需要較為莊重。

而職場的自我介紹，可再細分為求職時與錄取後。求職時的自我介紹是為了讓面試官了解自己，以增加錄取機會。錄取後的自我介紹，則多用於業務的處理，例如新人主動向客戶介紹自己。以下為求職英文自我介紹時的要點與禁忌：

不可不知的要點

1. 注重禮貌：因為面試是你與面試官的首次碰面，留意基本禮節（例如：早安、謝謝）可替自己加分不少。
2. 用字淺顯：英文思考重視想法，只要概念有表達清楚，用字可以簡單。
3. 速度適中：自我介紹目的是讓對方聽懂，因此速度不宜太快。
4. 預先演練：沙盤推演可能被詢問的問題，實際上場時方可從容回答。
5. 見好就收：講得久不一定等於講得好。若已表達的差不多，便可進行結尾。

不可不知的禁忌

1. 負面資訊：沒有人是完美的，但面試時應當表現出自己的優點，避免提及自己的缺點。

2. 自以為是：有自信是好事，但自信過度會讓人產生反感。

3. 流水帳：雖然自我介紹就是要讓面試官更了解自己，但這並不代表你需要把自己的生平都告訴他。

4. 固執己見：面試官可能會對自我介紹的內容不表認同，此時若你選擇與其針鋒相對，只會大大降低錄取的可能性。

5. 過度吹噓：稍微包裝自己的經歷與特質是必要的，但若加油添醋過了頭，很容易被專業人士戳破謊言，得不償失。

Unit
01

Unit
02

Unit
03

Unit
04

Unit
05

Unit
06

Unit
07

Unit
08

Unit
09

Unit
10

Unit
11

腦部暖身 一點都不難對話

請將以下六個單字填入空格內。

(a) interview   (b) courses   (c) major

(d) assistant   (e) creative   (f) Manager

In the office, you are informed to have this ____1____.

HR：Good morning Mr. Lin. I am James, the ____2____ of human resource. Please take a seat.

You：Thank you, and this is my resume.

HR：Please introduce yourself in English.

You：Good morning, I am Jason Lin. I graduated from Benson University, and my ____3____ is art and design. The ____4____ I took help me learn a lot. I am a ____5____ person, so I like to try different materials. My previous job was the ____6____ in ABC Company.

HR：Thank you! Why do you want to work in our company?

You：The reason is that your Company is famous for its creativity.

HR：Thank you. We will inform you the result in three days

翻譯

在辦公室裡，你接獲通知進行面試。

人資：早安，林先生。我是人資部門的主管 James。請坐。

　你：謝謝，這是我的履歷。

人資：請以英文自我介紹。

　你：早安，我是 Jason 林。我畢業於班森大學，主修藝術與設計。過去所修習的課程讓我廣泛理解此領域的知識。我是個有創意的人，所以我喜歡嘗試不同的材料。我的前一份工作是在 ABC 服

Unit
01

Unit
02

Unit
03

Unit
04

Unit
05

Unit
06

Unit
07

Unit
08

Unit
09

Unit
10

Unit
11

裝公司擔任助理。

人資：謝謝。為何會想到本公司工作呢?

　你：因為貴公司以創意聞名。

人資：謝謝。我們會在三天內通知您結果。

單字

- **be famous for** ph. 以⋯聞名
- **graduate** [ˋgrædʒʊˌet] v. 畢業
- **inform** [ɪnˋfɔrm] v. 通知
- **introduce** [ˌɪntrəˋdjus] v. 介紹
- **material** [məˋtɪrɪəl] n. 材質

答案

1. (a)　2. (f)　3. (c)　4. (b)　5. (e)　6. (d)

會說也會寫一：求職自我介紹講稿撰寫

撰寫求職用的自我介紹講稿時，除了介紹自己的背景與經歷外，最重要的就是如何讓自己與這個職缺產生連結。若是首次求職的社會新鮮人，因為其工作經歷相對較不豐富，因此重點可放在自己過去所學、自身性格、證照等。

❶Good morning, I am Jason Lin. ❷I graduate from Mark University, and my major is Information Techology. ❸The courses I took help me learn professional knowledge in this field. ❹I am a careful person, so I always check the details of the program I design. ❺My hobby is playing chess, because I can train my logical thinking through this game. ❻My previous job was the assistant in ABC Computer Company. ❼I have worked there for two years, and I learned how to debug. ❽I think I can make good use of what I have learned in the past in this job.

翻譯

早安，我是 Jason 林。我畢業於馬克大學，主修資訊工程。期間所修習的課程讓我學會許多專業知識。我是個細心的人，所以我會仔細檢查自己設計的程式。我的興趣是下西洋棋，因為我下棋能讓訓練我的邏輯思考。我的上份工作是在 ABC 電腦公司擔任助理。在那邊工作的兩年，我學會如何除錯。我自認可以將過去所學用在這份工作。

解析

一份完整的自我介紹講稿大致會有以下 8 個部分，包括：

❶問好：Good morning/afternoon/evening 早／午／晚安
❷學歷與主修：I graduate from 學校名稱／I am the graduate of 學校名稱；I major in 學科／My major is 學科.

❸說明所學：The courses/trainings help me learn+ 知識／技能 .

❹人格特質：I am a/an 形容個性的形容詞 .（例：careful ）

❺興趣：My hobby/personal interest is 興趣類別 .（例：basketball）

❻過去工作例：My previous job is 職位 in 公司名稱 .

❼年資：I have worked there for two years.

❽發揮所學：I think I can make good use of what I have learned in the past in this job

　　以上是基本的自我介紹講稿架構，熟悉此架構後，可在學歷主修部分再增加敘述目前已獲得的專業證書〈Ex. I scored 550 in TOEIC test〉。過去工作部分也可以敘述自己在每份工作中所獲得的成長，增加整個自我介紹的豐富度。

Unit
01

Unit
02

Unit
03

Unit
04

Unit
05

Unit
06

Unit
07

Unit
08

Unit
09

Unit
10

Unit
11

會說也會寫二：向新客戶自我介紹講稿

　　向客戶做自我介紹時，主要是要讓客戶了解你是誰，屬於哪個部門。因此新進人員應該主動上前招呼，並適當回應客戶的提問。詳細說明如下：

1. 招呼：

例 Nice to meet you, Mr. Mike. I am Jason, the new sales representative. I am responsible for the sale of our products in Japan. Here is my business card.

幸會，麥可先生。我是 Jason，新到職的業務。我負責公司在日本的產品銷售。這邊是我的名片。

2. 客戶可能的提出的問題：

❶ 關於其他同事：

例一 What happened to Leo?

Leo 還好嗎？

例二 Does Mary still work here?

瑪莉還有在這工作嗎？

❷ 關於長官：

例一 Could I talk to Manager Huang now?

我現在能跟黃經理談談嗎？

例二 Is Mr.Lin available now?

林先生現在有空嗎？

❸ 關於業務進度：

例一 How is the progress of the project now?

專案目前進度如何？

例二 May I know who is responsible for this project now?

我可以請問現在專案的負責人是誰嗎？

解析 |||||||||||||||||||||||||||||||||||||||||||||||||||||

Unit
01

Unit
02

Unit
03

Unit
04

Unit
05

Unit
06

Unit
07

Unit
08

Unit
09

Unit
10

Unit
11

1. 招呼：由於客戶對於新進人員不熟悉，新人的自我介紹要有以下幾個重點：a. 姓名 b. 職位 c. 所屬部門與職務

   告知客戶以上資訊後，再主動進行名片交換，如此一來，客戶對你就有基本的認識。

2. 如何回覆客戶詢問：

   ❶ 關於同事：不論清楚來龍去脈與否，不做評論為上策。

      例 What happened to Leo?

      Leo 還好嗎？

      ▶ I am not sure. He had left before I entered this company.

      ▷ 我不確定，他在我到職前就已離職。

   ❷ 關於長官：若不知道長官是否願意與客戶碰面，應當向秘書或助理確認，而非逕自帶客戶前往長官的辦公室。

      例 Could I talk to Manager Huang now?

      我現在能跟黃經理談談嗎？

      ▶ I will check his schedule for you, so please wait for few seconds.

      ▷ 我替您查一下他的行程，請稍等。

   ❸ 關於業務進度：公司可能不見得願意讓所有客戶都知道工作進度，因此不要隨意回答。

      例 How is the progress of the project now?

      專案目前進度如何。

      ▶ I am not sure. I will convey your message to the person in charge of your Project.

      ▷ 我不確定，但我會轉答您的訊息給處理人員。

現在你會說 ||||||||||||||||||||||||||||||||||||||||||||||||

請依句意填入 A-H。

A. When will I know the result of this interview

B. I would always start the conversations whenever I visit a new customer

C. This is my resume

D. I have worked in DEF Company for three years

E. I graduated from St. Kevin University

F. You company is famous for its good employee welfare

G. my major is International Trade, and these are the related certificates I have

H. My previous job was a sales in AMG Company

A：Good morning Mr. Lin, please take a seat.

B：Good morning. _____1_____.

A：Now let's begin the interview with the self-introduction.

B：I am John Lin. _____2_____, and _____3_____. I am an outgoing person, so _____4_____. _____5_____, so I have learned many sales skills from my colleagues. Also, _____6_____.

A：Why do you want to work in our company?

B：_____7_____.

A：Thank you.

B：_____8_____.

A：We will inform you in a week.

答案 ....

1. (C)　2. (E)　3. (G)　4. (B)　5. (H)　6. (D)　7. (F)　8. (A)

單字小筆記 ....

• **employee welfare** [͵ɛmplɔɪ`i`wɛl͵fɛr] 員工福利

• **colleague** [kɑ`lig] *n.* 同事

現在你會寫

1. 我畢業於 Hess 大學，主修企管。

_____

_____

中式英文出沒 ▶ I am graduate from Hess University, I major is Business Management.

錯在哪 ▶ graduate 已經是動詞，所以要刪掉 be 動詞。此句若 major 當作名詞用，那麼 I 要改成所有格 My。major 做動詞用，則改成 I major in...。

正解 ▶ I graduated from Hess University, and my major is Business Management.或 I graduated from Hess University, and I majored in Business Management.

2. 我的前份工作是在 ABC 公司擔任業務助理一職，所以有許多安排會議（arrange a meeting）的經驗。

_____

_____

中式英文出沒 ▶ My previous job position is sales assistant in ABC Company, so I have many experience arrange a meeting.

錯在哪 ▶ Job 本身就已經包含職位的意思，因受中文影響加上 position ，反而形成文法錯誤。要敘述自己有某方面 的經驗，應於 experience 後加上 in + Ving。

正解 ▶ My previous job is a sales assistant in ABC Company, so I have many experiences in arranging a meeting.

Unit 01

Unit 02

Unit 03

Unit 04

Unit 05

Unit 06

Unit 07

Unit 08

Unit 09

Unit 10

Unit 11

02 Unit 工作錄取

挑戰難度 ★★☆☆☆

真的你學過

　　當你接獲通知錄取一份工作時，通知的形式可能會是書面或電話聯絡，許多人可能會擔心自己會因為沒弄清楚內容，而錯過這份工作。但事實上，只要懂得抓出英文錄取通知中的關鍵資訊，其他內容多為客套或是應酬用語。針對關鍵資訊加以回覆，就毋須擔心會搞砸了。

單元重點及學習方向

❶ 學會運用**主詞**＋will 來表達未來將進行的動作。

❷ 學會 as（如同…）做為連接詞時的用法。

❸ 學會 as（以…的身分）做為介係詞時的用法。

❹ 應用本單元字彙、片語與句型練習接獲錄取通知的回答方式。

必 check 句型

1. **You will** be responsible for the sale of our new products.

   你將負責銷售我們的新產品。

2. **I will** reply you as soon as possible.

   我將盡快回覆您。

3. **As** we discussed, **you will** work **as** the engineer in our company.

   如同我們先前所談，你將在本公司擔任工程師。

4. **As** I promised, **you will** get the paycheck of your salary next Monday.

   如同我所承諾，你將於下週一收到薪水支票。

Ⓐ 你有學過的單字

1. **acceptance** [ək`sɛptəns] *n.* 接受
2. **confirm** [kən`fɝm] *v.* 確認
3. **competitor** [kəm`pɛtətɚ] *n.* 競爭者
4. **discuss** [dɪ`skʌs] *v.* 討論
5. **decision** [dɪ`sɪʒən] *n.* 決定
6. **decline** [dɪ`klaɪn] *v.* 拒絕
7. **employment** [ɪm`plɔɪmənt] *n.* 工作
8. **news** [njuz] *n.* 消息
9. **full-time** [`fʊl`taɪm] *adj.* 全職的
10. **reply** [rɪ`plaɪ] *n.* 回覆

Unit 01
Unit 02
Unit 03
Unit 04
Unit 05
Unit 06
Unit 07
Unit 08
Unit 09
Unit 10
Unit 11

小試身手 ||||||||||||||||||||||||||||||||||||||

1. You beat the other _____ and won this job.
   你擊敗其他競爭者贏得這份工作。

2. I am happy to _____ your _____ as the assistant of the Marketing Department in our company.
   我高興能跟您確認您將擔任本公司行銷部助理之事宜。

3. It is really a good _____ to me.
   對我來說這真是個好消息。

4. You will work as the _____ sales as we _____ in the interview.
   如同我們於面試時所討論，你將擔任全職業務。

5. Please send us your _____ by next Monday.
   請您於下週一前回覆。

解答 ···

1. competitors
2. confirm; employment
3. news
4. full-time; discussed
5. reply

句型喚醒你的記憶 ||||||||||||||||||||||||||||||||||

1. **You will** be responsible for selling books.
你將負責書籍銷售。

You + will 意思為「你將…」，用於指示對方未來將進行之動作。

例 You will get the report next Monday. 你將於下週一拿到這份報告。

2. **I will** inform you my decision as soon as possible.
我將盡快告知您我的決定。

I + will 意思為「我將…」，用於說明自己下一步將進行的動作。

例 I will visit my customer next week. 我下週將前往拜訪客戶。

3. **As I** promised, you will get your salary next week.
如同我所保證地，你將於下週拿到薪水。

As 作為連接詞使用時，意思為「如同…」，可用於說明條件或是前提。

例 As we discussed, you will get the salary paycheck next week.
如同我們所討論的，你將於下週拿到薪水支票。

4. You will **work as** designer in our company
你將在本公司擔任設計師一職。

As 做介係詞用時，意思為「以…的身分」，可用於說工作性質與職位。

例 You will work as the assistant in our company. 你將於本公司擔任助理一職。

Unit 01
Unit 02
Unit 03
Unit 04
Unit 05
Unit 06
Unit 07
Unit 08
Unit 09
Unit 10
Unit 11

知多少？多知道一點總是好

　　完成英文面試過後，接下來就是等待錄取與否。通知錄取的方式可能是該公司人員透過電話親自連絡，或是以郵件告之。在接獲通知後，該公司通常也都會給你一段考慮的時間，也可能會有一些相關文件與資料需要你去填寫與準備，因此不論最後是接受或是拒絕這份工作，都應注意以下的要點與禁忌：

不可不知的要點

1. 基本禮貌：對於獲得此工作應表示感謝。
2. 明確回覆：不論接受與否，都應讓對方清楚知道你的決定。
3. 保留未來合作之可能性：職場上沒有絕對的事，本次未進入該公司服務，不代表未來不會，因此不宜把話說死。

不可不知的禁忌

1. 資料填寫不完整：除口頭確認外，多數公司還需要再跑文件流程，倘若資料填寫不完整，會對自身權利造成影響。

2. 未按照規定時間回覆：一般而言，錄取你的公司都會給予一段時間進行考慮，超過這段時間未給予回應，可能就會視同你已放棄資格，因此在獲得錄取通知後，當於期限內回覆，以保障自身權益。

3. 未注意報到日期：求職面試後，會陸續接到多家公司的錄取通知。如果沒有仔細注意報到日期，可能會因為等待另一間公司的面試結果，而錯失已錄取之職缺。

　　若能遵守以上要點，避免上述禁忌，方可在求職路上，替自己開創更多機會，並於開始進入某一公司工作前，給予對方一個好印象。

Unit 01
Unit 02
Unit 03
Unit 04
Unit 05
Unit 06
Unit 07
Unit 08
Unit 09
Unit 10
Unit 11

腦部暖身 一點都不難對話

請將以下六個單字填入空格內。

(a) news　　　　　(b) acceptance　　　　(c) as

(d) offer　　　　　(e) confirm　　　　　(f) full-time

You received a phone call.

Jason： Good afternoon, this is Jason from ABC Company. Is this Mr. Leo?

Leo： This is Leo speaking.

Jason： Mr. Leo, I am so happy to ____1____ your employment **as** the ____2____ sales representative in International Sales Department. **You will take over** Williams' duty to sell our products to Europe.

Leo： Good ____3____ to me.

Jason： ____4____ we discussed in the interview few days ago, this ____5____ **comes into effec** on January 1, so please inform us your decision by this Friday.

Leo： Ok. Do I need to fill any documents for ____6____?

Jason： Yes, **I will** send you few documents through the e-mail address you provide to me.

Leo： Thank you. **I will make a decision** as soon as possible and send the document back.

Jason： I see. I **look forward to** your reply.

翻譯

你接到電話。

Jason：早安，我是 ABC 公司的 Jason，請問是 Leo 先生嗎？

Leo：我就是。

Jason：Leo 先生，於此很高興跟您確認您將於外貿部任全職銷售代表一職。

　Leo：真是個好消息。

Jason：如同幾天前於面試時所談，你將從一月一日開始上班，因此請於本週五前回覆我們。

　Leo：了解。接受這份工作需要填寫任何文件？

Jason：是需要填寫的。我會把這些文件寄到您所提供的信箱。

　Leo：謝謝。我會儘快決定並且將填寫好的文件寄回。

Jason：了解。期待您的回覆。

單字

- **take over** [`tek ˌovɚ] *ph.* 接任
- **comes into effect** [ˌkʌmz `ɪntuifɛkt] *ph.* 生效
- **make a decision** [ˌmekə dɪ`sɪʒən] *ph.* 做決定
- **look forward to** [ˌlʊk` fɔrwɚd ˌtu] *ph.* 期待

答案

1. (e)　2. (f)　3. (a)　4. (c)　5. (d)　6. (b)

Unit
01
Unit
03
Unit
04
Unit
05
Unit
06
Unit
07
Unit
08
Unit
09
Unit
10
Unit
11

會說也會寫一：接受工作 ||||||||||||||||||||||||||||

You receive an e-mail from the company you interviewed few days ago. The content is as followed:

Dear James,

We are very happy to inform you that you are qualified to get this positon. You will work as [1]the full-time programmer in our Software Department. As we discussed in the interview, [2]this offer come into effect on March 1. Please [3]send us your reply by next Monday. Please find the [4]acceptance form in the attachment. If you have any questions, please feel free to ask.

Sincerely yours,

Jason Lai

Software Department Manager

翻譯

你收到前幾天去面試的公司來信。

信件內容如下：

親愛的詹姆士先生：

　　我們很高興通知您，您錄取此職位。您將於本公司的軟體部門擔任全職軟體工程師。如同我們先前所討論，上班日為三月一日，故最晚請於下週一告知是否接受此工作。請下載附件中的接受表。如有任何問題歡迎詢問。

謹

賴傑森

軟體部門經理

解析

此封來信中有以下四項重要訊息：

❶你所錄取的職位：full time programmer
❷何時開始工作：March 1
❸回覆截止日期：next Monday
❹需填寫之文件類型：acceptance form

　　因此回覆時，應先充分了解上述四點，再決定是否接受此工作。若決定接受，則可參考以下範例進行回覆：

Dear Jason Lai,
以全名稱呼，表示禮貌
First of all, thank you for providing this opportunity. I am so excited
　　　　　　　對獲得此份工作表示感謝
when I opened this e-mail. Here I will accept this offer and please find
　　　　　　　　　表示接受此份工作
the filled acceptance form as attached. Also, I want to express my
　　表示已完成文件填寫
gratitude again.

I really look forward to being a part of you.

Sincerely yours,
James

Unit
01

Unit
02

Unit
03

Unit
04

Unit
05

Unit
06

Unit
07

Unit
08

Unit
09

Unit
10

Unit
11

會說也會寫二：拒絕工作

You receive an e-mail form the company you just interviewed.

Dear James,

We are very happy to inform you that you are qualified to get this positon. You will work as ❶the full-time programmer in our Software Department. As we discussed, ❷this offer will come into effect on March 1. Please ❸send us your reply by this Monday.

Please find the ❹acceptance form in the attachment. If you have any questions, please feel free to ask.

Peter Hu,
Software Department Manager

翻譯

你收到先前去參加面試的公司來信。

親愛的詹姆士：

　　於此我們很高興能告知您，您獲得這份工作。您將擔任本公司軟體部門的全職軟體工程師。如同先前所討論的，您將於三月一日開始上班，因此請於下週一前回覆是否接受此職缺。

　　接受表請詳見附件。如有任何問題歡迎詢問。

胡彼得
軟體部門經理

解析

此封來信中有以下四項重要訊息：

❶ 你所錄取的職位: full time programmer
❷ 何時開始工作: March 1
❸ 回覆截止日期: next Monday
❹ 需填寫之文件類型: acceptance form

　　因此回覆時，應先充分了解上述四點，再決定是否接受此工作。若決定拒絕，則可參考以下範例進行回覆：

Dear Mr. Hu,
以姓氏稱呼，表示禮貌
First of all, thank you for providing this opportunity. However, I
　　　　　　對獲得此份工作表示感謝
have accepted the offer provided by the other company few days ago.
　　　　　　表示拒絕此份工作
Thus, I have to give up the occupation I get. I will fill and return
the document needed to finish the procedure. I sincerely hope we
　　　　　　表示已完成文件填寫
still have a chance to work together in the future.

Sincerely yours,
James

Unit
01

Unit
02

Unit
03

Unit
04

Unit
05

Unit
06

Unit
07

Unit
08

Unit
09

Unit
10

Unit
11

39

 現在你會說 ||||||||||||||||||||||||||||||||||

請依句意填入 A-E。

A. this offer will come into effect on January 1

B. I will make a decision soon and send back the document

C. You will take over Williams' duty to sell our products to Europe

D. Good news to me

E. This is Leo speaking

Jason：Good afternoon, this is Jason from ABC Company. Is this Mr. Leo?

Leo：＿＿＿1＿＿＿.

Jason：Mr. Leo, I am so happy to confirm your employment as the full-time Sales Representative of International Sales Department. ＿＿＿2＿＿＿.

Leo：＿＿＿3＿＿＿.

Jason：As we discussed in the interview few days ago, ＿＿＿4＿＿＿, so please inform us your decision by this Friday.

Leo：OK. Do I need to fill any documents for acceptance?

Jason：Yes, I will send you few documents to the e-mail address you provide.

Leo：Thank you. ＿＿＿5＿＿＿.

Jason：I see. I look forward to your reply.

答案

1. (E)　2. (C)　3. (D)　4. (A)　5. (B)

現在你會寫 ||||||||||||||||||||||||||||||||||||||||||||||

Unit
01

Unit
02

Unit
03

Unit
04

Unit
05

Unit
06

Unit
07

Unit
08

Unit
09

Unit
10

Unit
11

1. 我很感激您提供這個機會給我。

_____

_____

中式英文出沒 ▶ I really thank you give me this opportunity.

　錯在哪 ▶ thank you for＋Ving（動名詞）才是正確用法，所以 thank you give...應更正為：thank you for giving...

　正解 ▶ Thank you for giving me this opportunity.

2. 就像我們面試時所討論的，你將從十二月一日開始上班。

_____

_____

中式英文出沒 ▶ As like we discussed in the interview, your offer comes into effect on December 1.

　錯在哪 ▶ as 與 like 都可以做為連接詞使用，有如同、就像的意思。因此在此範例中只需擇其一使用即可。

　正解 ▶ As/Like we discussed in the interview, your offer will come into effect on December 1.

職前訓練

挑戰難度 ★★☆☆☆

 **真的你學過**

　　錄取工作之後，接下來就是接受職前訓練。職前訓練的內容包含公司環境介紹、基本業務熟悉與相關業務交接。這些內容乍聽之下好像非常複雜，但事實上只要熟悉英文的方位與事件主從或順序概念的敘述方式，就能很快抓到職前訓練的重點，讓自己快速進入狀況

單元重點及學習方向

❶ 運用 before 與 after 來區分先後順序。
❷ 運用 to V 來表達目的。
❸ 運用 how to 來詢問步驟。
❹ 應用本單元之字彙、片語與句型練習接獲錄取通知的回答方式。

 必 check 句型

1. **Before** you use this machine, please read the manual in detail.
   操作本機器前,請先詳閱操作手冊。
2. **After** you log in the system, please update the user information.
   登入系統後,請更新使用者資料。
3. **To help** you get familiar with your duty more quickly, I will give you some lectures.
   為了讓你能盡快熟悉業務,我會幫你上課。
4. Can you tell me **how to** use the tool?
   可以請你告訴我如何使用這個工具嗎?

 你有學過的單字

1. **ask** [æsk] *v.* 詢問
2. **lecture** [`lɛktʃɚ] *n.* 課程
3. **employee** [ˌɛmplɔɪ`i] *n.* 員工
4. **familiar** [fə`mɪljɚ] *adj.* 熟悉的
5. **understand** [ˌʌndɚ`stænd] *v.* 了解
6. **practice** [`præktɪs] *n.* 練習
7. **operate** [`ɑpəˌret] *v.* 操作
8. **submit** [səb`mɪt] *v.* 繳交
9. **process** [`prɑsɛs] *n.* 程序
10. **quantity** [`kwɑntətɪ] *n.* 數量

Unit 01
Unit 02
Unit 03
Unit 04
Unit 05
Unit 06
Unit 07
Unit 08
Unit 09
Unit 10
Unit 11

小試身手 ||||||||||||||||||||||||||||||||||||||||||||||||

1. Please check the details before you _____ the report.

   繳交報告前請先檢查細節。

2. .I don't know how to _____ this machine.

   我不知道如何操作此機器。

3. I am not _____ with my duty.

   我對我的業務內容不熟悉。

4. Now I _____ how to use the system.

   現在我懂如何操作這個系統了。

5. Can you tell me the _____ of application?

   能請你告訴申請的程序嗎？

解答 ....

1. submit

2. operate

3. familiar

4. understand

5. process

句型喚醒你的記憶 ||||||||||||||||||||||||||||||||

Unit
01
Unit
02
Unit
03
Unit
04
Unit
05
Unit
06
Unit
07
Unit
08
Unit
09
Unit
10
Unit
11

1. **Before** I start to practice, can I ask one more question?
   在我開始練習之前，可以再問一個問題嗎？
   Before 意思為「在…之前」，可用於區分事情的前後順序。
   例 Before I start the lecture, I will give you some reference.
   　 在我上課之前，我會先給你一些參考資料。

2. **After** this training, you will have a test.
   完成訓練之後，你將接受測驗。
   After 意思為「在…之後」，可用於區分事情的前後順序。
   例 After the employee training, you need to submit a report.
   　 員工訓練後，你必須交一份報告。

3. **To understand** the process more, I read the manual.
   為了要更了解流程，我閱讀手冊。
   To V 意思為「為了…」，可用於說明進行某動作的目的。
   例 To finish the lecture early, please focus on this chart.
   　 為了能夠及早上完本課程，請注意此圖表。

4. Can you tell me **how to** use this system?
   能請你告訴我如何使用本系統嗎？
   How to 意思為「如何…」，可用於說明或詢問步驟。
   例 Can you teach me how to check the details of this report?
   　 可以請你教我如何確認報告內的細節嗎？

知多少？多知道一點總是好 ‖‖‖‖‖‖‖‖‖‖‖‖‖‖‖‖‖

　　進入公司後，接下來就是要熟悉環境、學習基本業務，並可能承接離職人員之業務。關於熟悉環境的部分，雖然這對你的工作表現可能影響有限，但若能快速建立熟悉度，就不必大小事都請教同事。

不可不知的要點 ‖‖‖‖‖‖‖‖‖‖‖‖‖‖‖‖‖‖‖‖‖‖‖

以下的要點可幫助你快速掌握各設施或人員的位置：
1. 找出一個參考點〈例：你的座位〉，以此為中心點記憶各設備位置。
2. 記住同事的業務職掌，碰上相關問題可向其詢問討教。

　　而在基本業務學習的部分，公司肯定希望你越快進入狀況越好，因此學習效率就是此處的重點。把握以下要點將可讓你更快熟悉業務內容：

1. 善用公司內的參考資料，縮短摸索時間。
2. 整理屬於自己的筆記，提高記憶與理解程度。
3. 持續更新內容，保持資料的正確性與即時性。

最後，關於業務承接的部分，其重點在於執掌的釐清與物品的清點。一般來說，當有人員離職，其職務與相關物品會先由其他同事暫代與保管，直到新進同仁到任才逐步交接。新人進行業務承接若能把握以下要點，方可事半功倍：

1. 善用檢查清單，可避免遺漏與縮短核對時間。
2. 依職掌與代理人員進行交接，清楚掌握業務內容。

Unit

01

Unit

02

Unit

03

Unit

04

Unit

05

Unit

06

Unit

07

Unit

08

Unit

09

Unit

10

Unit

11

腦部暖身 一點都不難對話

請將以下六個單字填入空格內。

(a) operate   (b) process   (c) lecture

(d) submit   (e) fill   (f) familiar

Jason：Good Morning everyone, I am Jason, the new sales representative.

Brown：Morning Jason, I am Brown, the Manager of International Sales Department. Welcome to join our team. Mary will help you to get ____1____ with the environment and later Emily will teach you how to ____2____ our machine and system.

Mary：Mr. Jason, please follow me.

Jason：OK.

Mary：First of all, let me show you where your seat is. You will sit between me and John. Then, I will tell you where the ____3____ room is.

Jason：Thank you. Can I ask one question here?

Mary：Sure, what do you want to know?

Jason：Where is the machine?

Mary：It is next to the conference room. Emily will teach you the ____4____ of operation later.

Jason：I got it.

Mary：Now let's go back to your seat. I will help you to ____5____ the form you have to ____6____.

翻譯

Jason：各位早安，我是 Jason，今天剛來報到的新業務。

Brown：早安，我是外貿部的經理 Brown。歡迎加入我們的團隊。
　　　　Mary 會帶你熟悉環境。稍後 Emily 會教你如何操作機器與系
　　　　統。

Mary：Jason 先生，請跟我走。

Jason：好的。

Mary：首先，讓我告訴你你的座位在哪。你坐在我和 John 中間。接
　　　　下來我要告訴你上課教室在哪。

Jason：謝謝。我可以問個問題嗎？

Mary：當然可以，你想問的是？

Jason：機器是在哪邊呢？

Mary：就在會議室旁邊。稍後 Emily 會在那教你如何操作機器。

Jason：我了解了。

Mary：現在我們先回到你的座位。我會協助你填寫你要繳交的表格。

單字

- **join** [dʒɔɪn] *v.* 參加
- **show** [ʃo] *v.* 指示
- **seat** [sit] *n.* 座位
- **between** [bɪ`twin] *prep.* 在…之間
- **operation** [ˌɑpə`reʃən] *n.* 操作

答案

1. (f)　2. (a)　3. (c)　4. (b)　5. (e)　6. (d)

會說也會寫一：如何填寫資料表

Example:

Employee ID Card Application Form

Document No.	ABC-12345---- (a)
Application date	January 1 2014----❶
Department	International Sales----❷
Applicant Name	Jason Lai ❸
Reason ---❹	■ New employee □ Position/Department changing □ Lost □ Others
Applicant signature: ----❺ Jason Lai	□ Approved □ Rejected ＿＿＿＿＿＿＿ ---- (b)

翻譯

範例：

新進員工 ID 卡申請表

文件編號	ABC-12345
申請日	2014 年 1 月 1 日
部門	外貿部
申請人姓名	Jason Lai
申請事由	□ 新進員工 □ 職務／部門變動 □ 卡片遺失 □ 其他
申請人簽名： Jason Lai	□ 審核通過□ 審核未通過 ＿＿＿＿＿＿＿

解析 ||||||||||||||||||||||||||||||||||||||||||||||||||||||||||||

Unit
01

Unit
02

Unit
03

Unit
04

Unit
05

Unit
06

Unit
07

Unit
08

Unit
09

Unit
10

Unit
11

　　本報表中一共有一個部分代表編號，五個部份需要填寫，兩個部分代表審核結果。以下針對其內容做進一步說明：

（a）文件編號：ABC-12345（每份申請表的獨立編號）

❶申請日期：January 1 2014（通常會是你報到的日期）
❷部門：International Sales（你所在的部門）
❸申請人姓名：Jason Lai
❹申請事由：■ New employee（由於你是新進員工，故選擇此選項）
❺申請人簽名：Jason Lai（簽名表示對這份申請表負責）

　　完成上述五個部分後，便可將申請表送交審核。如審核通過，審核人便會勾選■ Approved（審核通過）部分，並於下方（b）＿＿＿＿＿＿的簽名欄部分簽名負責，接下來就剩等待實際拿到 ID 卡。假使審核人員覺得填寫內容有問題，便會勾選■ Rejected（審核未通過），將你的申請表退回。

附註

申請事由中尚有以下三種情況，以下針對各個情況做進一步說明：
□ Position/Department changing 職務／部門變動：
　　當員工更換部門或是業務調整時，勾選此項目。
□ Lost 卡片遺失：
　　當員工遺失 ID 卡要再重新申請時，勾選此項目。
□ Others 其他事由：
　　若為其他申請緣由，勾選此項目。

會說也會寫二：如何填寫業務與物品交接表

Example:

Work and tool Handover Form
Date:_____ ---❶

	Company name- （2-a）	Description --- （2-b）	V— （2-c）
Customer list---❷	1.DEF	12/6：Project meeting Contact: Ray （14-2688-1234）	V
	2.Joe & Josh	12/20：Monthly meeting Contact: Joe （12-888-9765）	V
Item list---❸	Item name – （3-a）	Description – （3-b）	
	Laptop	1 set （with mouse）	V
	Smart Phone	1 set （include recharger）	V
		Signature _____	---❹

翻譯

範例：

業務與物品交接表
交接日期_____

	公司名稱	業務進度	
客戶列表	DEF 公司	12/6：專案會議 連絡人：Ray （002-2688-1234）	V
	Joe & Josh 公司	12/20：月會 連絡人：Joe（002-888-9765）	V
物品列表	物品名稱	概況	
	筆電	一組（含滑鼠）	V
	智慧型手機	一組（含充電器）	V
		簽名 _____	

解析

本交接表共分為以下四個部分：

❶ 交接日期（Date）:進行交接的時間。

❷ 客戶列表：

2-a 公司名稱（Company name）:你未來將接手的客戶名稱。

2-b 業務進度（Description）:目前的業務狀況、行程與聯絡窗口。

2-c 已交接（V）：標註 V 代表已確認交接，若業務未完成交接，或是物品上有缺漏，則該欄位應保持空白。

❸ 物品清單：

3-a 物品名稱（Item name）：你所接受的物品名稱。

3-b 概況（Description）：物品的數量與狀況。

❹ 簽名（Signature）：交接完成後於下方簽名，表示對此文件負責。

附註

　一般而言，交接表多為一式兩份。一份會在交接人手上，一份在被交接人手上。本範例僅列出被交接人的部分。另一份文件的內容與範例皆相同，唯一差別在於簽名。當交接方與被交接方皆完成簽署，代表交接程序已經完成。

Unit 01
Unit 02
Unit 03
Unit 04
Unit 05
Unit 06
Unit 07
Unit 08
Unit 09
Unit 10
Unit 11

 現在你會說 ||||||||||||||||||||||||||||||||||||

請依句意填入 A-E。

A. This lecture is about our system
B. What should I do if I forget to update the information
C. And then, choose option one to update user information
D. What to do next
E. Mr. Jason, now I will start the employee training

Emily：I will start the practice now. ____1____.

Jason：I will concentrate on yours words.

Emily：Before you enter this system, you need to key in the account and password you just get. ____2____. It may take you few minutes, so I will stop here and let you start the practice.

Jason：____3____?

Emily：You can key in all the information by yourself. It takes more time, so please memorize this process.

Jason：I got it. ____4____?

Mary：Choose option three for practice. You need to check the detail of a deal and find the mistake to finish this practice.

Jason：____5____.

答案

1. (E)　2. (C)　3. (B)　4. (D)　5. (A)

 現在你會寫 ||||||||||||||||||||||||||||||||||||

1.在繳交報告之前,請你檢查一下細節。

_____

_____

中式英文出沒 ▶ Before submit the report, please you check the detail.

錯在哪 ▶ 此句的時間分界落在 submit the report,因此 you 應調整位置,移往 before 之後,方為正確用法。

正解 ▶ Before you submit the report, please check the detail.

2.為了熟悉業務,所以我問了好幾個問題。

_____

_____

中式英文出沒 ▶ To get familiar with my duty, so I ask many questions.

錯在哪 ▶ 將 to v 移到句首是為了強調目的,因此若將其還原正常句型置於 I ask many questions 之後,就會發現其實 so 是受到中文影響而多加上去的。

正解 ▶ To get familiar with my duty, I asked many questions。

Unit 01
Unit 02
Unit 03
Unit 04
Unit 05
Unit 06
Unit 07
Unit 08
Unit 09
Unit 10
Unit 11

電話聯絡

挑戰難度 ★★☆☆☆

真的你學過

在職場上，電話聯絡是基本的技能之一，卻也是許多人的夢魘。許多平常敢開口說英文的人，一接起電話卻是手足無措。會產生這樣的落差，往往是因為擔心自己沒聽清楚或沒聽懂，可能給予對方錯誤回應。但事實上，只要掌握電話用語的常用基本句型，加上有效的訊息記錄方式，用英語講電話不再是件令人害怕的事。

單元重點及學習方向

❶ 學會如何運用 would like 表達請求。
❷ 學會如何運用助動詞 can/could 表達請求。
❸ 學會如何運用動詞 let 表達請求。
❹ 應用本單元之字彙、片語與句型練習電話英語。

必 **check** 句型 ||||||||||||||||||||||||||||||

1. I **would like** to speak to Mr. Lin.
   我想跟林先生講電話。
2. **Can** I ask how to spell your name?
   請問如何拼您的大名呢？
3. **Could** you repeat your number for?
   能再重複一次您的電話號碼嗎？
4. **Let** me confirm your message again.
   讓我再次確認您的留言內容。

 你有學過的單字 ||||||||||||||||||||||||||||||

1. **connection** [kə`nɛkʃən] *n.* 收訊
2. **number** [`nʌmbɚ] *n.* 號碼
3. **name** [nem] *n.* 名字
4. **set** [sɛt] *v.* 安排
5. **spell** [spɛl] *v.* 用字母拼寫
6. **take** [tek] *v.* 執行（…的動作）
7. **leave** [liv] *v.* 留下
8. **repeat** [rɪ`pit] *v.* 重複
9. **reconfirm** [ˌrikən`fɝm] *v.* 再確認
10. **poor** [pʊr] *adj.* 不良的

Unit
01

Unit
02

Unit
03

Unit
04

Unit
05

Unit
06

Unit
07

Unit
08

Unit
09

Unit
10

Unit
11

小試身手

1. The _____ is really bad. Could you say it again?

   收訊非常不好，可以請你再說一遍嗎？

2. May I ask how to _____ your name?

   請問如何拼您的大名呢？

3. Let me _____ your message.

   讓我再次確認您的留言內容。

4. Would you like to _____ a message?

   您要留言嗎？

5. May I _____ you message?

   需要我幫您留言嗎？

解答

1. connection
2. spell
3. reconfirm
4. leave
5. take

句型喚醒你的記憶 ||||||||||||||||||||||||||||||||||||||||

1. **I would like** to set a date for the department meeting.
   我想要安排部門會議的時間。
   Would like 意思為「想要…」，可用於表達意願。
   例 I would like to call Jason to confirm the detail.
   我想打電話給 Jason 確認細節。

2. **Could you** repeat the number you just said?
   能再重複剛剛你所說的號碼嗎？
   Could 意思為「能夠…」，語氣上較為禮貌，故適用於許多正式場合。
   例 Could you pass along my message to Jason?
   能夠請你幫我把這些訊息傳達給 Jason 嗎？

3. **Can I** take a message for you?
   要我替您傳達訊息嗎？
   Can 意思為「能夠…」，雖然在語氣不如 could 禮貌。但仍適用於多數正式場合。
   例 Can you send me the report by tomorrow?
   能夠請你在明天之前把報告寄給我嗎？

4. **Let me** reconfirm your message.
   讓我再次跟你確認留言內容。
   Let 意思為「讓…」，可用於表達下一步動作的進行。
   例 Let me check the detail of this report.
   讓我檢查一下這份報告的細節。

Unit 01

Unit 02

Unit 03

Unit 04

Unit 05

Unit 06

Unit 07

Unit 08

Unit 09

Unit 10

Unit 11

知多少？多知道一點總是好 ||||||||||||||||||||||||||||||||

　　一般的電話聯絡，對象可能是自己的朋友或是家人，在用字或是語氣上不必太拘謹。但英文商務電話屬於公務用途，因此撥打或接聽應當注意以下的要點與禁忌，方可避免出糗：

不可不知的要點 ||||||||||||||||||||||||||||||||

1.專注於來電者。
2.主動表明身分。
3.確認對方是否有時間接聽。
4.善用語音信箱。

不可不知的禁忌

1. 要求特別待遇。
2. 讓對方空等。
3. 於非上班時間撥打商務電話（跨時區或是緊急情況除外）。
4. 擱置所接收訊息未加以轉達。

　　另外，接聽電話時有時需要同步將對方所傳達的訊息記錄下來，以便轉達給相關人員。此時如何篩選與整理資訊就是一門學問，把握以下的原則，方可有效記錄資訊：

1. 標注來電時間與來電人員姓名與公司名。
2. 寫下欲傳達事件的參與人員、時間、地點。
3. 若有多個事件，以事件做區分。
4. 善用箭號標明從屬或順序。

　　若能按照上述要點記錄電話內容，不論是以筆記或口頭方式轉述，都可以清楚表達此通電話是於何時由何公司的何人所打來，傳達了哪些訊息，以及各訊息間的關聯性。

Unit 01
Unit 02
Unit 03
Unit 04
Unit 05
Unit 06
Unit 07
Unit 08
Unit 09
Unit 10
Unit 11

腦部暖身 一點都不難對話 ||||||||||||||||||||||||||

請將以下六個單字填入空格內。

(a) spell   (b) certainly   (c) pass along

(d) voicemail   (e) returns   (f) reached

Jason：Good morning, you have _____1_____ ABC Company. This is Jason speaking. How may I help you?

Kartivana：Good morning, **I'd like to** talk to Kelly Wang.

Jason：She is away from her desk at the moment. May I take your message or **would you like** to leave her a _____2_____.

Kartivana：**Let** me give you a message. This is Kartivana from DEF Company. I want to discuss the project starting next week.

Jason：OK **Can I ask** how to _____3_____ you name, please?

Kartivana：Of course, it's K-A-R-T-I-V-A-N-A, K as in King.

Jason：Thanks. And your number, please?

Kartivana：It is (045) 558-6213. Please ask her to call back soon.

Jason：_____4_____. To confirm, this is Kartivana of DEF Company at (045) 558-6213, and you want to talk about the project starting next week, correct?

Kartivana：That's it. Thank you.

Jason：I will _____5_____ this message when Ms. Kelly _____6_____.

翻譯

Jason：早安，這裡是 ABC 公司的辦公室，我是 Jason，請問您有什麼需要呢？

Kartivana：早安，麻煩請 Kelly 女士接電話。

Jason： Kelly 女士目前不在座位上，要我幫您留言，還是您要語音留言？

Kartivana： 麻煩你留個口信給她。我是 DEF 公司的 Kartivana，想要找她討論下週開始的專案計畫。

Jason： 沒問題，可以請教您的大名怎麼拼嗎？

Kartivana： 當然，K-A-R-T-I-V-A-N-A。K 是 King 的 K。

Jason： 謝謝。麻煩也請告訴我您的電話號碼好嗎？

Kartivana： 電話是（045）558-6213，請轉告她盡快回電。

Jason： 一定會的。再跟您確認一下，您是 DEF 公司的 Kartivana，電話是（045）558-6216，要討論下週的專案計畫，對嗎？

Kartivana： 沒錯，謝謝。

Jason： 等到 Kelly 女士一回來，我就馬上替您轉達。

單字

- **be away from** [bɪəˈwefrɑm] *ph.* 遠離
- **take a message** [tekəˈmɛsɪdʒ] *ph.* 替…留言
- **give sba message** [gɪvəˈmɛsɪdʒ] *ph.* 留言給…
- **correct** [kəˈrɛkt] *adj.* 正確的

答案

1. (f)　2. (d)　3. (a)　4. (b)　5. (c)　6. (e)

Unit 01　Unit 02　Unit 03　Unit 04　Unit 05　Unit 06　Unit 07　Unit 08　Unit 09　Unit 10　Unit 11

會說也會寫一：如何記錄關於單一事件之來電

Now is about **❶**3 pm. You just answered a call.

Mary：This is **❷**Mary from ABC Company, may I speak to Mark?

Jason：This is Jason speaking. Mark is in a meeting right now. May I take your message?

Mary：Let me give you a message. **❸**Our company has a new project in Japan, and we want to discuss the details face to face with Mark next week. We will be available next Monday morning, Tuesday afternoon, and Friday morning. Please tell Mark to call back after he checks his schedule. If we have no time to meet this week, I will change my schedule.

Jason：I will pass on this message to Mark.

Mary：Thank you.

翻譯

現在時間約下午三點，你接到一通來電。

Mary：我是 ABC 公司的 Mary，能請 Mark 接電話嗎？

Jason：您好，我是 Jason，Mark 目前正在開會，需要我替您留言嗎？

Mary：請幫我傳達以下訊息：我們公司在日本有一項新的專案計畫想於下週與 Mark 面對面討論細節。我們有空的時間是星期一早上、星期二下午與星期五早上。請 Mark 確認過他的行程後回電給我們。如時間皆無法配合，我會更動我這邊的行程來配合 Mark。

Jason：我會把此訊息傳達給他。

Mary：謝謝。

解析 |||||||||||||||||||||||||||||||||||||||||||||||||||||||||

範例中包含以下幾個重要訊息：

1. 來電時間：3 pm
2. 來電者身分：Mary from ABC Company
3. 事件：discuss the details of the new project in Japan with Mark

　　若要以文字記錄的方式將訊息傳達給 Mark，可參考以下範例：

To: Mark
When: 3 pm
Who: Mary from ABC Company

Message
Title: The discussion of the new project in Japan next week
Details:

1. Our available time: Monday morning, Tuesday afternoon, and Friday morning.
2. Please call back after check your schedule.
3. We can change our schedule for this meeting.

　　上述範例清楚標示來電時間與來電人身分，並以重點方式記錄訊息，可讓接受訊息的人很快理解內容，做出適當回覆。

Unit 01
Unit 02
Unit 03
Unit 04
Unit 05
Unit 06
Unit 07
Unit 08
Unit 09
Unit 10
Unit 11

會說也會寫二：如何記錄關於多個事件之來電 ||||||

Now is about ❶10 am, and Jason is answering a call.

Hanks：This is ❷Hanks from DEF Company. Is Mr. Nicklaus free to talk now?

Jason：This is Jason specking. Mr. Nicklaus is not in the office this morning. Do you want to leave a message?

Hanks：Please pass on the following messages to him: ❸I have three things needed to discuss with Nicklaus. The first one is the new project in China. We need to check some details. The second one is the date of our monthly meeting. We need to find the time when both of us are free. The third one is also about the monthly meeting. We have to decide the place of this meeting.

Jason：I will inform Nicklaus when he comes back.

Hanks：Thank you

翻譯

現在約上午十點，你接到一通來電。

Hanks：您好，我是 DEF 公司的 Hanks，能請 Nicklaus 接電話嗎？

Jason：Nicklaus 今天早上不會進公司，您要留言嗎？

Hanks：請幫我傳達以下訊息：我有三件事要跟他討論。第一件事情是關於在中國的新專案，我們需要討論細節。第二件是關於月會，我們需要找出彼此都有空的時間，第三件也是關於月會，要決定月會在哪邊舉行。

Jason：等他進公司我會把訊息傳達給他。

Hanks：謝謝。

解析 ||||||||||||||||||||||||||||||||||||||||||||

Unit
01

Unit
02

Unit
03

Unit
04

Unit
05

Unit
06

Unit
07

Unit
08

Unit
09

Unit
10

Unit
11

範例中包含以下幾個重要訊息：

❶來電時間：10 am

❷來電者身分：Hanks from DEF Company

❸事件：(1) new project in China

　　　　(2) monthly meeting

　　若要以文字紀錄的方式將訊息傳達給 Mark，可參考以下範例：

> To: Nicklaus
> When: 3 pm
> Who: Hanks from ABC Company
>
> Message
> Title 1: the new project in China
> Details: the discussion of the details
>
> Title 2: monthly meeting
> Details: find the time we are available
> 　　　　decide place of this meeting

　　上述範例清楚標示來電時間與來電人身分，並以重點方式記錄訊息，可讓接受訊息的人很快理解內容，做出適當回覆。

 現在你會說 ||||||||||||||||||||||||||||||||||||||||||||||

請依句意填入 A-E。

A. I will pass on this message when Emily returns

B. May I take a message or would you like her voicemail

C. Please ask her to call back soon

D. Can I ask how to spell you name, please

E. Good morning, you have reached ABC Company

Jason：_____1_____. This is Jason speaking. How may I help you?

Kartivana：Good morning, I'd like to talk to Emily.

Jason：She is not in the office at the moment. _____2_____.

Kartivana：Let me give you a message. This is Kartivana from DEF Company. I want to discuss the project starting next week

Jason：OK... _____3_____?

Kartivana：Of course, it's K-A-R-T-I-V-A-N-A, K as in King.

Jason：Thanks. And your number, please?

Kartivana：It is (045) 558-6213. _____4_____.

Jason：Certainly. To confirm, this is Kartivana of DEF Company at (009) 555-4321, and you want to talk about the project next week, correct?

Kartivana：That's it. Thank you.

Jason：_____5_____.

答案 ....

1. (E)　2. (B)　3. (D)　4. (C)　5. (A)

現在你會寫

1. 能請你再重複一次您的電話號碼嗎？

_____

_____

中式英文出沒 Could you repeat you phone number again？

錯在哪 repeat 即有重複之意，若受中文影響，加上 again 來表達再一次之意，反而使句子累贅。

正解 Could you repeat your phone number?

2. 請讓我來確認一下這次會議的時間與地點。

_____

_____

中式英文出沒 Let me to check the place and date of this meeting

錯在哪 let ＋ 主詞其後應加上原形動詞 v，若受到中文的「來」影響，使用 to v，便形成文法錯誤。

正解 Let me check the place and date of this meeting.

Unit 01
Unit 02
Unit 03
Unit 04
Unit 05
Unit 06
Unit 07
Unit 08
Unit 09
Unit 10
Unit 11

Part 2

面對客戶

05 Unit 客戶聯繫

挑戰難度 ★★★☆☆

真的你學過

　　了解如何接聽電話後，接下來公司可能就會指派你聯絡外國客戶。聯絡客戶時經常需要與其多次重複確認行程，許多人會擔心經過如此頻繁的訊息往來，可能會有訊息接受錯誤的情況發生。但事實上，只要善用英文中的疑問句，就能讓對方傳達給你的訊息具有條理性。再透過對照自身行程，就可做出有效的行程安排。

單元重點及學習方向

❶ 運用 which 開頭的疑問句請對方從中做出選擇。
❷ 運用 when 開頭的疑問句請對方挑選時間。
❸ 運用 prefer 與 better 請對方從選項中做出決定。
❹ 運用本單元的單字、片語與句型來練習如何聯絡客戶並安排與確認行程。

 **必 check 句型** ||||||||||||||||||||||||||||||||||||

1. **Which** date is **better** for you?
   你比較偏好哪個時間？
2. **When** will you be available?
   你何時有空？
3. **Which** place do you **prefer**, Hotel A or B?
   你比較想選擇 A 飯店還是 B 飯店？
4. I **prefer** to have a meeting in the conference room with the round table.
   我偏好在有圓桌的會議室裡開會。

 你有學過的單字 |||||||||||||||||||||||||||||||||||

1. **adjust** [əˋdʒʌst] *v.* 調整
2. **arrange** [əˋrendʒ] *v.* 安排
3. **clarify** [ˋklærəˏfaɪ] *v.* 釐清
4. **choice** [tʃɔɪs] *n.* 選擇
5. **check** [tʃɛk] *v.* 檢查
6. **list** [lɪst] *v.* 列出
7. **spare** [spɛr] *v.* 分出
8. **option** [ˋɑpʃən] *n.* 選項
9. **schedule** [ˋskɛdʒʊl] *n.* 行事曆
10. **postpone** [postˋpon] *n.* 延後

Unit 01
Unit 02
Unit 03
Unit 04
Unit 05
Unit 06
Unit 07
Unit 08
Unit 09
Unit 10
Unit 11

小試身手

1. We need to _____ the date of the meeting.

   我們必須調整會議日期。

2. I _____ some time to check the details with my team members.

   我安排一些時間跟成員們檢查細節。

3. Next Monday is not a good _____ for this meeting

   下週一不適合開會。

5. Please _____ the time you are free.

   請列出你有空的時間。

6. My schedule is full, so I have to _____ this business trip.

   我的行程太滿了，所以必須延後出差。

解答

1. adjust
2. arranged
3. option
4. list
5. postpone

句型喚醒你的記憶 |||||||||||||||||||||||||||||||||||

Unit
01
Unit
02
Unit
03
Unit
04
Unit
05
Unit
06
Unit
07
Unit
08
Unit
09
Unit
10
Unit
11

1. **Which** place is **better** for this monthly meeting?

哪個場地比較適合本次月會呢？

Which... is better 意思為「哪個比較好」，讓對方從兩個選項中挑出他／她喜歡的那個。

例 Which team is better for this project? 哪個團隊比較適合此專案？

2. **When** will you be in your office?

你何時會在辦公室？

When 意思為「何時」，用於詢問對方時間。其回答會是一個時間點或是時段，例如 after 3 pm。

例 When will you return this report? 你何時會將此報告寄回？

3. **Which** time do you **prefer**, 9:00 or 13:00?

你比較偏好上午九點還是下午一點呢？

Which... do you prefer 意思為「你比較偏好…」，用於讓對方從多個選項中做出選擇。

例 Which hotel do you prefer to live in this list?

你比較偏好住清單中所列的飯店的哪一間？

4. **I prefer to** check the details of the report with my team members.

我偏好與我的小組成員一同檢查報告細節。

I prefer to...意思為「我比較偏好…」，可用於表示自己的對多個選項所做出的選擇。

例 I prefer to have the meeting in the morning. 我偏好早上開會。

知多少？多知道一點總是好 ||||||||||||||||||||||||||||||||

　　聯絡客戶的主要目的就是與其討論與確認某些事項，其中行程的確認是經常需要做的。由於我們自己與對方可能都已安排好未來一週或甚至一個月的行程，因此當彼此需要碰面時，就必須對照行程表，找出大家都有空的時間。甚至當雙方無法找出共同的空閒時間時，有一方就必須更動自己的行程。為了要讓這樣討論更具效率，在安排行程應注意以下要點與禁忌：

不可不知的要點 ||||||||||||||||||||||||||||||||||||||||

1. 明確列出自己的可行時間：選項越多越好安排。
2. 仔細詢問對方的可行時間：選項越多越好安排。
3. 善用表格、行事曆、軟體等輔助工具進行資訊的對照：可以快速進行對照、做出最佳安排。

不可不知的禁忌

1. 行程未保留彈性調整的空間：遇到突發狀況時將可能會無法進行臨時應變，整個行程接受影響。

2. 未給予對方充足的回應時間：處理訊息需要一定的時間，太過倉促容易忙中有錯。

3. 多次變更時段：會讓對方無所適從，且同時留下壞印象。

　　若在安排行程時能把握上述要點中的第一與第二點，方可快速列出雙方的資訊，再透過輔助工具來對照並檢查資訊，方可做出安排，讓我方與對方可以及早將其列入行程表內。

Unit
01

Unit
02

Unit
03

Unit
04

Unit
05

Unit
06

Unit
07

Unit
08

Unit
09

Unit
10

Unit
11

請將以下六個單字填入空格內。

(a) immediately   (b) works   (c) book

(d) open   (e) prefer   (f) ahead

Jason： I think we need to sit down face to face before we move
_____1_____ on the details of this project.

Andy： Agree. Have you got a free minute this week?

Jason： Let me check my schedule. It looks like I can **do** on
Tuesday morning and Friday afternoon. **Which**
_____2_____ for you?

Andy： Tuesday is out for me because I have a business trip to
Hong Kong on that day, and I will come back to Taiwan
on Wednesday. Friday is a good **option** for me. The
morning is wide _____3_____ .

Jason： **When** can we start the meeting in that morning?

Andy： How does eight o'clock **sound**? Or you _____4_____ a
later time?

Jason： Eight is great. I'll _____5_____ the conference room
before I leave the office today.

Andy： **Terrific**. I will inform the rest of the team members
_____6_____ through e-mail.

翻譯

Jason：我想我們得先面對面坐下來好好談談，才能繼續此專案的細節。

Andy：我也同意，你這週可以撥出一點時間嗎？

Jason：讓我查一下行事曆，我好像星期二跟星期五有時間，這兩天您可
以嗎？

Andy：星期二我不行，那天我出差到香港，星期三才回國。星期五可以，我整個早上都有空。

Jason：我們那天早上早點要碰面呢？

Andy：你看八點鐘如何？或是你想要再晚一點？

Jason：八點很好，我今天下班離開辦公室前會先訂好會議室。

Andy：好極了，我會用 e-mail 立即通知專案的其他同仁。

單字

- **do** [du] *v.* 適合
- **option** [`ɑpʃən] *n.* 選項
- **sound** [saʊnd] *v.* 聽起來
- **terrific** [tə`rɪfɪk] *adj.* 非常好的

Unit
01

Unit
02

Unit
03

Unit
04

Unit
05

Unit
06

Unit
07

Unit
08

Unit
09

Unit
10

Unit
11

答案

1. (f)　2. (b)　3. (d)　4. (e)　5. (c)　6. (a)

會說也會寫一：善用行事曆規劃行程

Jason：I think we need to meet face to face before we move ahead on this project.

Andy：Agree. Have you got a free minute this week?

Jason：Let me check my schedule through my i-Pad. It looks like I can do on Tuesday morning, Thursday afternoon and Friday afternoon. Which works for you?

Andy：Thursday is out for me because I will be in Hong Kong on that day. Tuesday could work, but I need to reconfirm the schedule with my sesretary. Friday is a good option for me.

Jason：Friday seems to be the best choice for us. When can we start the meeting in that afternoon?

Andy：How does two o'clock sound? Or do you have other preferences?

Jason：Two is great. I'll book the conference room before I leave the office today.

Andy：Terrific. See you them

翻譯

Jason：專案繼續進行之前，我想我們需要面對面談談。

Andy：同意。你這週有空嗎？

Jason：讓我用i-Pad來看看我的行程表。看來我星期二早上、星期四下午與星期五下午有空。這三個時段哪個你有空？

Andy：星期四沒空，我那天人在香港。星期二早上也許可以，但我要再跟秘書同事確認。星期五確定可以。

Jason：看來星期五下午是最恰當的時間。我們要約下午幾點呢？

Andy：兩點如何，或是您有偏好的時間？

Jason：兩點好了，我下班前會預定會議室。

Andy：太棒了，到時候見。

 解析

此段對談的主題要進行安排會面，因此我們可以在談話的同時，透過週計畫表（紙本或是運用手機、電腦內的行事曆功能）來記錄雙方可行的時段，從中找出適合的時間。記錄方式可參考以下之範例：

Your（Jason's）weekly schedule:

	Mon	Tues	Wed	Thurs	Fri
Morning	Meeting（with Erik）	**Andy might be free**	Project discussion	Product release	Project Meeting
Afternoon		Visit customer	Visit Customer		**Andy is free**

從這張行事曆中，可以清楚看星期五下午是唯一已確定可行的會面時間，因此雙方最後選擇這個時段。

由於此範例僅一位對象確認時間，這種對照所產生的效果可能不太明顯，但當你是與多位對象商討會面時間，這種資料彙整方式就能省去你非常多的資料整理時間，並讓你能夠立刻和對方討論是否需要變更行程。

會說也會寫二：如何利用行事曆確認行程 ||||||||||

Jason：I think we need to confirm the date of the monthly meeting next week today.

Paul：Totally agree.

Jason：Let me check my schedule first. It seems my schedule is full on next Monday and Thursday. I will be available on the remaining three days.

Paul：I am free on Monday, Tuesday, and Friday. It seems Friday is a good option for us.

Paul：We have to check Andy's schedule, too. As he told me, he will be free on Friday only. He will be on a business trip to Japan in the rest four days.

Jason：Great. Friday is the best choice for all. I'll book the conference room before I leave today.

Paul：See you all at that time.

翻譯

Jason：我想我們需要確認月會要在下星期幾舉行？

Paul：完全同意。

Jason：讓我先看看我自己的行程表。看來我只有星期一與星期二行程全滿，其他三天都有空。

Paul：我是星期一、星期二與星期五有空。這樣看來星期五是個合適的選項。我們也需要確認一下 Andy 的行程。如同他告訴我的，他只有星期五有空，其他四天他在日本出差。

Jason：太好了，星期五是我們的最佳選擇。我下班前會先去預訂會議室。

Paul：到時候見了。

解析

此段對談的主題要進行安排會面，因此我們可以在談話的同時，透過週計畫表（紙本或是運用手機、電腦內的行事曆功能）來記錄雙方可行的時段，從中找出適合的時間。紀錄方式可參考以下之範例：

Your（Jason） weekly schedule:

	Mon	Tues	Wednes.	Thurs.	Fri.
Morning	Meeting (with Erik)	Meeting With Jenny **Paul is free**		Product release	**Andy is free. Paul is free**
Afternoon	Meeting (with Sam)	Project Meeting **Paul is free**		Project Meeting	**Andy is free. Paul is free**

從這張行事曆中，可以清楚看星期五下午是唯一三人都可行的會面時間，因此雙方最後選擇這個時段。

另外，由於是與多位對象商討會面時間，這種資料彙整方式能幫你省去非常多的資料整理時間，從中找出大家都可以的時段。

Unit 01
Unit 02
Unit 03
Unit 04
Unit 05
Unit 06
Unit 07
Unit 08
Unit 09
Unit 10
Unit 11

83

現在你會說

請依句意填入 A-E。

A. My schedule is too full to spare some time for a meeting this week

B. Do you think 2 pm is a good choice

C. I'll book the conference room before I leave today

D. Tuesday is not a good option for me

E. I think we need to arrange a meeting to continue our discussion

Jason：＿＿＿＿1＿＿＿＿.

  Paul：Totally agree. Have you got a free minute this week?

Jason：Let me check my schedule. ＿＿＿2＿＿＿.

  Paul：That's alright. We can postpone this meeting to next week. I am free on Tuesday morning and Friday afternoon.

Jason：＿＿＿3＿＿＿ because I have to host a product release. Friday is good enough, and I am wide open on that day.

  Paul：I will drop by your company right after my lunch time next Friday, so ＿＿＿4＿＿＿?

Jason：Two is great. ＿＿＿5＿＿＿.

  Paul：Terrific. See you at that time.

答案

1. (E)   2. (A)   3. (D)   4. (B)   5. (C)

 **現在你會寫**

1. 對你來説，星期一和星期五哪一天好？

_____

_____

中式英文出沒 ▶ Which day is good for you, Monday or Friday?

錯在哪 ▶ 此處 Which 問句是希望對方從兩個選項中擇一，因此
形容詞應使用比較級，故應把 good 改成 better。

正解 ▶ Which day is better for you, Monday or Friday?

2. 我和 Paul 的報告，你比較喜歡哪一份？

_____

_____

中式英文出沒 ▶ Which report do you prefer more, mine or
Paul's?

錯在哪 ▶ prefer 已有比較之意，此處受到中文影響，加上了比
較級 more，反而使語意累贅。

正解 ▶ Which report do you prefer, mine or Paul's?

Unit 01
Unit 02
Unit 03
Unit 04
Unit 05
Unit 06
Unit 07
Unit 08
Unit 09
Unit 10
Unit 11

06 Unit 準備會面

挑戰難度 ★★★☆☆

 **真的你學過** ||||||||||||||||||||||||||||||||||

　　聯絡客戶後安排行程後，接下來就是在雙方所約定的時間碰面之前做最後的確認。透過這道程序，雙方對於行程的變更都能有足夠的應變時間。但因為當中包含大量訊息交換，有時會讓許多人感到頭痛。但事實上，只要透過問句分類詢問，就可以快速且有效地完成行前確認。

單元重點及學習方向 |||||||||||||||||||||||||||||||||||

❶ 運用 When will you... 句型詢問行程。

❷ 運用 If you want to..., please (let)... 句型詢問是否變更行程。

❸ 運用 Let's meet at... 句型與對方約定碰面地點。

❹ 應用本單元之字彙、片語與句型練習如何與客戶碰面與接待客戶。

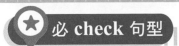 必 **check** 句型 ||||||||||||||||||||||||||||||||||||||||||||

1. **When will you** arrive in Taiwan?
   您會於何時抵台?

2. **If you want to** change the date of the meeting, **please** inform me.
   如果你想變更開會日期,請告知我。

3. **If you want to** cancel next week's meeting, please let me know in advance.
   如果你想取消下週會議,請提早告知我。

4. **Let's meet at** the lobby of the airport.
   讓我們在機場大廳碰面。

 你有學過的單字 ||||||||||||||||||||||||||||||||||||||||||||

1. **arrival** [ə`raɪvl] *n.* 抵達
2. **breakdown** [`brek͵daʊn] *n.* 故障
3. **cancel** [`kænsl̩] *v.* 取消
4. **departure** [dɪ`partʃɚ] *n.* 離開
5. **delay** [dɪ`le] *v.* 延遲
6. **flight** [flaɪt] *n.* 班機
7. **postpone** [post`pon] *v.* 延後
8. **trafic** [`træfɪk] *n.* 交通
9. **transfer** [træns`fɚ] *v.* 轉機
10. **transport** [`træns͵pɔrt] *n.* 交通

Unit 01
Unit 02
Unit 03
Unit 04
Unit 05
Unit 06
Unit 07
Unit 08
Unit 09
Unit 10
Unit 11

小試身手

1. If you want to _____ this meeting, please let me know.
   若您想取消本次會議，請告知我。

2. My _____ is cancelled due to the bad weather.
   我的班機因天候不佳而取消了。

3. I will _____ in Tokyo.
   我將於東京轉機。

4. My estimated _____ time is 4:30 PM.
   我預計於下午 4 點 30 分離開。

5. The _____ is good in Taipei.
   台北的交通系統很完善。

解答

1. cancel
2. flight
3. transfer
4. departure
5. transport

句型喚醒你的記憶

Unit
01

Unit
02

Unit
03

Unit
04

Unit
05

Unit
06

Unit
07

Unit
08

Unit
09

Unit
10

Unit
11

1. **When will you** leave Taiwan?

   你何時離台呢？

   When will you... 意思為「你何時…」，可用於詢問對方行程。

   例 When will you meet Mr. Huang? 你何時會與黃經理碰面？

2. **If you** want to postpone the meeting to next week, **please** notify me in advance.

   如果你想把會議延後到下週舉行，請先通知我。

   If you..., please.... 意思為「如果你…，請…」，可用於詢問對方是否針對行程進行變更。

   例 If you want to add one more topic to this meeting, please inform the rest team members.如果你想在本會議中增加討論主題，請通知其他成員。

3. **If you** want to have a brief discussion before the next week's meeting, **please let** Mary and I know.

   如果你想在下週會議前先進行一次討論，請告知我和 **Mary**。

   If you...., please let... 意思為「如果你…，請讓…」，可用於詢問對方是否變更行程，並規定其後續處理/通知方式。

   例 If you want to cancel this meeting, please let me know. 若你想取消本次會議，請先讓我知道此消息。

4. **Let's meet at** the exit of the train station.

   讓我們約在車站出口碰面。

   Let's meet at... 意思為「讓我們約在…碰面」，可用於與對方確認會面地點。

   例 Let's meet at the exit of this building. 讓我們約在此棟建築物的出口碰面。

知多少？多知道一點總是好 ▌▌▌▌▌▌▌▌▌▌▌▌▌▌▌▌▌▌▌▌▌▌▌▌▌▌

　　行前確認的目的有二，一是為了檢視既定行程是否可行，二是讓雙方有時間應變臨時變更。若能把握以下的要點，避開下列之禁忌，將可快速且有效地完成確認：

不可不知的要點 ▌▌▌▌▌▌▌▌▌▌▌▌▌▌▌▌▌▌▌▌▌▌▌▌▌▌▌▌▌▌

1. 掌握抵達與離開時間：

   確認上述兩個時間是行前確認最重要的部分。一旦這兩個時間有所變更，將會牽動所有行程的安排。

2. 按事件或人員進行分項：

   行程確認的細項可能非常多而繁雜，一次確認同類型項目可避免重複或是遺漏，例如先行確認所有參加專案會議人員行程，確認無誤後再行檢視其他部分。

3. 保留彈性與提供備案：

   當班機有所延誤時，客戶抵台的時間可能延後數小時甚至是一天，因此確認行程時，應包含可運用之彈性時間範圍，以及交通或不可抗力因素，好讓既定行程無法進行時，雙方能有其他替代方案選擇。

不可不知的禁忌

1. 未預留應變時間處理變更需要連繫時間，因此不論是我方或對方要調整行程，都應提早告知，以利對方進行應變。

2. 變換連繫窗口訊息傳達越多次，就越容易產生誤差或是遺漏，因此進行行程確認最好維持單一窗口，以避免訊息傳達錯誤。

腦部暖身 一點都不難對話 |||||||||||||||||||||||||||

請將以下六個單字填入空格內。

(a) estimated   (b) pass   (c) lunch

(d) marketing   (e) reconfirm   (f) restaurant

Jason：Before you visit Taiwan, could I ___1___ the schedule with you?

Ken：Of course. Let's begin the arrival time of my flight.

Jason：You will take China Airline from San Francisco. The flight number is TW1205 and ___2___ to land in Taiwan at 10 AM this Monday.

Ken：Correct. It may take me another 30 minutes to ___3___ the Customs, so could we meet in the lobby at 10: 30 AM.?

Jason：I got it. Since your arrival time will soon be ___4___ time, we will pick you up to the ___5___ after we meet.

Ken：Thanks a lot.

Jason：Secondly, let's reconfirm the time of the meeting with our partners. This meeting is scheduled to be held in our conference room at 1 PM. Right?

Ken：Right.

Jason：Let's check the last schedule. You will have a project discussion with our ___6___ team at 4 PM.

翻譯

Jason：在您訪台之前，能與您再次確認行程嗎？

Ken：當然可以。讓我們先從班機抵達時間開始吧！

Jason：您將搭乘華航編號 TW1205 班機於舊金山起飛，預計於本週一上午十點抵台。

Ken：沒錯。過海關可能要再花個 30 分鐘，所以我們可以約 10 點半在機場大廳碰面。

Jason：了解。由於您的抵達時間接近中午，與您碰面後會直接載您前往餐廳一同用餐。

Ken：非常感謝。

Jason：接下來，讓我們確認與合作夥伴開會的時間。這個會議訂在下午一點於本公司會議室舉行。

Ken：沒錯。

Jason：再來確認最後一個行程，你將於下午四點與本公司的行銷團隊進行專案計畫的討論。

單字 ....

- **land** [lænd] *v.* 降落
- **Customs** [ˋkʌstəmz] *n.* 海關
- **lobby** [ˋlɑbɪ] *n.* 大廳
- **partner** [ˋpɑrtnɚ] *n.* 夥伴

Unit
01

Unit
02

Unit
03

Unit
04

Unit
05

Unit
06

Unit
07

Unit
08

Unit
09

Unit
10

Unit
11

答案 ....

1. (e)　2. (a)　3. (b)　4. (c)　5. (f)　6. (d)

會說也會寫一：行程表撰寫 |||||||||||||||||||||||

How to write a schedule:
1. The date: March 1, 2014
2. The time: 9 AM—11 AM
3. Activity: Meeting with ABC Company
4. The participants: Jason, Mark, Leo
5. Descriptions: about new product
6. Notes: bring iPad

Example:

Date: March 1, 2014

Time	Activity	Participant	Description	Notes
9-11	Meeting with ABC Company	Jason, Mark, Leo	About new product	bring iPad
11-12	Meet James	Jason	Project meeting	

翻譯

如何撰寫行程表
1. 日期：2014 年 3 月 1 日
2. 時間：9 點-11 點
3. 行程：與 ABC 公司開會
4. 參加人員：Jason, Mark, Leo
5. 簡述：關於新產品
6. 附註：帶 iPad

範例

日期：2014 年 3 月 1 日

時間	行程	參與人員	簡述	附註
9-11	與 ABC 公司開會	Jason, Mark, Leo	關於新產品	帶 iPad
11-12	與 James 碰面	Jason	專案會議	

 解析 ||||||||||||||||||||||||||||||||||||||||||||||||||

　　本範例行程表共包含以下六個部分，各部分可達到不同的提醒作用。以下針對其作用做進一步說明：

1. 日期：2014 年 3 月 1 日。

　可用於區分每日行程，避免標註錯誤。

2. 時間：9 點-11 點。

　列出各行程時間後，方可看出空檔時間有哪些。

3. 行程：與 ABC 公司開會。

　可提醒自己是否需要移動地點。

4. 參加人員：Jason、Mark、Leo。

　列出參加人員可達相互提醒之效。

5. 簡述：關於新產品。

　說明此行程的重點為何。

6. 附註：帶 iPad。

　可用於提醒應攜帶物品。

　　本範例因篇幅限制，僅列出上午的行程來加以說明，實際使用時應包含下午與晚上時段。以下提供空白參考範例：

Time	Activity	Participant	Description	Notes
9-11				
11-12				
13-15				
16-18				
17-20				
21-22				

Unit 01
Unit 02
Unit 03
Unit 04
Unit 05
Unit 06
Unit 07
Unit 08
Unit 09
Unit 10
Unit 11

會說也會寫二：因應變更，調整既有行程表

How to adjust the schedule and have a revised version:

Example: Dennis wants to meet Jason at 10 AM.

Jason's schedule:

Time	Activity	Participant	Description	Notes
8-10	Meeting with ABC Company	Jason, Mark, Leo	About new product	bring iPad
10-12	Meet James	Jason	Project meeting	

Revised Schedule:

Time	Activity	Participant	Description	Notes
8-10	Meeting with ABC Company	Jason, Mark, Leo	About new product	bring iPad
10-12	Meet James	Jason	Project meeting	
14-16	Meet Dennis	Jason, Dennis	Meeting	

翻譯

如何調整行程產生新行程表：

範例：Dennis 想與 Jason 於上午十點碰面。

Jason 的行程表：

時間	行程	參與人員	簡述	附註
8-10	與 ABC 公司開會	Jason, Mark, Leo	關於新產品	帶 iPad
10-12	與 James 碰面	Jason	專案會議	

修正版行程表：

時間	行程	參與人員	簡述	附註
8-10	與 ABC 公司開會	Jason, Mark, Leo	關於新產品	帶 iPad
10-12	與 James 碰面	Jason	專案會議	
14-16	與 Dennis 碰面	Jason, Dennis	會議	

解析

　　了解如何撰寫行程表後，接下來就是運用此行程表與客戶確認行程，或是從中增加或調整行程。以下說明如何增加行程：

　　範例中 Jason 上午共有兩個行程。分別是：

1. 8-10 點：與 ABC 公司代表開會
2. 10-12 點：與 James 開會

　　由兩個行程使 Jason 早上已無法再增加行程。因此除非此會面極其重要且無法改至其他時間，否則為了自己作業上的方便，一般會將臨時加入的行程排至自己的空檔時間。以本範例為例，Jason 就把與 Dennis 要求的 10 點，改安排在下午兩點到四點。

　　能進行這樣的安排是因為客戶端也能相互配合，但如果行程的變更是出自於不可抗力因素，則其調整方式也會有所不同。以下透過範例加以說明：

情況：James 的班機臨時被取消，無法於上午抵台。

處理方式一：延後至下午空檔時段/取消本次會議。

時間	行程	參與人員	簡述	附註
8-10	與 ABC 公司開會	Jason, Mark, Leo	關於新產品	帶 iPad
10-12				
14-16	與 Dennis 碰面	Jason, Dennis	會議	
16-18	與 James 碰面	Jason, James	專案會議	

處理方式二：取消本次會議。

時間	行程	參與人員	簡述	附註
8-10	與 ABC 公司開會	Jason, Mark, Leo	關於新產品	帶 iPad
10-12				
14-16	與 Dennis 碰面	Jason, Dennis	會議	

Unit 01
Unit 02
Unit 03
Unit 04
Unit 05
Unit 06
Unit 07
Unit 08
Unit 09
Unit 10
Unit 11

現在你會說

請依句意填入 A-E。

A. The flight number is TW1205 and estimated to land in Taiwan at 11 AM this Monday

B. It may take me another 30 minutes to pass the customs

C. Let's check the latest schedule

D. we can have lunch first after we meet

E. Let's begin the arrival time of my flight

Jason：Before you visit Taiwan, could I reconfirm the schedule with you?

Ken：Of course. _____1_____.

Jason：You will take China Airline from San Francisco. _____2_____.

Ken：Correct. _____3_____, so we can meet in the lobby at 11: 30 AM.

Jason：I got it. Since your arrival time will soon be the lunch time, I think _____4_____.

Ken：Thanks a lot.

Jason：Secondly, let's reconfirm the time of the first meeting. This meeting is scheduled to be held in our conference room at 1 PM. Right?

Ken：Right.

Jason: _____5_____. We will have a project discussion with our marketing team at 4 PM.

答案

1. (E)   2. (A)   3. (B)   4. (D)   5. (C)

現在你會寫 ||||||||||||||||||||||||||||||||||||

1.請問你何時抵達機場？

_____

_____

中式英文出沒 ▶ When will you arrive the airport?

錯在哪 ▶ 若要表達抵達某一地點，應使用 arrive in/at 而非
arrive。
arrive ＋ at 用來表示抵達較小的地〈例:車站〉，
arrive ＋ in 則用於抵達較大的地方〈例:國家〉

正解 ▶ When will you arrive at the airport?

2.如果想延後本次會議，請事先告知。

_____

_____

中式英文出沒 ▶ If want to postpone this meeting, please notify
first.

錯在哪 ▶ 中文主受詞皆省略仍可理解句意。但英文無法做這樣
的省略。因此應先把句子還原為「如果你想延後本次
會議，請事先告知我」，就不會遺漏主受詞。

正解 ▶ If you want to postpone this meeting, please
notify me in advance.

07 Unit 客戶接待

挑戰難度 ★★★☆☆

真的你學過

　　自機場接到客戶後，除公事上的洽談，若各行程間橫跨用餐時間，則應提早預訂餐廳，以減少等候用餐的時間。由於餐廳必須確認多個事項，讓許多人視預定餐廳為畏途，但事實上，只要掌握好敘述時間與人數的句型，再加上幾個提出要求問句，就可以完成餐廳的預定。

單元重點及學習方向

❶ 運用 Can I book/reserve a table with... 句型向餐廳訂位。
❷ 運用 May I have/ask... 句型來表達詢問之意。
❸ 運用 What should I..., if... 句型來表達詢問之意。
❹ 應用本單元之字彙、片語與句型練習如何預定餐廳。

 **必 check 句型** ||||||||||||||||||||||||||||||||||||

1. **Can I** book a table for four?
   我能預訂四個人的座位嗎？

2. **May I ask** few questions about my reservation tomorrow?
   我可以問幾個關於明日訂位的問題嗎？

3. **May I have** the reservation number?
   我可以知道我的訂位編號嗎？

 **你有學過的單字** ||||||||||||||||||||||||||||||||||||

1. **book** [bʊk] *v.* 預定

2. **check** [tʃɛk] *v.* 檢查

3. **contact** [`kɑntækt] *n.* 連絡

4. **customize** [`kʌstəmˌaɪz] *v.* 客製化

5. **have** [hæv] *v.* 獲得

6. **immediate** [ɪ`midɪɪt] *adj.* 立即的

7. **ingredient** [ɪn`gridɪənt] *n.* 成分

8. **keep** [kip] *v.* 保留

9. **open** [`opən] *adj.* 營業的

10. **reservation** [ˌrɛzɚ`veʃən] *n.* 預約

小試身手

1. Can I _____ a table for two?

   可以預定兩個人的座位嗎？

2. May I have your _____ number?

   可以留下您的連絡電話嗎？

3. Please keep this _____ for me.

   請保留此預約。

4. Our _____ hour is from 9 AM to 5 PM.

   我們從早上九點營業到下午五點。

5. I need your _____ reply.

   我需要您的立即回覆。

解答

1. book

2. contact

3. reservation

4. opening

5. immediate

句型喚醒你的記憶 ||||||||||||||||||||||||||||||||||||||||

1. **Can I book a** round **table with** ten seats?

   我能預定十個座位的圓桌嗎？

   Can I book a table with＋座位數意思是「我能預定…個座位嗎？」，
   可用於詢問餐廳的訂位情況。

   例 Can I book table with two seat? 我能預訂兩人的座位嗎？

2. **May I ask** one question about the food you serve?

   我能問一個關於您們供應的餐點的問題嗎？

   May I ask... 意思為「我能問…」，可用於詢問對方問題。

   例 May I ask few questions about the food I ordered? 可以詢問幾
   個關於我所點的餐點的問題嗎？

3. **May I have** your service e-mail address?

   可以告訴我你們的客服信箱嗎？

   May I have... 意思為「我能知道…」，可用於表達詢問之意。

   例 May I have the name of this waiter? 我可以知道這位服務生的姓
   名嗎？

4. **What should I** prepare **if** I want to bring my pet to your
   restaurant?

   若要攜帶寵物進入您的餐廳，請問我該準備哪些東西？

   What should I..., if...意思為「若要…我應該…」，可用詢問對方處理
   某事所需進行的步驟。

   例 What should I do if I want to have a customized hamburger?
   若需要特製漢堡，我該如何做？

Unit
01

Unit
02

Unit
03

Unit
04

Unit
05

Unit
06

Unit
07

Unit
08

Unit
09

Unit
10

Unit
11

知多少？多知道一點總是好 ||||||||||||||||||||||||||||

　　若需要與客戶一同用餐，提早預約餐廳除可省去現場等候的時間外，若有特殊需求，也可先行讓餐廳知道，尤其評估是否接受請求。當以英文進行餐廳預訂時，若能掌握以下要點，避免觸及下列禁忌，方可按照自身需求完成訂位，並提高餐廳接受你的特殊需求的可能。

不可不知的要點 ||||||||||||||||||||||||||||||||||

1. 事先查詢餐廳相關資訊：
   多數餐廳會將其相關資訊公布在網站上供顧客進行查詢，若有意於該餐廳用餐，事先了解其營業時間與餐點內容，可以縮短詢問時間，更快完成訂位程序。
2. 清楚告知訂位時間與人數：
   準確告知預計時段與前往用餐的人數給餐廳能縮短核對時間，縮短整體花費的時間，對顧客與餐廳都是好事。
3. 附上特殊需求之事由本著互相尊重之原則，若顧客先行說明特殊需求之緣由，除其需求極為不合理外，多數餐廳會盡可能滿足其需求。

不可不知的禁忌

1. 長話不短說：

   餐廳的訂位電話是供所有顧客使用，因此長時間占線是非常自私的行為。因此電話訂位時，應該清楚扼要的講重點。

2. 一再變更訂位：

   處理訂位需要一定的作業時間，因此當顧客多次變換時段與人數，會造成餐廳作業上的不便，也讓餐廳對你留下不良印象。

3. 提出不合理之要求：

   此處的不合理意指影響其他顧客權益與超出服務範圍。舉例來說，在沒有包廂的餐廳要求其他顧客不得聊天，就是影響其他顧客權益。在美式餐廳要求中式食物，則屬超出服務範圍。

Unit 01
Unit 02
Unit 03
Unit 04
Unit 05
Unit 06
Unit 07
Unit 08
Unit 09
Unit 10
Unit 11

腦部暖身 一點都不難對話

請將以下五個單字填入空格內。

(a) seconds   (b) serve   (c) postpone

(d) contact   (e) provide

Jason： **Can I book a table with four seats** at 6:30 PM tomorrow?

Operator： Let me check our system for you, please wait for few
_____1_____ .The time you book is available. May I
have your name and _____2_____ number, sir?

Jason： Sure. Jason with the number of 0912-345-678.

Operator： Thank you, sir. Let me repeat the information you
_____3_____ . You are Jason with number of 0912-345-
678. Your reservation is at 6:30 PM tomorrow.

Jason： Correct. **May I ask** do you _____4_____ vegetarian food?

Operator： Yes, we do. We have vegetarian noodles and salad.

Jason： I got it.

Operator： We would like to remind you that the reservation will
be cancelled if you are late more than 15 minutes.

Jason： Ok. **What should I do if I want to** _____5_____ my
reservation?

Operator： Please call us one hour before the time of your
reservation.

Jason： Thank you.

翻譯

Jason： 我能預訂明天晚上 6 點半四個人的座位嗎？

接線生： 讓我替您確認一下，請稍帶片刻。你所預約的時段目前尚有空
位，可以請您提供大名與聯絡電話嗎？

Jason： 當然可以。Jason，連絡電話是 0912-345-678。

接線生： 謝謝。讓我重覆您剛提供的資訊。您是 Jason，您的連絡電話是 0912-345-678。您預定的時間是下午六點半。

Jason： 沒錯。可以再請問你們有提供素食嗎？

接線生： 有提供素食，有素食麵與沙拉可選擇。

Jason： 了解。

接線生： 於此提醒您，若遲到超過 15 分鐘，將會取消您的預約。

Jason： 好的。那如果要延後預約時間呢？

接線生： 請於一小時前來電告知變更。

Jason： 謝謝。

單字 ....

- **tomorrow** [tə`mɔro] *n.* 明天
- **repeat** [rɪ`pit] *v.* 重複
- **vegetarian** [ˌvɛdʒə`tɛrɪən] *adj.* 素食的
- **remind** [rɪ`maɪnd] *v.* 提醒

答案 ....

1. (a)   2. (d)   3. (e)   4. (b)   5. (c)

Unit 01
Unit 02
Unit 03
Unit 04
Unit 05
Unit 06
Unit 07
Unit 08
Unit 09
Unit 10
Unit 11

會說也會寫一：填寫線上訂位資訊 ||||||||||||

Example:

Opening hours---❶
Lunch: 11:30~15:00 (Last Order 14:00)
Dinner: 18:00~22:30 (Last Order 21:30)

Online reservation---❷

Date –（a）	12/13□check availability
Time –（b）	19:30□check availability
Party size –（c）	4
Name –（d）	Jason
Contact number –（e）	0912-345-678
Description –（f）	We want the table by the window

翻譯

範例：

營業時間
午餐：11:30~15:00（最後點餐 14:00）
晚餐：18:00~22:30（最後點餐 21:30）

線上訂位

日　　期	12/13□訂位情況
時　　間	19:30□訂位情況
人　　數	4
訂位人姓名	Jason
連絡電話	0912-345-678
特殊需求	我們想要靠窗的座位

本範例中的線上訂位，共包含兩部分：

❶營業時間（open hours）：

在本範例中，營業時間可細分為中餐時段與晚餐時段，午晚餐之間時有一段休息時間的。也正因如此，特別標註了兩個時段的最後點餐時間。以中餐時段為例，兩點的時候服務生會詢問客人是否需要點餐，如不需要可再繼續用餐至三點。

❷線上預約表單（online reservation）：

在本範例表單中，需填寫的部分共有六項

（a）日期：在大多數的線上訂位系統，都可透過行事曆功能來查詢每日的訂位狀況。

（b）時間：確定好日期之後，就可再透過時間拿查詢自己要預訂的時段是否已經額滿。

（c）人數：確認日期與時段後，接下就是填入人數，以便餐廳進行座位安排。

（d）訂位人姓名：此欄位的作用在於客人實際前往用餐時，方便系統搜尋訂位資料。

（e）連絡電話：留下連絡電話的目的大致有以下兩種。一是當客人遲到時，餐廳可以詢問是否需要展延或取消。二是方便餐廳於訂位當日與客人做最後確認。

（f）特殊需求：此欄位可填入你的一些特定要求。在本範例中，訂位人希望座位靠近窗戶，故於此特別註明。

註

　　雖名為特殊需求，但這並不代表餐廳會全盤接受客人的要求，一般而言，餐廳可能會接受特製食物、特殊座位安排等較易執行的需求。影響其他顧客權益之要求可能就會遭餐廳拒絕。

Unit
01

Unit
02

Unit
03

Unit
04

Unit
05

Unit
06

Unit
07

Unit
08

Unit
09

Unit
10

Unit
11

會說也會寫二：線上預定特製餐點

Example:

Contact US—**❶**

We will reply you need within 3 hours.

For on immediate reply, please call 003-123321 in our

opening hours **❷**

From – （a）	123456@yahoo.com
To – （b）	Exeellentsteak@jpgroup.com
Reservation No.--- （c）	R141120
Name— （d）	Jason
Description— （e）	Due to the religion reason, I will need two customized sandwiches. Please don't put pork in these two sandwiches. The rest ingredients are ok. Thank you for your kindness.

翻譯

範例：

聯絡我們

我們將於三小時內回覆您。

如需立即回覆，請於營業時間內撥打 003-123321。

從	123456@yahoo.com
自	Exeellentsteak@jpgroup.com
訂位編號	R141120
訂位人姓名	Jason
需求	由於宗教因素，我需要兩份特製三明治。這兩份三明治不加豬肉。其餘食材皆可。感謝您的協助。

解析 |||||||||||||||||||||||||||||||||||||||||||||||||||||

要求餐廳特製餐點時，就可能需要填寫類似本範例的表單，本表單共可分為兩部分，以下針對各內容作更進一步的說明：

❶聯絡我們：

此處主要是告知顧客線上客服的回覆速度，在本範例告中，標榜的是三小時內一定會回覆。並另建議需要馬上得到回覆的顧客改打客服電話進行詢問。

❷特殊需求表單：

（a）從：此欄位填入顧客的信箱，以便客服瞭解需求後，進行回覆。

（b）自：此欄位固定為該餐廳的客服信箱，用於接受顧客線上填寫的特殊需求表單。

（c）訂位編號：填寫此編號主要是為了方便訂位資料的查詢。

（d）訂位人姓名：填寫姓名字可讓客服人員更快找到顧客的訂位資訊，做出適當回應。

（e）特殊需求：此欄位用於填寫需求內容。填寫時盡可能清楚且具體描述你的需求。以本範例為例，Jason 以宗教需求為事由，希望餐廳能特製作兩個不加豬肉的三明治。

註

雖名為特殊需求，但本著相互尊重的原則，其確切內容不應太過離譜。舉例來說，當我們前往美式餐廳用餐，若要求餐廳調整漢堡食材，尚屬合理。但倘若要求餐廳提供飯食或麵食，就屬不合理需求，這類型的需求也會被餐廳所拒絕。

Unit 01
Unit 02
Unit 03
Unit 04
Unit 05
Unit 06
Unit 07
Unit 08
Unit 09
Unit 10
Unit 11

 **現在你會說** ||||||||||||||||||||||||||||||||||||||||||||||

請依句意填入 A-E。

A. May I have your name and contact number, sir

B. Let me repeat the information you provided

C. Please call us one hour before the time of your reservation

D. We have vegetarian noodles and salad

E. Can I book a table with four seats at 6:30 PM tomorrow

Jason： _____1_____?

Operator： Let me check it for you, please wait for few seconds. The time you book is still available. _____2_____?

Jason： Sure. Jason with the number of 0912-345-678.

Operator： Thank you, sir. _____3_____. You are Jason with the number of 0912-345-678. Your reservation is at 6:30 PM tomorrow.

Jason： Correct. May I ask do you serve vegetarian food?

Operator： Yes, we do. _____4_____.

Jason： I got it.

Operator： I'd like to remind you that the reservation will be cancelled if you are late more than 20 minutes.

Jason： Ok. What should I do if I want to postpone my reservation?

Operator： _____5_____.

Jason： Thank you.

答案 ....

1. (E)　2. (A)　3. (B)　4. (D)　5. (C)

 現在你會寫 ||||||||||||||||||||||||||||||||||||

1.我能預定 6 人座的座位嗎？

_____

_____

中式英文出沒 ▶ Can a book a 6 seats table?

錯在哪 ▶ 英文中表示幾人座的方式為 a table with ..seats。把 a 6 seats table 修正為 a table with 6 seats 即為正確句型。

正解 ▶ Can I book a table with 6 seats?

2.若需要特製餐點，應該怎麼做？

_____

_____

中式英文出沒 ▶ What should do if need customized food?

錯在哪 ▶ 中文省略主詞不至於影響理解，但英文若全數省略會形成文法錯誤，因此需將主詞還原。

正解 ▶ What should I do if I need customized food?

Unit
01

Unit
02

Unit
03

Unit
04

Unit
05

Unit
06

Unit
07

Unit
08

Unit
09

Unit
10

Unit
11

與客戶用餐

挑戰難度 ★★☆☆☆

真的你學過

　　若你將外國客戶接送至公司時，時間已接近用餐時段，或本來就排定與該客戶有一整天的行程，基於地主之誼，一般來說都會邀請客戶一同用餐。但很多人都對如何點菜感到頭痛，深怕因為自己的疏忽，而使這頓飯吃的不愉快。事實上，只要善用問句讓客戶做出選擇並留意文化差異，方可賓主盡歡。

單元重點及學習方向

❶ 運用 What kind of... 句型讓客戶做出選擇。

❷ 運用 Do you want to... /How would you like 句型讓客戶做出選擇。

❸ 運用 I would like to order... 句型進行點餐。

❹ 應用本單元之字彙、片語與句型練習詢問客戶意見後進行點餐。

 必 **check** 句型 ||||||||||||||||||||||||||||||||||||

1. **What kind of** food do you like?

   你喜歡哪種類型的食物？

2. **How would you like** your steak?

   你牛排要幾分熟？

3. **Do you want to** have a cup of coffee?

   你想要喝杯咖啡嗎？

4. **I would like to order** two steaks and one sandwich.

   我要點兩份牛排與一份三明治。

 你有學過的單字 ||||||||||||||||||||||||||||||||||||

1. **beef** [bif] *n.* 牛肉

2. **noodle** [`nudl] *n.* 麵條

3. **.meal** [mil] *n.* 餐點

4. **medium** [`midɪəm] *adj.* 五分熟的

5. **medium rare** [`midɪəm,rɛr] *n.* 三分熟

6. **rice** [raɪs] *n.* 米飯

7. **steak** [stek] *n.* 牛排

8. **special** [`spɛʃəl] *n.* 特餐

9. **soup** [sup] *n.* 湯

10. **wine** [waɪn] *n.* 酒

Unit 01
Unit 02
Unit 03
Unit 04
Unit 05
Unit 06
Unit 07
Unit 08
Unit 09
Unit 10
Unit 11

小試身手

1. I would like to order a _____ noodle.
   我要點一碗牛肉麵。

2. What kind of _____ do you want?
   你想吃哪種餐點？

3. How would like your _____?
   你牛排要幾分熟？

4. What is today's _____?
   今日特餐是？

5. Do you want to drink some red _____?
   你要喝點紅酒嗎？

解答

1. beef
2. dish
3. steak
4. special
5. wine

句型喚醒你的記憶 |||||||||||||||||||||||||||||||

1. **What kind of** tea do you like the most?

你最喜歡哪種類型的茶呢？

What kind of 意思為「哪種類型的…」，用餐時可用其詢問對方喜歡的食物類型。

例 What kind of wine do you like? 你想要喝哪種酒呢？

2. **How would you like** your salad?

你沙拉要怎樣的呢？

How would you like＋食物名稱意思為「你想要…（何種食物）？」或「你想要…（料理食物的方式）」？

例 How would you like your soup? 請問湯品有任何喜好嗎？

3. **Do you want to** have some bubble milk tea?

你想喝泡沫奶茶嗎？

Do you want to 意思為「你想要…」，可用於詢問對方意願。

例 Do you want to have some soup? 你想喝湯嗎？

4. **I would like to order** two beef noodles and one fried rice.

我要點兩份牛肉麵跟一份炒飯。

I would like to order 意思為「我想要點…」，可用於向服務生點餐。

例 I would like to order a hamburger and one cup of coffee. 我想要點一份漢堡跟一杯咖啡。

知多少？多知道一點總是好

　　進入餐廳後，接下來就是進行點餐。但由於是與外國人一同用餐，點餐時應留意以下幾個要點，避免觸及禁忌，才不會因為一時的疏忽，因為這頓飯在客戶心中留下不好的印象。以下針對要點與禁忌做進一步說明

不可不知的要點

1. 考量飲食習慣：各地區食物都有其習慣的調味與烹煮方式，除客戶表示想嘗試某類型的料理外，可選擇料理方式與客戶國家接近的食物，讓客戶能夠吃得習慣。

2. 注意餐具使用習慣：中餐習慣使用筷子，西餐慣用刀叉。用餐前應主動詢問外國客戶是否需要刀叉。

3. 注意文化差異：不同地區有不同的用餐文化。例如西餐飲用湯品是於主餐之前，而中餐則剛好相反。留意這些小細節，可讓客戶感受到你對這頓商務用餐的用心。

不可不知的禁忌

1. 忽略宗教因素：某些人會因為宗教因素選擇不吃某些食材（例如：回教徒不吃豬肉；印度是牛為聖獸），若與客戶用餐時忽略此點，讓客戶在不知情的情況下破戒，是非常失禮的行為。

2. 飲酒過量：在許多國家的餐飲文化中，酒都是重要的一環。適當的飲酒能讓用餐氣氛更加愉快，但飲酒過量容易酒後失態，因此與客戶用餐時，飲酒應有分寸。

3. 忽略素食需求：不論是因為何種因素選擇吃素，我們應尊重其選擇。選擇餐廳或餐點若未將此列入考量，使菇素的客戶用餐時受到種種限制，是非常不禮貌的。

　　以上所提出的要點與禁忌無法涵蓋所有情況，但在點餐時秉持多替客戶考量的原則，方可讓接下來的用餐氣氛愉快。

Unit
01

Unit
02

Unit
03

Unit
04

Unit
05

Unit
06

Unit
07

Unit
08

Unit
09

Unit
10

Unit
11

腦部暖身 一點都不難對話 ||||||||||||||||||||||||||||||||

請將以下六個單字填入空格內。

(a) having   (b) bottle   (c) menu

(d) prepare   (e) have   (f) have booked

In a steakhouse

Jason： I _____1_____ a table for four online with the name of Jason.

Waiter： Ok, let me check our system. Your seats are at 4B zone, please follow me.

Jason： Thanks. James, Leo here we go.

Waiter： Thank you for _____2_____ dinner in our restaurant. Today's special is 10 oz. rib. All meals in the _____3_____ are available.

Jason： I would like a special. How about you James, Leo?

James： A 6 oz. Fillet, please.

Leo： An 8 oz. Sirloin, please.

Waiter： How would you like your steak, sir?

James： Medium-rare, please

Leo： Medium, please.

Jason： Do you want to _____4_____ some wine?

James & Leo： Why not? You choose one for us.

Jason： I would like to order a _____5_____ of Burgundy.

Waiter： Anything else, sir?

Jason： One salad.

Waiter： Thank you sir. We will start to _____6_____ your meals.

翻譯

在一間牛排館內。

Jason： 我用 Jason 的名稱在網路上預訂了四人的座位。

服務生： 好的，請讓我進入系統確認一下。您的座位是在 4B 區，麻煩請跟我來。

Jason： 謝謝。James、Leo 我們一同入席吧。

服務生： 很感謝各位蒞臨本餐廳享用晚餐，本日特餐為 10 盎司肋排。菜單上所有餐點都有供應。

Jason： 我要點一份特餐。James、Leo 你們呢？

James： 一份 6 盎司菲力。

Leo： 一份 8 盎司沙朗。

服務生： 請問你要幾分熟呢？

James： 3 分熟，謝謝。

Leo： 5 分熟，謝謝。

Jason： 你們會想喝點酒嗎？

James & Leo： 有何不可，替我們選瓶酒吧！

Jason： 我要開一瓶勃根地紅酒。

服務生： 還有需要其他餐點嗎？

Jason： 再一份沙拉。

服務生： 謝謝。我們會開始準備您的餐點。

Unit
01

Unit
02

Unit
03

Unit
04

Unit
05

Unit
06

Unit
07

Unit
08

Unit
09

Unit
10

Unit
11

單字

- **steakhouse** [`stek͵haʊs] *n.* 牛排館
- **oz (ounce)** [aʊns] *n.* 盎司
- **fillet** [`fɪlɪt] *n.* 菲力牛排
- **sirloin** [`sɝˏlɔɪn] *n.* 沙朗牛排
- **Burgundy** [`bɝˏgəndɪ] *n.* 勃根地

答案

1. (f)　2. (a)　3. (c)　4. (e)　5. (b)　6. (d)

會說也會寫一：看懂西餐菜單來點餐 ||||||||||

Menu

Salad

Fruit/vegetable

Soup

Today's special/mushroom soup

Main course

US Fillet 6 oz $ 560

Austrian T-bone 8 oz $ 600

Rib 8oz $ 580

Drinks

Tea/coffee/Juice

Example

I would like order a fruit salad, today's special, Austrian T-bone medium, and an iced tea.

翻譯

Menu

沙拉

水果／蔬菜

湯

本日嚴選/蘑菇湯

主餐

美國菲力 6 盎司 $560

澳洲丁骨 8 盎司 $ 600

肋排 8 盎司 $580

飲料

茶／咖啡／果汁

範例

我要點水果沙拉、本日例湯、澳洲丁骨 5 分熟與冰茶。

解析

　　西餐菜單常以套餐（set/combo）方式呈現，我們點餐時按照每一部分進行選擇方可完成點餐。本範例的套餐組合共分為以下幾部分：

1. 沙拉（salad）：蔬菜／水果沙拉
2. 湯品（soup）：本日嚴選／蘑菇湯
3. 主餐（main course）：菲力、沙朗、肋排
4. 飲料（drink）：茶／咖啡／果汁

　　此菜單也代表了簡易西式飲食的用餐順序。最開始是先食用沙拉，更為精緻的餐廳可能會在加上開胃菜（appetizer），許多廚師也會在開胃菜上展現巧思，讓客戶感受自己的廚藝。若覺得開胃菜非常精緻，可使用 dedicate 來形容，例如：This appetizer is so delicious and dedicate（這道開胃菜真是美味又精緻）。

　　而在主餐部分，特別是肉類，服務生會像我們詢問熟度。熟度共可分為以下幾種：

1. Raw：生的。未經烹調的牛肉。
2. Rare：一分熟。單面微微煎過，近乎全生的牛肉。
3. Medium-rare：三分熟。表面煎熟，內部微溫並帶些微粉紅。
4. Medium：五分熟。表面煎熟，肉呈粉紅。
5. Medium-well：七分熟。部分已呈暗紅。
6. Well-down：全熟。完全煎熟，有時微焦。

　　根據上述熟度分類。當我們要點五分熟的沙朗，可參考以下例句：

I would like to order a medium sirloin.

　　吃完主餐後，通常還會有甜點（dessert）與飲料（drink），飲料通常又會在分成 iced/hot（冰／熱）。享用完這兩道餐點後，西餐的一餐基本上就算用餐完畢。

Unit 01
Unit 02
Unit 03
Unit 04
Unit 05
Unit 06
Unit 07
Unit 08
Unit 09
Unit 10
Unit 11

會說也會寫二：看懂中餐菜單來點餐 | | | | | | | | | | | |

Menu

Soups
Chicken soup $80
Beef soup $90
Dishes
Mapo Tofu $120
Fried rib $200
Hot pepper chicken $180
Rice
Ham Fried rice--60
White rice-- $10

Example

I would like to order two chicken soups, one Mapo topu, one fried ribs, and two white rice

翻譯

Menu

湯品
雞肉湯 $80
牛肉湯 $90
主菜
麻婆豆腐 $120
炸肋排 $200
辣椒雞 $180
飯類
火腿炒飯 $60
白飯 $10

範例

我要點兩碗雞肉湯、一份麻婆豆腐、一份炸肋排與兩碗白飯。

解析 ||||||||||||||||||||||||||||||||||||||||||||||||||||||

　　中菜菜單的品項相對西餐來說，是更加豐富多元的。另外中餐用餐也比較不強調順序性。本範例先針對湯品、菜類、飯類做簡單說明。

1. 湯品（soup）：牛肉湯、雞肉湯。
2. 主菜（cuisine）：麻婆豆腐、炸肋排、辣椒雞。
3. 飯類：白飯、火腿炒飯。

　　由於中菜的種類變化萬千，翻譯上也出現眾多版本，過去多數會將烹調手法與食材名稱都納入，此翻譯原則的優點是內容詳盡，但缺點是過於冗長。現今由於中文的日漸崛起，許多菜色直接採音譯，以下列舉出幾種具代表菜色做進一步說明：

1. 炒飯（fired rice/chao-fan）：

   fired rice 中的 fried 代表烹調手法油煎，rice 代表飯。Chao-fan 則使用音譯，後者因為中文的強勢崛起，也逐漸為西方所接受

2. 宮保雞丁（chicken cubes with peanuts/spicy diced chicken/Kung Pao Chicken） chicken cubes with peanuts 敘述了本道菜的食材有雞肉丁與花生，spicy diced chicken 則說明調味方式是辣味。Kung Pao Chicken 則需了解宮保的意涵。

　　比較兩種菜名翻譯方式，過去點一份炒飯加上一份宮保雞丁，常用的英文句子可能會是：I would like to order a chicken cubes with peanuts and a fried rice.

　　但現在越來越多情況會是：I would like to order a chao-fan and a Kung Pao chicken. 當菜名音譯越來越為西方所接受時，未來以英文點菜時，將會更加容易。

Unit 01
Unit 02
Unit 03
Unit 04
Unit 05
Unit 06
Unit 07
Unit 08
Unit 09
Unit 10
Unit 11

125

 現在你會說 ||||||||||||||||||||||||||||||||||||||||||

請依句意填入 A-E。

A. All dishes in the menu are available

B. Fried rice is better

C. Mapo Tofu could be a good choice

D. What kind of food do you prefer

E. I have booked a table for four online with the name of Jason

In a Chinese restaurant

Jason：_____1_____.

Waiter：Let me check it for you. Your seats are at 2C zone, please follow me.

Jason：Thank you!

Waiter：_____2_____. When you are ready to order, please let me know.

Jason：Do you have any restriction in eating?

Amy：I don't eat beef.

Jason：I got it. Let's take a look of the menu. _____3_____

Ben：I like spicy food. Do you have any recommendation?

Jason：_____4_____. This cuisine mixed hot pepper with Tofu.

Ben：It sounds great. I want this.

Jason：About the main meal, do you prefer plain rice or fried rice?

Amy：_____5_____.

Jason：OK.

答案

1. (E)　2. (A)　3. (D)　4. (C)　5. (B)

 現在你會寫

1. 你想喝杯酒嗎？

_____

_____

中式英文出沒 ▶ Do you want drink a glass of wine?

錯在哪 ▶ 中文的「想要…」對應的英文應該是 want to ，而非 want 。修正此文法錯誤即為正確的句子。

正解 ▶ Do you want to drink a glass of wine?

2. 我想要點一碗牛肉麵跟兩盤炒飯。

_____

_____

中式英文出沒 ▶ I would like order one beef needles and two fried rice.

錯在哪 ▶ 中文的「想要…」翻譯成英文時正確用法應是 would like to V... ，故若修正為 would like to order，即為正確的句子。

正解 ▶ I would like to order one beef needles and two fried rice.

Unit 01
Unit 02
Unit 03
Unit 04
Unit 05
Unit 06
Unit 07
Unit 08
Unit 09
Unit 10
Unit 11

餐間閒聊

挑戰難度 ★★☆☆☆

真的你學過

　　點完餐之後，在等待送餐與用餐過程中皆會與外國客戶以英語交談。此時的對話雖然大多無關公事，但卻也讓許多人感到頭痛。其原因在於若遲遲不開啟話題，會讓彼此有些尷尬，但當不小心開錯話題時，可能又會破壞和諧的用餐氣氛。事實上，只要避開關於隱私或是爭議話題，並善用問句掌控場面，餐間閒聊不再是一種困擾。

單元重點及學習方向

❶ 運用 Are you interested in + Ving... / What kind of... do you like 句型詢問對方是否喜歡做某事。
❷ 運用 Are you a fan of...句型來詢問對方是否熱愛某人事物。
❸ 運用 How do you feel about... 來詢問對方對事物的感受。
❹ 應用本單元之字彙、片語與句型練習如何進行餐間閒聊。

 **必 check 句型** ||||||||||||||||||||||||||||||||||||||||||||

1. **Are you interested in** watching movie?

   你喜歡看電影嗎？

2. **What kind of** sports do you like?

   你喜歡哪種類型的運動呢？

3. **Are you the fan of** Jeremy Lin?

   你是林書豪的球迷嗎？

4. **How do you feel about** the weather in Taiwan?

   你覺得台灣的天氣如何？

 **A 你有學過的單字** ||||||||||||||||||||||||||||||||||||||||||||

1. **actor** [`æktə-] *n.* 男演員

2. **actress** [`æktrɪs] *n.* 女演員

3. **fan** [fæn] *n.* 粉絲（支持者）

4. **leading** [`lidɪŋ] *adj.* 主要的

5. **humid** [`hjumɪd] *adj.* 潮濕的

6. **tourist** [`tʊrɪst] *n.* 遊客

7. **recommend** [ˌrɛkə`mɛnd] *v.* 推薦

8. **role** [rol] *n.* 角色

9. **popular** [`pɑpjələ-] *adj.* 受歡迎的

10. **weather** [`wɛðə-] *n.* 天氣

Unit 01
Unit 02
Unit 03
Unit 04
Unit 05
Unit 06
Unit 07
Unit 08
Unit 09
Unit 10
Unit 11

129

小試身手

1. Are you the _____ of Michael Jackson?

   你是 Michael Jackson 的粉絲嗎？

2. I like the _____ he played in this show.

   我喜歡他在這齣戲所演出的角色。

3. Who is the _____ actor in this movie?

   這部電影的主角是誰呢？

4. Did you watch that _____ sci-fi movie?

   你看了那部受歡迎的科幻電影？

5. How do you feel about the _____ in Taipei?

   你覺得台北的天氣如何？

解答

1. fan
2. role
3. leading
4. popular
5. weather

130

句型喚醒你的記憶 ||||||||||||||||||||||||||||||||||||

1. **Are you interested in** playing basketball?
你喜歡打籃球嗎？
Are you interested in +Ving 意思為「你喜歡…嗎？」，可用於詢問對方的喜好。
例 Are you interested in watching baseball games? 你喜歡看棒球賽嗎？

2. **What kind of movie do** you like the most?
你最喜歡哪種類型的電影呢？
What kind of... do you like 意思為「你最喜歡哪種類型的…呢？」，可用於詢問的喜好。
例 What kind of book do you like? 你喜歡哪種類型的書呢？

3. **Are you the fan of** Marvel movie?
你是漫威的影迷嗎？
Are you the fan of... 意思為「你是…的迷（支持者）嗎？」，可用於詢問對方對於某事物的喜好程度。
例 Are you the fan of Harry Potter movie? 你是哈利波特電影的影迷嗎？

4. **How do you feel about** the hotel you lived yesterday?
昨天下榻的飯店你覺得如何？
How do you feel about 意思為「關於…你覺得如何？」。可用於詢問對方意見與感受，藉此開啟話題。
例 How do you feel about the traffic in Taipei? 你覺得台北的交通狀況如何？

Unit 01
Unit 02
Unit 03
Unit 04
Unit 05
Unit 06
Unit 07
Unit 08
Unit 09
Unit 10
Unit 11

知多少？多知道一點總是好 ||||||||||||||||||||||||||||

　　相較於其他國際商務行程，與外國客戶用餐應該是氣氛最輕鬆的一個。在用餐時，西方人傾向不談公事，因此談話的主題可以比較多元。但畢竟商務用餐仍屬正式場合，當中仍有許多我們應當把握的要點與避免的禁忌。若能做好這些細節，賓主盡歡並不是難事。以下先針對要點部分進行說明。

不可不知的要點 ||||||||||||||||||||||||||||||||||||

1. 保有開放性：餐間閒聊是為了保持場面熱絡，因此選擇可自由表述的主題，例如個人興趣、喜好的電影類型等，讓我方與客戶都能暢所欲言。
2. 留意文化差異：相同的事物可能在不同的文化中可能具有完全相反的意涵，餐間閒談時應特別留意這樣的差異性，以免無意中冒犯對方。
3. 恰當的遣詞用字：餐間閒聊雖然氣氛輕鬆，但還是要注重基本的禮儀，要避免使用粗俗不雅的字眼，以表示對客戶的尊重。

　　而在禁忌的部分，主要是為了避免引起爭端，破壞愉快的用餐氣氛，以下舉出三個例子加以說明：

不可不知的禁忌

1. 討論隱私：西方高度重視隱私權，因此除非對方主動提起，否則盡量不以家庭、婚姻做為談話主題。
2. 種族歧視：種族是個相當敏感的話題，任何具有歧視性的字眼，都不應出現在商務用餐的場合中。
3. 討論政治：每個人對於政治情勢可能持有不同看法，有時甚至極度堅持己見，因此用餐時應避免此類話題，以免挑起爭端，影響用餐氣氛。

　　若在餐間閒聊時能把握上述原則，避免觸及爭議性話題，方可使整個用餐過程愉快而熱絡。

Unit
01

Unit
02

Unit
03

Unit
04

Unit
05

Unit
06

Unit
07

Unit
08

Unit
09

Unit
10

Unit
11

腦部暖身 一點都不難對話 |||||||||||||||||||||||||||||

請將以下六個單字填入空格內。

(a) taste   (b) leading   (c) features

(d) release   (e) role   (f) popular

Jason：**Are you interested in** watching movie?

Mark：I watch movie very often.

Jason：Me, too. Did you see the ____1____ movie named "Interstellar"?

Mark：Not yet. Can you tell me the storyline in general?

Jason：Of course. It is about the space trip. The ____2____ actor is sent to other planet to find the resources that we need.

Mark：It sounds great. I should watch it when I have free time.

Jason：It seems you love sci-fi. **Are you a fan of** any actor or actress ?

Mark：I am the fan of Robert Downey Jr[1]. I like the ____3____ Tony Stark he played in Iron Man.

Jason：His performance is great. He successfully interprets the ____4____ of this role.

Mark：I can't wait the ____5____ of new Marvel movie.

Jason：So do I. We do have a similar ____6____ in movie.

翻譯

Jason：你喜歡看電影嗎？

Mark：我喜歡且經常看電影。

Jason：那你去看現在正夯的「星際效應」了嗎？

Mark：還沒，可以大概跟我說明一下劇情嗎？

Jason：沒問題。這部電影是關於星際旅行。主角被送到其他星球去尋找地球所需的資源。

Mark：聽起來很不錯。等我有空我應該去看這部電影。

Jason：聽起來你喜歡看科幻電影。你是哪位演員的影迷？

Mark：我是小勞勃道尼的影迷，我喜歡他在鋼鐵人裡 Tony Stark 的角色。

Jason：他的表演真的很棒，成功詮釋那個角色的特點。

Mark：我很期待新的漫威電影的上映

Jason：我也是。我們喜好的電影還真相似。

註

英文名字中出現 Jr.代表以下意涵：父母替子女取與自己相同的名字。兒女被加上 Jr.後，翻譯時可譯為「小⋯」或是「二世」。例如：Robert Downey Jr.。

單字

- **storyline** [ˋstorɪˌlaɪn] *n.* 劇情
- **planet** [ˋplænɪt] *n.* 星球
- **sci-fi (science fiction)** [ˋsaɪənsˋfɪkʃən] *n.* 科幻
- **interpret** [ɪnˋtɝprɪt] *v.* 詮釋

Unit 01
Unit 02
Unit 03
Unit 04
Unit 05
Unit 06
Unit 07
Unit 08
Unit 09
Unit 10
Unit 11

答案

1. (f)　2. (b)　3. (e)　4. (c)　5. (d)　6. (a)

會說也會寫一：如何準備討論電影 |||||||||||||||||

Something you can say about Movie:
1. Name: Fury, The Lord of Ring
2. Type: sci-fi, Romance,War, Comedy....
3. Storyline: the space trip, love story, WWI
4. Actors/actress: Prat Pitt, Robert Downey Jr, Anne Hathaway
5. Director: An Li, John Woo Yu-Sen

Example

I like ❶sci-fi movies and I just saw a movie named XXXXX. ❷The main storyline of this movie is about the space trip. ❸The leading actor is sent to other planet to get the precious resource which we need. ❹The director of this movie is XXX, so we can see some special ideas in this work. ❺It is really a good movie, so I recommend it to you.

翻譯

關於電影你可以說：
❶片名：怒火特攻隊、魔戒。
❷類型：科幻、浪漫、戰爭、喜劇等。
❸劇情：星際旅行、愛情故事、一次世界大戰。
❹演員：布萊德彼特、小勞勃道尼、安海瑟威。
❺導演：李安、吳宇森。

　　我喜歡科幻電影，最近才剛看了一部叫 XXXXX 的電影。該片的劇情是在講述星際旅行。主角被送到其他星球去取得我們所需要的珍貴資源。本片的導演是 XXX，所以我們能在片中看到很多特別的想法。這是一部很棒的電影，所以我推薦你去看。

 解析

當與客戶在用餐時討論到電影時，可以從以範例中的四個面向加以切入，最後再加上一句推薦語。這樣的介紹已很有系統，且具延續性。不會一説完就讓話題中止，以下為四個面向的進一步説明：

1. 片名與類型：讓對方馬上知道名稱與類型
    例 Fury is a war movie. 怒火特攻隊是一部戰爭片。
2. 主要劇情：讓對方大致了解故事的走向為何，可開啟後續的討論。
    例 The storyline is about a mission in WWII. 該片劇情是在敘述二戰時期的一項軍事任務。
3. 演員：有些人因為是某演員的影迷而選擇觀上該片，因此可以介紹主角是由誰擔綱演出。
    例 Brad Pitt is the leading actor and he leads a tank squad in this movie. 本片由布萊德彼特領銜主演，片中他帶領一支坦克部隊。
4. 導演：導演有時也是吸引觀眾進場看電影的原因，因此介紹本片的導演可讓談話的廣度增加。
    例 The director of this movie is David Ayer. 本片的導演為大衛艾亞。
5. 推薦語：介紹完你喜歡的電影，最後別忘了推薦給客戶。
    例 It is a good movie, s o I recommend it to you. 這是部好電影，所以我推薦給你。

透過以上的四個面向，當你來用餐時，若客戶開啟一個關於電影的話題，你就不用擔心自己會開不了口了。若對當中的某一面向瞭解程度較深，方可多著墨於此，與客戶多交換看法，讓餐間的閒聊話題不斷。

Unit
01

Unit
02

Unit
03

Unit
04

Unit
05

Unit
06

Unit
07

Unit
08

Unit
09

Unit
10

Unit
11

會說也會寫二：如何討論天氣

Something you can say about weather and scenery(tourism):
Principle: Make comparisons and provide choices.
About weather you can say:
1. Type: snow, rain, typhoon…
2. Seasons: spring, summer, fall, winter.
3. Temperature: high/low, specific figure
About scenery (tourism) you can say:
4. Landmarks: Taipei 101, National Palace Museum
5. Tourist attractions: Sun Moon Lake, Ali Mountain

Example

❶~❸Taiwan rarely snows, so the temperature is much higher than that in your country during winter. The temperature seldom drops below 10 centigrade. ❹~❺If you like to take pictures of landmarks, Taipei 101 is the place you must visit. If you prefer outdoor places, you can go to Sun Moon Lake.

翻譯

關於天氣你可以說：
原則：做比較。
❶類型：下雨、下雪、颱風等。
❷季節：春、夏、秋、冬。
❸溫度：高/低、明確的溫度。
關於風景（景點）你可以說：
❹地標：台北101、故宮。
❺景點：日月潭、阿里山。
　　台灣甚少下雪，所以冬天的溫度比你所居住的國家高。台灣冬天氣溫甚少低於攝氏10度。如果你喜歡和地標合照，一定要去台北101，如果你

偏愛戶外，可以去日月潭。

Unit
01

Unit
02

Unit
03

Unit
04

Unit
05

Unit
06

Unit
07

Unit
08

Unit
09

Unit
10

Unit
11

解析

當餐間閒聊的話題是天氣或是旅遊時，若把握以下的大原則，並由範例中的幾個面向作切入，就能侃侃而談，不會一下子就覺得無話可說。

聊天氣的大原則就是比較法。懂得比較台灣與外國客戶的國家在氣候上的差異，然後再加上一些自身的觀感，就可以創造許多的意見交換。以下針對三個面向與比較法做進一步說明：

1. 類型：先將討論主題縮小，讓彼此可以環繞此主題聊天，不必思考如何開啟下一個話題。

　例 Taipei rains a lot. 台北常下雨。

2. 季節：通常會以現在季節進行討論。

　例 It often rains in the winter time. 冬天時常常下雨。

3. 溫度：即便已經提出一個明確的數值，人們溫度的感受是相對的，因此討論到溫度時，常會跟對方的國家相比較。

　例 The temperature is higher compared to that in your country.
　與你居住的國家相比，台灣冬天氣溫較高。

若要把話題轉到旅遊觀光上，提供多個選擇或建議可讓話題有延續性，以下針對範例的兩個面向做進一步說明：

4. 地標：代表性建物話題性也高，以這些地點為話題的開端，可讓客戶對台灣更有印象。

　例 If you like to take pictures of landmarks, Taipei 101 is the place you must visit. 如果你喜歡拍拍地標，一定要去台北101。

5. 景點：對於喜歡戶外活動的客戶，可以介紹知名的風景區，讓他們依照喜好安排行程。

　例 If you prefer outdoor places, you can go to Sun Moon Lake.
　如果你偏愛戶外，可以去日月潭。

現在你會說 ||||||||||||||||||||||||||||||||||||||||||||

請依句意填入 A-E。

A. Can you tell me the storyline in general

B. He successfully interprets the features of roles he plays

C. Are you a fan of any actor or actress

D. We do have a similar taste in movie

E. Yes, I watch movie very often

Jason：Are you interested in watching movie?

Mark：＿＿＿＿1＿＿＿＿.

Jason：Me, too. Did you see the popular movie named "Fury"?

Mark：Not yet. ＿＿＿＿2＿＿＿＿?

Jason：Of course. It is about the war. The leading actor is sent to Germany to complete the mission in WWII.

Mark：It sounds great. I should watch it when I have free time.

Jason：It seems you love war movie. ＿＿＿＿3＿＿＿＿?

Mark：I am a fan of Brad Pitt.

Jason：＿＿＿＿4＿＿＿＿.

Mark：I can't wait the release of his new movie.

Jason：So do I. ＿＿＿＿5＿＿＿＿.

答案

1. (E)　2. (A)　3. (C)　4. (B)　5. (D)

現在你會寫 |||||||||||||||||||||||||||||||||||||||||||

1. 你喜歡聽流行音樂嗎？

_____

_____

中式英文出沒 ▶ Are you interested in listen to popular music?

錯在哪 ▶ be interested in +Ving 才是正確用法，因此要將 listen 修正為 listening。

正解 ▶ Are you interested in listening to popular music?

2. 你覺得台北的天氣如何？

_____

_____

中式英文出沒 ▶ How do you feel about Taipei's weather?

錯在哪 ▶ 若受到中文的影響，可能會將台北的天氣翻譯為 Taipei's weather，但使用 the weather in Taipei 才 為正確用法。

正解 ▶ How do you feel about the weather in Taipei?

Part 3

產品銷售

10 Unit 推銷產品

挑戰難度 ★★★☆☆

真的你學過

　　了解如何接待客戶後，接下來就是向客戶介紹公司的產品或服務。許多人都會認為一定要能言善道且英文基礎深厚，才能用英文進行產品推銷，但事實上，只要懂得運用英文中強調句型與比較句型，就能凸顯出公司產品的特點，讓客戶願意花錢購買，使你成為一名業績長紅的銷售人員。

單元重點及學習方向

❶ 運用 What makes sth... is... 句型來強調產品特色。
❷ 運用 We provide/produce... 句型來介紹自家產品。
❸ 運用 The advantage(s)of... is/are... 句型來說明自家產品優點。
❹ 運用本單元的單字、片語與句型來練習如何聯絡客戶並推銷產品。

 **必 check 句型**

1. **What makes** our product popular **is** its low price.
　價格低廉是我們產品受歡迎的原因。
2. We **provide** customized service.
　我們提供客製化的服務。
3. We **produce** the automobile parts.
　我們生產汽車零件。
4. **The advantages of** our product **are** durable and cheap.
　我們產品的優點是便宜且耐用。

 **你有學過的單字**

1. **briefing** [`brifɪŋ] *n.* 簡報
2. **feature** [fitʃɚ] *n.* 特色
3. **competiveness** [kəm`pɛtətɪvnɪs] *n.* 競爭力
4. **leading** [`lidɪŋ] *adj.* 頂尖的
5. **order** [`ɔrdɚ] *n.* 訂單
6. **place** [ples] *v.* 開出
7. **purchase** [`pɝtʃəs] *v.* 採購
8. **promotion** [prə`moʃən] *v.* 促銷
9. **reasonable** [`riznəbl] *adj.* 合理的
10. **quotation** [kwo`teʃən] *n.* 報價

Unit
01

Unit
02

Unit
03

Unit
04

Unit
05

Unit
06

Unit
07

Unit
08

Unit
09

Unit
10

Unit
11

小試身手

1. Let me start the _____ of our product
   讓我開始產品簡報。

2. The _____ of our product is easy to bring.
   本公司產品的特色就是便於攜帶。

3. You can get a discount if you _____ an order now.
   現再下訂可享折扣。

4. We have the _____ technology in this field.
   我們擁有業界最頂尖的技術。

5. Please send us the _____ because we are interested in your products.
   由於我們對貴公司的產品有興趣，煩請報價。

解答

1. briefing
2. feature
3. place
4. leading
5. quotation

句型喚醒你的記憶 |||||||||||||||||||||||||||||||||

Unit
01

Unit
02

Unit
03

Unit
04

Unit
05

Unit
06

Unit
07

Unit
08

Unit
09

Unit
10

Unit
11

1. **What makes** us different from other suppliers **is** our service.
良好的服務是我們優於其他供應商的地方。
What makes sth.... is... 意思「⋯的原因是⋯」，可用於説明產品特點或是強調差異性。
例 What makes we famous is our good service. 良好的服務使我們聲名遠播。

2. **We provide** many kind of services to our customers.
我們提供客戶許多不同的服務。
We provide... 意思為「我們提供⋯」，可用於説明公司的產品或服務的類型有哪些。
例 We provide customized parts to our customers. 我們提供客製化零件給客戶。

3. **We produce** the parts of bicycle.
我們生產自行車零件。
We produce... 意思為「我們生產⋯」，可用於説明公司的產品類型有哪些。
例 We produce digital cameras. 我們生產數位相機。

4. **The advantage** of our products is easy to use.
我們產品的優點就是操作容易。
The advantage of... 「⋯的優點是⋯」，可用於説明某事物的優點。
例 The advantage of our machine is durable. 我們公司生產的機器優點是耐用。

知多少？多知道一點總是好 |||||||||||||||||||||||

在現今資訊爆炸的時代，相同的產品透過不同行銷手法與話術包裝可能會產生不同的銷售情況，因此若能正確掌握客戶心理，使其認同產品或服務的價值，這筆交易成功的可能性也會大增。以下針對以英文推銷產品時應注意的要點與禁忌做進一步說明：

不可不知的要點 |||||||||||||||||||||||||||||||

1. 善用比較法：

由於客戶可能一天之內會聆聽多間廠商的產品推銷，提出自身產品與其他產品的差異性，可讓客戶對你的產品印象較為深刻。

2. 強調價值／效益：

商場上大家都在追求利潤，對於價格肯定會計較，當自身的產品價格比競爭對手高時，可改從後續性的角度切入，向客戶說明雖然首次的投資可能會較高，但後續的資金或物力投入較低，成本攤提後其實更為划算。

3. 創造關聯性：

透過網路，產品的各種資訊都會被揭露，客戶對當中的好與壞也自有拿捏。但是當我們能夠讓客戶認同產品背後的意象與後續效果，就更有機會完成交易。

不可不知的禁忌

1. 過度吹噓：

   雖然行銷本來就會稍加渲染產品的優點，但過於誇大反而會造成反效果，因此推銷產品時應有所本，才能真正打動客戶。

2. 重傷競爭對手：

   商場的競爭應回歸產品本身，相互攻訐只會形成惡性循環。

3. 亂給承諾：

   除非今天自己就是老闆，擁有最終決定權，否則別輕易承諾客戶，以免因為主管的不同意，使你失信於客戶。

Unit
01

Unit
02

Unit
03

Unit
04

Unit
05

Unit
06

Unit
07

Unit
08

Unit
09

Unit
10

Unit
11

腦部暖身 一點都不難對話 ||||||||||||||||||||||||||

請將以下六個單字填入空格內

(a) movable　　　(b) darkness　　　(c) demonstrate

(d) select　　　(e) carry　　　(f) try

In DEF Company's Conference room

Jason：Good morning, Andy.

Andy：Moring Jason, please start your briefing now.

Jason：Ok, Let me begin with name of our product. Our new product is called multifunction bicycle toolkit. **The advantages** of this product are easy to ___1___ and use. This toolkit is pocket size, so users don't have to worry about where to put it. Besides, we design a ___2___ light, so it can be used in the ___3___. Now, let me ___4___ how to use it. First of all, press the button and you can ___5___ the tool mode you want to use. If you want change the tool, press the button again to switch the mode.

Andy：It sounds great. May I have a ___6___?

Jason：Of course. If you have any questions, please feel free to ask.

Andy：OK. Thank you for your briefing today.

翻譯

Jason：Andy 早安

Andy：Jason 早安，請開始簡報吧。

Jason：沒問題。就先從產品名稱開始。我們的新產品叫做多功能自行車工具組。本產品的優點在於攜帶便利且方便使用。此工具組僅口

袋大小,所以使用者不必擔心沒地方放置。此外,本工具組附有照明裝置,因此即使在黑暗中也可使用。現在讓我展示如何使用本工具組。首先請按下按鈕選擇工具模式,再按一次按鈕可切換模式。

Andy:聽起來很不錯,我可以體驗一下嗎?

Jason:當然可以。體驗過程中如果有任何問題歡迎詢問。

Andy:好,感謝您今天的產品簡報。

單字

- **multi-function** [ˌmʌltɪˋfʌŋkʃən] *adj.* 多功能的
- **toolkit** [tulˌkɪt] *n.* 工具組
- **pocket** [ˋpɑkɪt] *n.* 口袋
- **switch** [swɪtʃ] *v.* 轉換

Unit 01
Unit 02
Unit 03
Unit 04
Unit 05
Unit 06
Unit 07
Unit 08
Unit 09
Unit 10
Unit 11

答案

1. (e)　2. (a)　3. (b)　4. (c)　5. (d)　6. (f)

會說也會寫一：開發信：介紹產品 |||||||||||

範例

Dear Mike,

❶We are ABC Company that produces bicycle parts in Taiwan. ❷We have known that you are the leading bike manufacturer in Denmark through the video you put in Youtube. ❸The advantages of our components are durable and light, and they perfectly match the image of your brand. The attachment is our latest parts in the market. ❹We have partners all over the world like Baint and Nelida.

❺If you want further information or are interested in our products, please feel free to contact us. ❻We look forward to cooperating with you in the future.

Sincerely yours,

Jason

 翻譯

親愛的 Mike：

　　我們是來自台灣生產自行車零件的 ABC 公司，我們從您放在 Youtube 上的影片得知您是丹麥地區自行車製造廠的龍頭。

　　本公司產品的優點是耐用質輕，此點於您的品牌形象完全相符。我們的合作夥伴遍及全球，例如 Baint 和 Nelida。

　　如您需要更多資訊或對本產品有興趣，請聯絡我們。期待未來能與您合作。

謹

Jason

解析 |||||||||||||||||||||||||||||||||||||||||||||||||||||||||

本範例開發信共可分為六大部分，以下針對各部分做進一步說明：

❶自我介紹：

由於開發信通常是投遞給從未接觸過的公司，因此需要自我介紹說明本公司的名稱與所在地區。例如：We are ABC Company that produces bicycle parts in Taiwan。

❷訊息來源：

此舉表示我方並非亂槍打鳥，是搜尋過相關資訊後才行投遞，如此可提高客戶閱讀完整封信件的意願。例如本範例的訊息來源就是 Youtube 影片。

❸產品優點：

寄送開發信無非就是希望客戶購買產品，因此凸顯自家產品的優點，並找出產品與客戶之連結性，交易成功機率會提高。

❹既有客戶：

提出既有客戶的功用在於證明本公司產品已獲得其他公司之認可，如果舊有客戶中包含知名一線大廠，一定要列出，可讓較為保守的新客戶放心與我方交易。

❺詢問窗口：

若客戶看完信件內容對公司產品有興趣，除了寄信時的信箱外，附上公司的其他聯絡方式，像是手機或是市話，都可提高完成交易的機率。

❻結尾應酬：

此處用語一般來說，主要都是表達希望能夠達成交易或是建立合作關係。

例如：We look forward to cooperating with you in the future. 期待未來能與您合作。

　　另外，由於客戶每天收到郵件數量可能多到驚人，因此開發的篇幅不宜過長，宜精簡扼要，讓客戶願意稍微花點時間看完內容。

Unit
01

Unit
02

Unit
03

Unit
04

Unit
05

Unit
06

Unit
07

Unit
08

Unit
09

Unit
10

Unit
11

會說也會寫二：開發信：介紹服務

範例

Dear James,

❶We are ABC Company that provides the website integration service from Taiwan. ❷We have known that your group owns several brands in Germany through the website of 2014 International Machine Exhibition.

❸Our main service is to help our customer to integrate the information in their official websites. The integrations include the re-arrangement of main page, the adjustment of search bar, and the improvement of picture display. The attached picture shows the best example. ❹The picture you see is the comparison. The one on the right is more eye-catching.

❺If you want to upgrade your website, please free to contact us through 030-123-456 or service@abc.com ❻We look forward to providing the best service to your company.

翻譯

親愛的 James：

我們是來自台灣提供網頁整合服務的 ABC 公司。我們透過 2014 年國際機械展的網站得知貴集團在德國擁有多個品牌。

我們協助客戶整合其官方網站的資訊。整合範圍包括主頁的重整，搜搜尋列的調整與圖片展示的修正。附圖為最佳實例。此圖為一張比較圖，可明顯看出右圖較能吸引目光。

如果您想升級網頁，請透過 030-123-456 或是 service@abc.com 與我們聯絡。我們期待提供您最好的服務。

本範例開發信共可分為六大部分，以下針對各部分做進一步說明：

❶ 自我介紹：

此處與會讀也會寫一的解析大同小異，主要是標出公司的名稱、服務內容與所在區域。

❷ 訊息來源：

開發信常見搜尋模式就是各大展覽的官網，該網站中會列出參加廠商的名稱與基本資料，可透過這些資訊再查詢欲投遞開發信公司的詳細資料。

❸ 產品優點：

不同於有形的商品可敘述外觀尺寸的具體數據，介紹服務時，可採先分大項弄再細則的方式。例如：本公司提供清潔服務，清潔類型包括廢棄物清運與辦公室清掃等。

❹ 既有客戶：

與推銷產品時相同，若已有合作之客戶，可簡介本公司服務在該客戶的實行狀況，藉此讓新客戶更了解服務的優點在哪，提高交易成功的可能性。

❺ 詢問窗口：

當客戶對公司產品有興趣時，多留下幾種連絡方式可使其更容易與我們聯絡，從而提升客戶的詢問與購買意願。

❻ 結尾應酬：

一般來說，結尾主要是要表達合作意願，常用的句型有 We look forward to + Ving 我們期待⋯ 與 We hope to hear from you soon. 我們期待能於近期獲得您的回覆。

　　不論是向客戶推銷有形的產品或是無形的服務，若能把握上述之重點，就能提高客戶開信的機率，而有完成交易或建立合作關係之可能性。

 **現在你會說** ||||||||||||||||||||||||||||||||||||||||||

請依句意填入 A-E。

A. The advantages of this product are easy to carry and use

B. Now, let me show you how to use it

C. May I have a try

D. If you have any questions, please feel free to ask

E. please start your briefing now

In DEF Company's Conference room

Jason：Good morning, Andy. Thank you for sparing your precious time.

Andy：Morning Jason, _____1_____.

Jason：OK, let me begin with name of our product. Our new product is called portable bicycle toolkit. _____2_____. It is about a pocket size, so users don't have to worry about where to put it when they are cycling. Besides, we design a movable light at the end, so it can be used in the dark environment. _____3_____. First of all, press the button and you can select the tool mode. If you want change the tool, press the button again to switch the mode.

Andy：It sounds great. _____4_____?

Jason：Of course. _____5_____.

Andy：OK. Thank you for your briefing today. The design concept is great and I think I will place the order soon.

答案

1. (E)　　2. (A)　　3. (B)　　4. (C)　　5. (D)

現在你會寫 |||||||||||||||||||||||||||||||||||||

1. 客製化的服務使我們受大眾歡迎。

_____

_____

中式英文出沒 ▶ What makes we popular is our customize service.

錯在哪 ▶ what make 中的 What 為主詞，故動詞 make 其後應加上受詞，故此處的我們應採用 us 而非 we。

正解 ▶ What makes us popular is our customized service.

2. 本公司產品優點在於質輕而耐用。

_____

_____

中式英文出沒 ▶ The advantages of our product lie in light and durable.

錯在哪 ▶ 若受到中文「在於」的影響，將其理解為「由…所決定」，就會曲解句意。此處的「在於」應理解為「是」才正確。

正解 ▶ The advantages of our product are light and durable.

Unit
01

Unit
02

Unit
03

Unit
04

Unit
05

Unit
06

Unit
07

Unit
08

Unit
09

Unit
10

Unit
11

談判

挑戰難度 ★★★★☆

真的你學過 ||||||||||||||||||||||||||||||||||||||||||||||

　　在商場上，不可能凡事皆盡如我意，當買賣雙方無法達成共識時，就需進行談判交涉。碰上這樣的場合，即使自認英文底子不錯的人，也開始擔心自己能否為公司爭取最大利益。但事實上，只要懂得運用英文疑問句、比較級等基本的文法，就可以清楚表達我方立場，與對方進行交涉。

單元重點及學習方向 |||||||||||||||||||||||||||||||||||||||||

❶ 運用 Is it possible to... 句型來討論可能性。
❷ 運用 Compared to..., our/we...句型來凸顯自家產品或服務的優勢。
❸ 運用 That is the... that we/you... 句型來表達立場。
❹ 運用本單元的單字、片語與句型來練習如何聯絡客戶進行談判與議價。

1. **Is it possible to** have a discount?
   價格可以再更便宜嗎?
2. **Compared to** the similar product of other brands in the market,
   our products are cheaper.
   與市售其他品牌的類似產品相比,我們的產品價格較低廉。
3. **That is** the lowest price that we can provide.
   此為我們所能提供的最低價。
4. **That is** the minimum amount you should order.
   此為你的最小訂購量。

1. **consensus** [kən`sɛnsəs] *n.* 共識
2. **concern** [kən`sɝn] *v.* 在乎
3. **compromise** [`kɑmprə͵maɪz] *v.* 妥協
4. **competitor** [kəm`pɛtətɚ] *n.* 競爭者
5. **cost-effective** [`kɑstə`fɛktɪv] *adj.* 划算的
6. **discount** [`dɪskaʊnt] *n.* 折扣
7. **favorable** [`fevərəbl] *adj.* 特惠的
8. **negotiation** [nɪ͵goʃɪ`eʃən] *n.* 協商
9. **relatively** [`rɛlətɪvlɪ] *adv.* 相對地
10. **reconsider** [͵rikən`sɪdɚ] *v.* 重新考慮

Unit 01

Unit 02

Unit 03

Unit 04

Unit 05

Unit 06

Unit 07

Unit 08

Unit 09

Unit 10

Unit 11

小試身手

1. What we _____ is the quality.

   我們在乎的是品質。

2. How many sets should we buy if we want to get a 10% _____ ?

   我們一次買多少組才能打九折呢？

3. We need some _____ to the unit price.

   我們在單價上需要一些調整。

4. We will provide you a _____ price.

   我們將提供您優惠價。

5. Please _____ this quotation.

   請重新考慮此報價。

解答

1. concern
2. discount
3. adjustments
4. favorable
5. reconsider

句型喚醒你的記憶 ||||||||||||||||||||||||||||||

1. **Is it possible to** lower the price a little bit?

可以再稍微降價嗎？

Is it possible to... 意思為「可以⋯嗎？」，可用於詢問某事的可能性。

例 Is it possible to get some free sample? 可以給我一些免費試用品嗎？

2. **Compared to** other brand, **we** have the best quality.

與他牌相比，我們的品質最好。

Compared to..., we 意思為「與⋯相比，我們⋯」，可用於比較兩者的差異性。

例 Compare to other computer brand, we have the longest warranty. 與其他電腦品牌相比，我們的保固期最長。

3. **That is the lowest** unit price **that we** can provide you.

此為我們所能提供的最低單價。

That is + 最高級（highest/lowest）that we... 意思為「此為我們所能⋯最高／最低的（單價）⋯」，可用於說明我方之立場。

例 That is the lowest price we can provide you. 此為我們所能提供的最低單價。

4. **That is the minimum** amount **that you** should order if you want to have 10% off.

此為享九折優惠的最低訂購量。

That is +（maximum/minmum）that you... 意思為「此為你們所需⋯最大／最小的（數量）⋯」，可用於要求對方配合之事項。

例 That is the maximum amount that you can purchase with this favorable price. 此為本優惠價所可購買之最大數量。

Unit
01

Unit
02

Unit
03

Unit
04

Unit
05

Unit
06

Unit
07

Unit
08

Unit
09

Unit
10

Unit
11

知多少？多知道一點總是好 ||||||||||||||||||||||||||

　　會進行商務談判主要是因買賣雙方無法達成共識，因此不論整個協商過程為何，最終的目的就是形成雙方都可接受的結果。為了達到這樣的結果，在過程中應注意以下要點與避免下列禁忌：

不可不知的要點 ||||||||||||||||||||||||||||||||||||

1. 堅守底限：

　　談判的其實就是做有限度的妥協，因此要先預設我方可接受的最低底線，若低於此限，應考慮放棄交易。

2. 換位思考：

　　當談判未能有所進展時，可從客戶的回應反向找出癥結點，調整談判策略，提高交易成功機率。

3. 適時讓步：

　　進行談判無非是是希望達成共識，因此倘若雙方一直處於僵局，我方可在不損及自身權益的前提下，給予對方一些利多。

不可不知的禁忌

1. 喪失理性：

   由於買買雙方可能都各有所堅持，理性思考才能突破僵局，出現情緒化字句反而會誤事。

2. 缺乏判斷：

   若客戶所派出的人員能夠善用談判技巧，會將對話導向他所預設的方向，若一時不察，依此方向繼續談判，我方的權益可能受損

3. 自作主張：

   除非今天你自己就是老闆，即便今天公司全權授權，也不宜做出超過事前推演範圍之外的承諾，以免產生後續問題。

Unit
01

Unit
02

Unit
03

Unit
04

Unit
05

Unit
06

Unit
07

Unit
08

Unit
09

Unit
10

Unit
11

腦部暖身 一點都不難對話 |||||||||||||||||||||||||||

請將以下六個單字填入空格內。

(a) get   (b) purchase   (c) raise
(d) restriction   (e) kind   (f) range

Jason：It seems we need further discussion on the minimum ____1____ amount in this deal.

Amy：Yeah! Our company really likes the idea of your products, but now we don't have enough capital due to some budget reason. **Is it possible to** adjust such ____2____?

Jason：It depends on the ____3____. According to our sales policy, we will provide a 10% discount if the customer purchases more than 1000 sets at once.

Amy：Can we lower the amount to 700 sets but still ____4____ the favorable price?

Jason：I have to say sorry to you, because we really can't provide you such discount with this amount. However, I can promise that you will have a better price if you ____5____ the amount a little bit.

Amy：If we raise the amount to 800 sets, what ____6____ of discounts can we have?

Jason：We can give you a 5 % discount with that amount.

Amy：Deal.

翻譯

Jason：看來我們需要再討論本次交易的最小採購量。

Amy：沒錯。我們公司非常喜歡貴公司產品的概念，但目前受限於預算

資金有些不足，可否降低限制呢？

Jason：這要看你想調降的幅度。根據本公司的銷售方針，客戶一次購買
1000 組才能享有九折優惠。

Amy：那有可能只購買七百組但仍享有九折優惠嗎？

Jason：這邊必須跟你說抱歉，我們無法在此採購數量提供此優惠價格。
但如果再稍微提高購買量，我保證能給你一些折扣。

Amy：如果買八百組可以享有多少折扣呢？

Jason：八百組的話可以給予九五折。

Amy：成交。

Unit
01

Unit
02

Unit
03

Unit
04

Unit
05

Unit
06

Unit
07

Unit
08

Unit
09

Unit
10

Unit
11

單字 ....

- **capital** [`kæpətl] *n.* 資金
- **budget** [`bʌdʒɪt] *n.* 預算
- **policy** [`pɑləsɪ] *n.* 方針
- **deal** [dil] *n.* 成交

答案 ....

1. (b)　2. (d)　3. (f)　4. (a)　5. (c)　6. (e)

會說也會寫一：商談單價 ||||||||||||||||||||||||||

範例

Dear Leo,

❶As we discussed in the phone, the unit price of this machine still have room for negotiation. Here let me respond your request.

❷The unit price you requested in this deal is 70 USD, ❸but this price is much lower than the most favorable price we provide to our customer with this purchase amount. The best price we can give is 80 USD.

❹Please reconsider this price and reply us soon.

Sincerely yours,
Jason

翻譯

親愛的 Leo：

　　如同我們在電話中所討論的，本次交易的單價尚有協商空間。於此讓我回覆你的要求。

　　你所要求的單價是 70 美金，但這個價格遠低於我們提供此採購量的最優惠價。我們最低只能降到 80 美金。

　　請再次考慮此價格，並盡快回覆是否接受此議價。

謹
Jaosn

解析

在寫信與客戶商議價格時，為了提高溝通的效率，避免多次的信件往返，通常內容通常會包含以下幾個部分：

❶初步的討論：

會進行議價表示買賣雙方在之前可能已經提出一個價格，但這個價格無法為對方所接受，寫信的目的也是在此前提下繼續協商。以此範例為例，Jason 表示將回應 Leo 提出的價格。

❷客戶提出的具體要求：

説明完寫信緣由後，接下來就是重述對方的要求。在本範例中，Leo 所提出的單價是 70 美金。

❸我方給予的回應：

敘述完對方的要求之後，接下來就是給予回應，這也是信件的核心。在這個部份我方會提出一個底限，並希望客戶接受。在本範例中，Jason 表示我方的最優惠價就是 80 美金。

❹請對方回覆：

此部分其實內容相當固定，主要都是希望客戶妥協，盡快回覆是否接受我方提出的價格。常用的句型有：

(a) Please reconsider... 請再考慮…

(b) Please accept... 請接受…

由於對方在收到此信後，也可能不接受我方的還價，又再提出一個折衷的新價格。當買賣雙方幾次重複上述流程後，就可能達成共識，使交易能夠進入下一個環節。

註

若經過多此信件往返仍對價格僵持不下，可改採提供贈品或是分期付款等利多，讓客戶妥協。

會說也會寫二：商談訂購量

Dear Dennis,

❶In your previous letter, you mentioned that you want to adjust the minimum purchase amount in this project. Here let me reply your request.

❷As you indicated, you want to lower the minimum purchase amount from 1000 sets to 900 sets this time but still have the same discount. In general, we won't provide any discounts to purchase below 1000 sets. ❸Considering you are one of the most important trade partners we have in USA, we still provide you a 10% discount if you buy 900 sets.

❹Please reply us soon. We do cherish the business relationship we have built.

Yours,
Jason

翻譯

　　你在前一封來信中提到你們公司想調整本次交易的最低採購量，於此針對你的要求加以回應。

　　如同你所提出的，你們希望將本次的最低採購量從 1000 組降至 900 組並享有原有之折扣。一般來說，單次採購量未達一千組，我們是不提供折扣的。但念在你們是本公司在美國非常重要的貿易夥伴之一，若一次購買 900 組，仍可享有九折優惠。

　　請盡速回覆，我們相當珍惜彼此所建立的夥伴關係。

謹
Jason

解析 ||||||||||||||||||||||||||||||||||||||||||||||||||||||||||||||||

　　交易時除協議單價之外，採購量也是一個需要討論的項目。一般來說，根據規模經濟（詳見註）的概念，一次購買的數量越大，可享有的折扣也越多，但到底買多少算多，需要買賣雙方的意見交換，才可能達成共識，以下針對範例信件中的四大部分作進一步說明：

❶初步的討論：

　　每間公司針對不同的購買量可能會給予相對應的折扣，此封信件就是此做為後續討論的前提。Jason 公司所提出最低採購數量是 1000 組。

❷客戶提出的具體要求：

　　客戶可能基於某些因素，不想一次採購這麼多產品，因而提出下修最低採購量的要求，但仍希望對方可以給予相同折扣。在本範例中 Dennis 就是希望少買 100 組，但仍享有買 1000 組的九折。

❸我方給予的回應：

　　一般而言，為保持一定的利潤，我方常會在客戶要求與我方底限中在取出一個中間值請對方考慮。但在某些情況下，特別是已固定合作許久之貿易夥伴，考量到後續的生意往來，會選擇接受對方之要求。在本範例中，就讓客戶只購買 900 組，但享有九折優惠。

❹請對方回覆：

　　此部分內容主要都是希望對方盡快接受我方條件，但也可能選擇接受對方要求。以本範例為例，我方基於雙方合作已久，讓客戶少買一百組，但享有原本的優惠。

註

　　規模經濟指的是當生產規模擴大時，因為購入原料的成本降低，生產過程也更具效率，使長期的平均成本會降低。在這樣的情況下，因為利潤提高，生產者就有給予客戶降價的空間。

 現在你會說 ||||||||||||||||||||||||||||||||||||||||||||||||

請依句意填入 A-E。

A. And you hope we can provide you a better price
B. Thank you for your consideration
C. Please tell me the lowest unit price you can provide
D. We won't make a deal without profit
E. I think we need to discuss the unit price of this purchase

Jason：_____1_____.

Mark：Yeah.

Jason：As you mentioned in meeting few days ago, your company needs 100 training machines next month. _____2_____.

Mark：Right. Since we have purchased certain amount, I want to know is it possible to lower the price from 300 USD to 210 USD per machine?

Jason：Thank you for showing interest in our product. However, the price you requested is too low _____3_____.

Mark：Since we are trade partners, let's compromise a little bit. _____4_____.

Jason：_____5_____. The most favorable unit price you can get is 240 USD.

Mark：I can accept this price.

答案

1. (E)　2. (A)　3. (D)　4. (C)　5. (B)

現在你會寫 |||||||||||||||||||||||||||||||||||||||||||||||

Unit
01

Unit
02

Unit
03

Unit
04

Unit
05

Unit
06

Unit
07

Unit
08

Unit
09

Unit
10

Unit
11

1.有可能調降產品價格嗎？

_____

_____

中式英文出沒 ▶ Is it possible to adjust and drop the price of the product?

錯在哪 ▶ 若受到中文的「調降」影響，將其理解「調整」與「降低」兩個部分，反而會是英文句子怪異難懂，「調降」用 lower 即可清楚表達意思。

正解 ▶ Is it possible to lower the price of the product?

2.此為享有折扣的最低採購量。

_____

_____

中式英文出沒 ▶ That is the minimum purchase amount have discount.

錯在哪 ▶ 「享有折扣的」若轉換成英文，在概念上是補充敘述，應以片語或子句的方式出現。因此應將 have 修正為 if you want to have 或是 to have。

正解 ▶ That is the minimum purchase amount if you want to have a discount./ That is the minimum purchase amount to have a discount.

簽約

挑戰難度 ★★★★★

真的你學過

　　與客戶協商達成共識之後，接下來就是雙方簽約，以保障彼此權益。但由於簽約牽涉法律層面，許多人都認為必須要有深厚的英文基礎才有辦法處理英文合約，但事實上，只要掌握合約中的重要元素，搭配簡易的敘述句型，簽約並沒有你想的這麼困難。

單元重點及學習方向

❶ 運用... is on the basis of/based on... 句型說明簽約的依據。

❷ 運用 Sth covers/includes... 句型來說明合約的涵蓋範圍。

❸ 運用 S + has/have the right to..., if... 來說明雙方的權利。

❹ 運用本單元的單字、片語與句型來練習與客戶商談簽約事宜。

 必 **check** 句型

1. The agreement **is** made **on the basis of** the new project.

   本合約是依照新專案所撰寫。

2. The contract **is based on** the consensus we reached in last meeting.

   本合約是依照上次會議所達成之共識所撰寫。

3. The contract **covers** the sales of the new product.

   本合約的內容涵蓋新產品的銷售。

4. The seller **has the right to** postpone the shipment **if** the buyer doesn't pay in time.

   如買方未及時付款，賣方有權暫緩出貨。

 A 你有學過的單字

1. **benefit** [`bɛnəfɪt] *n.* 利益
2. **legal** [`ligl] *adj.* 法律上的
3. **mutual** [`mjutʃʊəl] *adj.* 互相的
4. **obey** [ə`be] *v.* 遵守
5. **representative** [rɛprɪ`zɛntətɪv] *n.* 代表
6. **signature** [`sɪgnətʃɚ] *n.* 簽名
7. **terminate** [`tɝməˌnet] *v.* 終止
8. **party** [`pɑrtɪ] *n.* 當事人
9. **right** [raɪt] *n.* 權利
10. **violate** [`vaɪəˌlet] *v.* 違反

Unit
12

Unit
13

Unit
14

Unit
15

Unit
16

Unit
17

Unit
18

Unit
19

Unit
20

Unit
21

Unit
22

小試身手

1. The contract shall be made on the basis of _____ benefits
   合約應以互利為目的來撰寫。

2. Two parties should _____ the content of the contract.
   當事人雙方應遵守合約內容。

3. The _____ of each party signed the contract with a lawyer as a withess.
   當事人雙方的代表在律師的見證下簽約。

4. The seller has the right to _____ the agreement if the buyer refuses to provide related documents
   如買方不願提供相關文件，賣方有權終止合約。

5. The buyer has the _____ to return the product if they find the quality is worse than the sample.
   如買方發現貨品品質不如樣品，買方有權進行退貨。

解答

1. mutual
2. obey
3. representative
4. terminate
5. right

句型喚醒你的記憶 ||||||||||||||||||||||||||||||||||||

Unit
12

Unit
13

Unit
14

Unit
15

Unit
16

Unit
17

Unit
18

Unit
19

Unit
20

Unit
21

Unit
22

1. The contract **is on the basis of** the project meeting few days ago.

   本合約是根據數天前的會議所撰寫。

   ... is on the basis of... 意思為「依據…」，可用於說明事物的背景。

   例 The agreement is on the basis of the consensus we reached yesterday. 此合約是根據昨天所達成的共識來撰寫。

2. This purchase **includes** the cases and rechargers of smart phones.

   本次採購包含智慧型手機的充電器與手機殼。

   Sth includes... 意思為「某事物涵蓋…」，可用於敘述事物的範圍。

   例 The contact **includes** the purchase of the new machines and parts. 本合約包含新機器與零件的採購。

3. The contract **covers** the replacement of old parts.

   本合約涵蓋舊零件的替換。

   Sth covers... 意思為「某事物包涵…」，可用於敘述事物的範圍。

   例 The purchase covers the new training machines. 本次採購包含新的訓練機。

4. The seller **has the right to** cancel the shipment **if** the buyer refuses to the insurance fee.

   若買方不願支付保險費用，賣方有權取消出貨。

   ... has/have the right... if... 意思為「若…，則…有權…」，可用於說明當事人享有的權利。

   例 Buyers have the right to return the machine if it doesn't function well. 若機器無法正常運作，買方有權要求退貨。

知多少？多知道一點總是好 ‖‖‖‖‖‖‖‖‖‖‖‖‖‖‖‖‖‖‖‖

在商場上，口頭承諾只有一方事後反悔，往往因為舉證的困難言衍生往後的諸多事端，因此簽訂具有法律效力的合約就有其必要性。合約是將雙方所同意知事項文字化，並由雙方簽名以示負責。因此在完成簽署前應注意以下之要點，以避免產生後續問題。

不可不知的要點 ‖‖‖‖‖‖‖‖‖‖‖‖‖‖‖‖‖‖‖‖‖‖‖‖

1. 簽約雙方的名稱與相關資訊：

此部分會記載以下關於當事人的資訊：

(1) 簽約日期：此日期代表合約的生效日，因此要特別注意時間是否正確，以免影響後續權益。

(2) 公司名稱與所在地：此處的名稱須為公司之全衛+國家與城市名稱

(3) 適用法規：合約屬於法律文件，當產生糾紛會有以何國法律為準的問題產生，因此應於此列出各當事人的法源依據，並於合約內容中明定應以哪國為準。

2. 合約的涵蓋範圍：

法律保障合約所提及之內容，故於簽約之前務必要審視其範圍是否為雙方所同意。

3 雙方的權利與義務：

此部分為合約的核心，通常會有公司法務人員或是直接委請律師協助確認，故毋需太過擔心會有遺漏。

4 終止的客觀條件：

若簽約當事人有人違反合約內容，另一方應當有權終止此合約，以保障自身權益，故於簽約前檢查終止條件是否合理。

上述內容皆確認無誤後，才可由雙方代表正式進行簽署，使該合約產生法律上的效力。

Unit
12

Unit
13

Unit
14

Unit
15

Unit
16

Unit
17

Unit
18

Unit
19

Unit
20

Unit
21

Unit
22

腦部暖身 一點都不難對話

請將以下六個單字填入空格內。

(a) sign
(b) decide
(c) settling
(d) represent
(e) Group
(f) aspects

Jason：Since we have reached a consensus in many   1   , now let's discuss some details of the agreement.

Ken：Sure.

Jason：First of all, let's discuss when to   2   the contract. How about one week after the discussion today namely March 3.

Ken：Let me check my schedule. I am free on that day, so I can   3   our company to sign the contract with you.

Jason：It would be great. Now let's check the name, and you and I will use in the contract.

Ken：We will use DEF Company.

Jason：We will use ABC   4   .

Ken：About the governing law, it will be under the law of Taiwan as we discussed, right?

Jason：Correct. The reason why we have to   5   one legal source is for   6   the dispute, but I hope we never have to use it in the future.

Ken：I totally agree.

翻譯

Jason：因為我們已經在多方面達成共識了，現在就來討論一下簽約的細節吧！

Ken：當然好。

Jason：首先讓我們決定何時進行簽約。本次討論後的一週，也就是三月三日可以嗎？

Ken：讓我看一下行事曆。我那天有空，所以可以代表公司跟你們簽約。

Jason：太棒了。那現在讓我們來確認合約上我們所使用的名稱。

Ken：我們會使用 DEF 公司

Jason：我們採用 ABC 集團。

Ken：在準據法的部分。我們採先前所討論過的台灣法律為準對吧？

Jason：沒錯。決定一個法源依據，是為了解決爭端的，但我希望我們未來不會有機會用到此法。

Ken：完全同意。

Unit **12**
Unit **13**
Unit **14**
Unit **15**
Unit **16**
Unit **17**
Unit **18**
Unit **19**
Unit **20**
Unit **21**
Unit **22**

單字

- **namely** [ˋnemlɪ] *adv.* 即
- **governing** [ˋgʌvɚnɪŋ] *adj.* 管理的
- **source** [sors] *n.* 源頭
- **dispute** [dɪˋspjut] *n.* 爭議

答案

1. (f)   2. (a)   3. (d)   4. (e)   5. (b)   6. (c)

會說也會寫一：合約序文撰寫

範例

❶This agreement is made on January 1 2013, ❷by and between ABC Company, a company organized under the law of Taiwan (hereinafter referred as Party A) and DEF Company, a company organized under the law of Germany (hereinafter referred as Party B).

❸Whereas, Party A desires to sell the New Training machine to Party B. ❹In consideration of the mutual benefit, the Parties agree the following content:

翻譯

本契約於 2013 年 1 月 1 日，由台灣依法所設立之 ABC 公司（以下簡稱甲方）與德國依法所設立之 DEF 公司（以下簡稱乙方）所簽訂。

鑑於，甲方欲銷售新型訓練機給乙方，在考量雙方利益下，當事人同意以下事項:

補充

➤ hereinafter 為法律上的慣用字，意思為「在下文中」，意思上等於 after this agreement。

以下為組成公式：

here + 介係詞 = 介係詞 + this agreement

例：hereto = to this agreement = 至此

以此邏輯做推演，往後再看到其他 here + 介係詞的組合，也能夠了解它的意思，不再心生畏懼。

為避免產生後續爭議，一般而言，合約的序文至少會包含以下幾個部分：

❶簽約時間：

這個時間同時也代表了合約生效的時間，若以本範例為例，合約的生效日是 2013 年 1 月 1 日。

❷簽約當事人資訊：

此資訊內容又可再細分為以下三項：

・簽約當事人名稱：

　此名稱具有法律效力，若其他文件的名稱與之不同，多數情況會以合約上的名稱為準。以範例合約為例，雙方分別使用 ABC 公司與 DEF 公司作為代表。

・法源依據：

　寫明法源依據主要是怕未來萬一產生糾紛不知應該以哪一個國的法律為主，因此在序文部分先行寫出，再於合約內容中做詳細規範。以本範例為例，ABC 公司採台灣法，DEF 公司採德國法。

・簡稱方式：

　由於合約的內容可能非常多且牽涉大量專業用語，為便於書寫與閱讀完整的公司名稱通常只會出現在最開始的序文與最後的簽署部分，並於序文列出簡稱方式。以本範例為例，ABC 公司簡稱甲方，DEF 公司簡稱乙方。

❸簽約事由：

此部分用於說明為何要簽約，以本範例為例，因為甲方要賣新型訓練機給乙方，所以雙方簽約。

❹簽約依據：

此部分用於補充說明簽約事由，通常會以基於互利互信等角度做論述。以本範例為例，採用的是基於互利。

Unit
12

Unit
13

Unit
14

Unit
15

Unit
16

Unit
17

Unit
18

Unit
19

Unit
20

Unit
21

Unit
22

會說也會寫二：簽署

範例

❶In witness of this whereof, the authorized representative of the Parties have caused this agreement is to be signed in duplicated as of the date written above.

❷**Buyer**   **Seller**
DEF Company   ABC Company
By: _____（signature） By: _____（signature）
Name: James Huang   Name: Tom John
Title: sales Manager   Title: Purchase Manager
Date: Date:

翻譯

茲此特以立約為據，由雙方授權代表於上述之日期簽署本合約，並做成一式兩份。

買方   **賣方**
DEF 公司   ABC 公司
簽名：_____   簽名：_____
姓名：James Huang   姓名：Tom John
日期：_____   日期：_____

補充

duplicate 意思為分成兩分，若進行簽約時要求一式兩份，代表最後會有兩份具有雙方簽署的合約，以本合約為例，一份給賣方，一份給買方，兩份都具備相同的效力。

解析

審視完合約內容過後，最後就是簽署合約，完成此程序後合約也正式生效，為了確保其法律效力，簽署的內容通常包含以下幾個部分：

❶見證：

此部分通常包含兩大訊息：

・雙方派出互相可接受之代表。

・合約共一式幾分，若以本範例中的為一式兩份為例，即雙方共簽署兩份相同內容之合約，並各持一份。以此邏輯類推，一式三份或更多即代表須簽署相同內容的對應份數合約。

❷簽署人資料與簽名：

這邊的簽屬人資料指的是以下幾項：

・公司全銜：

此一名稱需與序文中所列完全相同，否則將喪失其法律效力。以此範例為例，買方為 DEF 公司，賣方為 ABC 公司，在序文中也必須是這樣的名稱。

・簽約代表姓名：

這部分會列出負責簽約的人是誰，以便與實際簽名負責的人相對照，確保法律上的效力。以本範例為例，ABC 公司的代表是 Tom John，DEF 公司的代表是 James Huang。

・職稱：

列出職稱除再次確認簽約人身分外，也可檢視代表的適切性。舉例來說，若客戶端是由總裁親自簽署，而我方卻派出業務員，客戶可能產生該業務員是否獲得完全授權之疑慮。

上述的簽署人資料做的都只是確認，真正使合約產生效力的是簽約代表的簽名，簽名的同時會附上日期，代表是於此日完成簽約。

Unit 12
Unit 13
Unit 14
Unit 15
Unit 16
Unit 17
Unit 18
Unit 19
Unit 20
Unit 21
Unit 22

 現在你會說 ||||||||||||||||||||||||||||||||||||||||||||

請依句意填入 A-E。

A. First of all, let's decide when to sign the contract
B. Now let's check the title you and I will use in the agreement
C. Why we discuss this is to choose one legal source for settling the dispute if needed
D. now let's discuss some details of the contract
E. We will use our group's name ABC Group

Jason：Since we have reached a consensus in many aspects, _____1_____.

Ken：Sure.

Jason：_____2_____. How about five days after the discussion today namely March 3?

Ken：Let me check my schedule through my mobile. I am free on that day, so I can be the representative of our company to sign the contract with you.

Jason：It would be great. _____3_____.

Ken：We will use GHJ Company.

Jason：_____4_____.

Ken：About the governing law, we will use Taiwan's law as we discussed, right?

Jason：Correct. _____5_____ but I hope it won't happen in the future.

Ken：I agree. And I sincerely hope that we can keep this partnership for long.

答案 ....

1. (D) 2. (A) 3. (B) 4. (E) 5. (C)

 現在你會寫

1. 本合約是根據上次專案會議的共識而來。

_____

_____

中式英文出沒 ▶ This contract is based on the consensus of the last project meeting to come.

錯在哪 ▶ 中文的「根據…而來」翻譯為英文時，其實運用 is based on 即能完整對應，加上 to come 是錯誤的。

正解 ▶ This contract is based on the consensus of last project meeting.

2. 本次交易包含新機採購與舊零件替換。

_____

_____

中式英文出沒 ▶ This deal includes new machine purchase and old parts replace.

錯在哪 ▶ 此處的「新機採購」與「舊零件替換」應理解為「新機的採購」與「舊零件的替換」。故須修正為 the purchase of new machine 與 the replacement of old parts。

正解 ▶ This deal includes the purchase of new machines and the replacement of old parts.

Unit
12

Unit
13

Unit
14

Unit
15

Unit
16

Unit
17

Unit
18

Unit
19

Unit
20

Unit
21

Unit
22

13 Unit 出貨事宜

挑戰難度 ★★★☆☆

 真的你學過

　　與客戶完成簽約確定所有事項之後，接下來就是按照合約內容出貨。在出貨前我方都會與客戶做最後確認，但由於這道手續較為繁瑣，很多人擔心因為英文不夠好，因而遺漏一些細節。事實上，只要善用條件句來確認時間、地點，就能輕鬆完成出貨。

單元重點及學習方向

❶ 運用 Upon + Ving, we will... 句型來表達每個環節的要點
❷ 運用 S will... before/by + 日期來確認出貨的時間。
❸ 運用 S should... unless... 句型來表達例外情況。
❹ 運用本單元的單字、片語與句型來練習與客戶確認出貨的相關事宜。

 必 **check** 句型

1. **Upon receiving** your payment, we will ship the product to you.
   一收到付款就會出貨給您。
2. The product **will** be delivered **before** this Friday.
   產品將於本週五前寄出。
3. The shipment **will** be made **by** this Monday.
   我們將於本週一前為您出貨。
4. The machine **should** arrive in USA by this Monday **unless** the flight is delayed.
   除非班機有延誤，否則機器會在本週一前抵美。

 A 你有學過的單字

1. **deliver** [dɪ`lɪvɚ] *v.* 運送
2. **express** [ɪk`sprɛs] *n.* 快遞
3. **insurance** [ɪn`ʃʊrəns] *n.* 保險
4. **payment** [ɪn`ʃʊrəns] *n.* 款項
5. **port** [port] *n.* 港口
6. **receive** [rɪ`siv] *v.* 收到
7. **shipment** [`ʃɪpmənt] *n.* 出貨
8. **trace** [tres] *v.* 追蹤
9. **urgent** [`ɝdʒənt] *adj.* 緊急的
10. **warehouse** [`wɛr͵haʊs] *n.* 倉庫

Unit
12

Unit
13

Unit
14

Unit
15

Unit
16

Unit
17

Unit
18

Unit
19

Unit
20

Unit
21

Unit
22

小試身手 ||||||||||||||||||||||||||||||||||||||||||

1. We will _____ the product you ordered through truck.
   我們將以卡車運送您所訂購之產品。

2. Your payment includes the _____.
   您的付款包含保險類用。

3. You will _____ the parts within one week.
   您將於一週內收到零件。

4. You can _____ the shipment through this system.
   您可以透過此系統追蹤出貨情況。

5. The product you ordered will arrive at your _____ five days later.
   您所訂購的產品將於五天後送達您公司倉庫。

解答

1. deliver
2. insurance
3. receive
4. trace
5. warehouse

句型喚醒你的記憶 ||||||||||||||||||||||||||||||||||||||||||

1. **Upon** receiving your order, **we will** process the paper work.

   一收到你的訂單，我們會進行文件作業。

   Upon...., we will... 意思為「一…我們就…」，可用於說明出貨時每一環節的達成要件。

   例 Upon receiving your payment, we will deliver the parts you ordered. 一收到貨款，我們就會出貨您所訂購的零件。

2. The product **will** arrive at the port **before** April 3.

   本產品將於四月三日前到港。

   ... will... before... 意思為「…將在…之前…」，可用於說明事情的先後。

   例 The replacement you ordered will arrive at the warehouse you chose in the order before March 15. 你所訂購的替換品將於三月十五日前送抵你於訂單中所選擇的倉庫。

3. The machine you ordered **will** arrive at your warehouse **by** this Monday.

   你所訂購的機器將於週一前抵達你公司倉庫。

   ... will... by... 意思為「…將在…前…」，可用於說明事情的確切時間點。

   例 The shipment will be made by this Thursday. 我們將於本星期四前為您出貨。

4. The parts **should** arrive in the city you requested in the order this Friday **unless** the flight is cancelled.

   除非飛班機取消，否則零件將於本週五抵達你訂單所要求的城市。

   ... should... unless 意思為「除非…否則…」，可用於說明發生例外情況的可能原因。

   例 The product should arrive at your city in time unless the express company sends them to the wrong place. 除非快遞公司送錯地點，否則產品應該要及時送抵你所在的城市。

Unit 12
Unit 13
Unit 14
Unit 15
Unit 16
Unit 17
Unit 18
Unit 19
Unit 20
Unit 21
Unit 22

知多少？多知道一點總是好 ▌▌▌▌▌▌▌▌▌▌▌▌▌▌▌▌▌▌

　　與客戶簽約後，接下來就是依約進行出貨。出貨前雙方一定會針對細節再做一次確認，此程序通常會包含已下幾個部分：

1. 出貨品項：

　　雖然合約貨訂單中都已載明購買的產品是什麼，但出貨前要再確認產品的編號（若為英文＋數字，更應仔細對照），以免寄錯東西，產生很多後續問題。

2. 出貨數量：

　　訂單或合約一定會清楚標示本次購買數量，出貨時若有數量短少，除要額外支出運送成本外，還可能有賠償問題產生。

3. 出貨／到貨時間：

　　由於貨品運送需要一定的時程，因此買賣雙方會約定產品應於何時自賣方國家出口，並於何時抵達賣方國家。出貨前雙方要確認這兩個時間，才不會影響彼此的權益。

4.出／收貨人：

不論是國際貿易慣例或是各國進出口法規，皆對進/出口人有所規定，因此買賣雙方應於出貨前再次確認出貨文件是否合格，以避免貨品生產好卻無法出口，或是已經出貨卻被卡在買方國家海關無法進口。

5.其他事項：

由於出貨也可能因為某些突發或不可抗力因素而有所延遲，雙方應於出貨前商討與確認相關的處置，以保障彼此權益。

　　執行上述的確認步驟後，方可大大降低出錯的機會，讓買賣雙方可以順利地完成交易。

腦部暖身 一點都不難對話 ||||||||||||||||||||||||||

請將以下六個單字填入空格內。

(a) made   (b) double   (c) repeat

(d) Indeed   (e) finished   (f) shipment

In a phone call.

Jason：Frank, Are you free now? Let's check the details of the
_____1_____.

Frank：I am free. Let's begin with name and amount that I
purchase. I buy ten X123 training machines from you.

Jason：Right. Ten machines are all ready to deliver. To make
sure you can receive them in time, here I _____2_____
the delivery and arrival time to you. The shipment will
be _____3_____ this Friday (March 1) from Taiwan and
will arrive in your country next Thursday (March 6).

Frank：All correct. And the ten machines are exported with
name of ABC Company, right?

Jason：I have _____4_____ checked about this. If the name is
different from that in the document needed, it will be a
big trouble for both of us.

Frank：_____5_____. Last thing to reconfirm is the tracking
number of the shipment. It should be XX-1234.

Jason：Right. Now we've _____6_____ the confirmation.

翻譯

Jason：Frank 你現在有空嗎？讓我們確認一下出貨事宜。

Frank：有空。就先從我購買的產品名稱與數量開始吧！我向你們公司購
買了十台 X123 型訓練機。

Jason：沒錯。十台機器都已準備出貨了。為了確保你能即時收到貨品，我再重複一次出貨與到貨時間。這十台訓練機將於本週五（三月一日）從台灣出貨，並於下星期四（三月六日）抵達你所在的國家。

Frank：沒錯。這十台機器是以 ABC 公司的名義出口的對吧？

Jason：針對這部分我有再三檢查。因為如果與所需提交的出口文件名稱不符的話，對你我都會造成很大的麻煩。

Frank：是阿！最後要確認的是追蹤碼。編號是 XX-1234。

Jason：沒錯。現在我們完成確認工作了。

單字
....

- **delivery** [dɪ`lɪvərɪ] *n.* 出貨
- **arrival** [ə`raɪvl] *n.* 抵達
- **export** [`ɪks`port] *v.* 出口
- **trouble** [`trʌbl̩] *n.* 麻煩

答案
....

1. (f)　2. (c)　3. (a)　4. (b)　5. (d)　6. (e)

Unit 12
Unit 13
Unit 14
Unit 15
Unit 16
Unit 17
Unit 18
Unit 19
Unit 20
Unit 21
Unit 22

會說也會寫一：出貨確認信 ||||||||||||||||||||||

範例

Dear Sam,

❶Since we're ready for the shipment, we'd like to reconfirm the details with you.

❷According to the agreement we signed, you ordered 100 WSA model machines from us in this purchase. The delivery time is scheduled on March 15 from Taiwan, Taichung while the arrival time is on March 25.

❸Please check all the above-mentioned details, and reply no matter what the mistakes you found to help us continue the following process.

Yours sincerely,

Jason

翻譯

親愛的 Sam：

　　由於我們已經準備好出貨，於此想與您再次確認相關細節。

　　根據我們雙方簽訂的合約，你於本次採購中，向我們購買 100 台 WSA 型機器。貨品將於三月十五日自台灣台中出貨。並於三月二十五日抵達你的國家。

　　請再次確認上述細節。無論是否發現錯誤，請給予回覆以利我方作業。

謹

Jason

解析 ||||||||||||||||||||||||||||||||||||||||||||||||||||||||||||||

Unit
12

Unit
13

Unit
14

Unit
15

Unit
16

Unit
17

Unit
18

Unit
19

Unit
20

Unit
21

Unit
22

　　於出貨前寫信向客戶再次細節時，為避免產生遺漏，信件內容大致會有一下三個部分：

❶寫信事由：

　　此部分主要是向客戶表達產品已經準備好，寫信是要雙方確認好相關的事項以便出貨。在本範例信件中，採用的就是上述脈絡。

❷出貨細節：

　　此部分也是確認信的核心。於此會針對以下項目進行全部或是部分確認：

・訂購品項與數量：

　　在本範例中，客戶訂購的是 100 台 WSA 型機器，因此出貨前 Jason 與其再次確認。

・出貨與到貨時間：

　　在本範例中，貨物預計於三月十五日自台中出貨，於十天後抵達客戶所在國家。

・進／出口人：

　　本範例雖然未對此進行確認，但為確保進出口文件的正確性，買賣雙方應多留意文件內容是否有誤，以免影響自身與客戶權益。

・運送追蹤碼：

　　運送追蹤碼是要客戶能夠了解當前的貨品用送狀況。一般而言，我方與貨運業者確認相關事宜後，就會獲得此組編號。

❸要求回覆：

　　這部分的內容是在要求客戶看完此信確認細節後，通知我方一切沒有問題，可以出貨了。

會說也會寫二：出貨變更信 ||||||||||||||||||||||||||

範例

Dear Leo,

❶We have prepared the product you ordered, so here let's check the details of the shipment.

❷As we agreed in the contract, you ordered 100 UDF model machines from us. And the 100 machines are scheduled to deliver this Monday (December 20). **❸**However, the shipment will be delayed at least one day since the cargo ship we booked has some mechanical problems needed to fix.

❹We will inform you the new arrival time once we got the news. Sorry for bringing inconvenience to you.

Yours,

Jason

翻譯

親愛的 Leo：

　　我們現在已經準備好你所訂購的產品，所以在出貨前再次與你確認細節。

　　同我們合約內容所示，你向本公司訂購 100 台 UDF 型機器。這些機器將於本週一，也就是十二月二十日出貨。但由於我們所預定的貨輪出現機械故障，需要時間修理，所以出貨至少會延遲一天。

　　當我們得知新的船隻出發時間，會再通知您，造成不便敬請見諒。

謹

Jason

解析 ||||||||||||||||||||||||||||||||||||||||||||||

在寫信與客戶核對出貨細節時，若只是單純確認不做變更，主要是透過重述合約或訂單內容，請客戶再次檢查。但當我方發現某個環節需要調整時，例如交通問題，其信件內容大致包含以下幾個部分：

❶寫信事由：

與一般出貨確認信相同，於此要先告知客戶產品已經準備好，以利後面解釋為何需要延遲出貨。

❷出貨細節：

此部分的主要內容已於會說也會寫一中介紹過，於此就不再贅述。在本範例中，客戶向我方訂購 100 台機器，機器將於本週一，也就是十二月二十日出貨。

❸變更內容：

變更出貨時間的原因經常來自交通因素，而這樣的延遲通常又出自突發狀況或是不可抗力因素。以本範例為例，由於貨輪突然出現機械故障，導致貨品無法依照預定時間離港。

❹致歉：

雖然在本範例中造成延遲的因素並非我方所能控制，但客戶無法按照既定時間收到貨物已成事實，因此基於禮儀，還是要向客戶致歉，並在影響排除之後，告知客戶新的運送與抵達時間。

註

影響貨運業者正常出貨的因素除器械故障外，還有不可抗力因素與人員罷工。針對這兩者，規格較高的運輸保險會將其涵蓋在內，因此倘若真的遭遇此情況，賣方也勿需擔心後續賠償。

Unit
12

Unit
13

Unit
14

Unit
15

Unit
16

Unit
17

Unit
18

Unit
19

Unit
20

Unit
21

Unit
22

 現在你會說 ||||||||||||||||||||||||||||||||||||||||||||

請依句意填入 **A-E**。

A. The parts I ordered should arrive in Germany on April 16
B. If we use the other name, the customs won't accept the document
C. Let's shift the focus to the legal aspect
D. You can key in this number to check where the parts are
E. Let's begin with the product name and purchase amount

Jason：The shipment is about to be made, so let's check the details.

Tony：Sure.

Jason：___1___. You buy 12000 parts from us according to the agreement.

Tony：Correct. I think all parts are ready, so let's reconfirm the arrival time first. ___2___.

Jason：Right. We have left some room for unexpected situations, so we believe you will receive the parts in time.

Tony：Good. ___3___. Do all the parts are exported with name of your company?

Jason：Definitely. ___4___.

Tony：I got it. Last thing to reconfirm is the tracking number of the shipment. It is kkk-7890.

Jason：Right. ___5___.

答案 ....

1. (E)　2. (A)　3. (C)　4. (B)　5. (D)

 **現在你會寫**

1.一收到款項，我們就會開始準備出貨。

_____

_____

中式英文出沒 ▶ Upon receive the payment, we will prepare the shipment.

錯在哪 ▶ upon 是介係詞，後面應加上動名詞 Ving，故此處應將 receive 修正為 receiving.

正解 ▶ Upon receiving the payment, we will prepare the shipment.

2.除非班機取消，否則貨物可以在本週三抵美。

_____

_____

中式英文出沒 ▶ The product should arrive USA this Wednesday unless the flight cancels.

錯在哪 ▶ 英文描述抵達某個大的地點（如國家）時，arrive in 方為正確用法。另本句中的班機是由航空公司取消，故應採被動式的 be cancelled。

正解 ▶ The product should arrive in USA this Wednesday unless the flight is cancelled.

Unit 12
Unit 13
Unit 14
Unit 15
Unit 16
Unit 17
Unit 18
Unit 19
Unit 20
Unit 21
Unit 22

處理客訴

挑戰難度 ★★★☆☆

真的你學過

　　在商場上，難免會碰到客戶對公司產品或服務不滿意，這可能來自客戶的主觀感受，也可能是產品或服務本身有某個環節出錯。客戶進行抱怨時難免帶有情緒性字眼，因此許多人視處理英文客訴為畏途。但事實上，只要善用重述的技巧，釐清客戶的抱怨重點，在自己的權限內給予回覆與承諾，方可消弭客戶的不滿。

單元重點及學習方向

❶ 運用 To make sure... 句型與對方確認事情。
❷ 運用 Let me explain...句型來解釋事情的原委。
❸ 運用 The solution/answer we provide... 句型來說明我方的回覆。
❹ 運用本單元的單字、片語與句型來練習處理客訴問題。

 必 **check** 句型 ||||||||||||||||||||||||||||||||||

1. **To make sure** I get the point of your suggestion, here I will repeat what you just said.
   為確定我有了解你的建議，讓我重述你剛所說的內容。

2. **Let me explain** why we set up this payment policy.
   讓我解釋為何要設立這樣的付款政策。

3. **The solution** we **provide** you now is free repair.
   我們提供給你的解決方法是免費維修。

4. **The answer** we **provide** you is that the model you asked is currently not available.
   我們給你的回覆是你所詢問的型號目前缺貨。

Ⓐ 你有學過的單字 |||||||||||||||||||||||||||||||||

1. **attitude** [ˋætətjud] *n.* 態度

2. **compensate** [ˋkɑmpənˌset] *v.* 補償

3. **convey** [kənˋve] *v.* 傳達

4. **impatient** [ɪmˋpeʃənt] *adj.* 不耐煩的

5. **improve** [ɪmˋpruv] *v.* 改善

6. **loss** [lɔs] *n.* 損失

7. **paraphrase** [ˋpærəˌfrez] *v.* 重述

8. **satified** [ˋsætɪsˌfaɪd] *adj.* 滿意的

9. **submit** [səbˋmɪt] *v.* 提交

10. **superivsor** [ˌsupɚˋvaɪzɚ] *n.* 主管

Unit
12

Unit
13

Unit
14

Unit
15

Unit
16

Unit
17

Unit
18

Unit
19

Unit
20

Unit
21

Unit
22

小試身手 ||||||||||||||||||||||||||||||||||||||||||||

1. The reason why I made this call is the bad _____ of your sales representative.

   我打這通電話是因為你的業務態度不佳。

2. We will send you a small gift to _____ your loss.

   我們會寄送小禮物來補償你的損失。

3. I will _____ your suggestion to our Marketing Department.

   我會把你的建議傳達給我們的銷售部門。

4. Let me _____ what you just said.

   讓我重述剛剛你所說的內容。

5. To make sure we can give you a clear reply, I have conveyed your question to my _____.

   為了給您清楚的答覆，我已將您的問題傳達給我的上司了。

解答 ···

1. attitude

2. compensate

3. convey

4. paraphrase

5. supervisor

句型喚醒你的記憶 |||||||||||||||||||||||||||||||||||||

Unit
12

Unit
13

Unit
14

Unit
15

Unit
16

Unit
17

Unit
18

Unit
19

Unit
20

Unit
21

Unit
22

1. **To make sure** I have gotten your question right, here **I** will repeat what you just said.

   為確保我有聽懂你的疑問，讓我重述你剛剛所說的內容。

   To make sure..., I... 意思為「為確保⋯，我⋯」，可用來與對方確認事項。

   例 To make sure I recorded your complaint right, here I read you what I just typed. 為確保有正確記錄你的抱怨內容，讓我口述我剛所鍵入的文字給你。

2. **Let me explain** why we sell you the product at this price.

   讓我向解釋為何賣你這個價格。

   Let me explain... 意思為「讓我解釋⋯」，可用於向對方說明事情的經過或原因。

   例 Let me explain why the shipment is delayed. 讓我向您解釋為何出貨會延遲。

3. **The solution we provide** is to send you the replacement within three days.

   我們所提供的解決方法是在三天內寄送替換品給你。

   The solution we provide... 意思為「我們提供的解決方法是⋯」，可用於回覆對方所提出的問題。

   例 The solution we provide is to send our engineer to you factory. 我們提供的解決方法就是派工程師到你們工廠。

4. **The answer we provide** to you is we accept credit card.

   我們的答覆是我們接受信用卡。

   The answer we provide... 意思為「我們的答覆是⋯」，可用於回答對方問題。

   例 The answer we provide is we only accept cash. 我們的答覆是僅收現金。

知多少？多知道一點總是好

在商場上，客訴的情況其實屢見不鮮，客訴的原因可能是產品或服務本身出現問題，也可能是客戶情緒性的發洩，但不論原因為何，在不傷及自身權益的前提下，本著以客為尊的態度，在處理客訴時應注意以下的要點與避免觸及下列之禁忌：

不可不知的要點

1. 釐清內容：

   為了要給與客戶正確的回覆，聆聽客戶抱怨時宜同步進行記錄，最後在重述其內容，以確保我方理解正確。

2. 重點式回覆：

   回覆客訴時，應針對其抱怨重點給予回應，過多的敘述性或是應酬性文字，會讓投訴人覺得我方沒有解決的誠意。

3. 瞭解自身權限：

   在很多客訴情況中，許多投訴人都會要求處理人員給予立即的承諾。面對這樣的狀況，處理人員應考量自己的裁量範圍，切記不要越權處理，以免造成部門甚至整個公司的困擾。

不可不知的禁忌

Unit
12

Unit
13

Unit
14

Unit
15

Unit
16

Unit
17

Unit
18

Unit
19

Unit
20

Unit
21

Unit
22

1. 非理性回覆：

   即便客戶的語氣與用字非常不好，此時若因此動氣，也以情緒性字眼回覆，就可能產生衝突，不但無法解決原本的問題，還增加新問題。

2. 時間資訊不明確：

   針對無法馬上給予回覆的客訴情況，若未告知預計的處理時間，這樣的不確定性同樣會讓投訴人認為公司是在敷衍。

腦部暖身 一點都不難對話 ||||||||||||||||||||||

請將以下六個單字填入空格內。

(a) record　　　　　(b) value　　　　　(c) function

(d) damage　　　　(e) within　　　　(f) inconvenience

You just received a phone call.

Jason：This Jason from ABC Company, how may I help you?

Caller：I bought ten power banks from your online store, but two of them don't ____1____ well when I received the package.

Jason：Sorry for bringing ____2____ to you. May I have your order number please?

Caller：P-12345.

Jason：Let me check our system, please wait for few seconds.

Caller：OK.

Jason：According to our ____3____, all of them passed the quality testing before shipment. As a result, the ____4____ happened during the shipment. We will send two new power banks to you ____5____ 3 day. Besides, we will provide you a 10 US dollar coupon for the next purchase as compensation. Hope you will still buy our products in the future.

Caller：I am satisfied with you reply. ABC Company does ____6____ customers' rights.

翻譯

Jason：我是 ABC 公司的 Jason，請問有什麼可以為您服務的嗎？

來電者：我在貴公司的線上商店購買了十顆行動電源，但當我收到包裹

時，有兩個是壞的。

Jason：對您造成不便非常抱歉，請問能告訴我您的訂單號碼嗎？

來電者：P-12345

Jason：讓我查詢系統資料一下，請稍待。

來電者：好的。

Jason：根據我們這邊的紀錄，所有產品都有通過品質測試，所以應該是在運送途中發生損壞。我們將於三天內寄送兩個新的行動電源給你。另外，我們將提供十美金的折價券做為補償，你可於下次購買時使用。希望您未來仍會購買本公司產品。

來電者：我能接受你的回覆，ABC 公司真的有重視顧客權益。

單字

- **power bank** [`pauɚ,bæŋk] *n.* 行動電源
- **store** [stor] *n.* 商店
- **package** [`pækɪdʒ] *n.* 包裹
- **coupon** [`kupɑn] *n.* 折價券

答案

1. (c) 2. (f) 3. (a) 4. (d) 5. (e) 6. (b)

Unit 12

Unit 13

Unit 14

Unit 15

Unit 16

Unit 17

Unit 18

Unit 19

Unit 20

Unit 21

Unit 22

會說也會寫一：回覆抱怨信 ||||||||||||||||||||||||||

範例

Dear James,

❶Thank you for informing us that you got the wrong part.
❷Here I apologize for our mistakes. The part you purchased in order AB123 is UVN model, but we sent you the VUN model instead. ❸We will send you the right type within four days. Please return the wrong part to our company and we will cover the expense. ❹Besides, we will provide you a 10% coupon so that you can use in next purchase as compensation.
❺Sorry for bringing you the inconvenience. Hope this mistake won't affect the relationship we have built.

Sincerely,

Jason

翻譯

親愛的 James：

感謝你告知我們寄錯零件給你這件事。

我代表公司對此錯誤向你道歉。你訂單 AB123 中所購買的零件是 UVN 型，但我們卻寄 VUN 型的給你。我們會在四天內寄正確的零件給你。請將寄錯的零件寄還給我們，我們會負擔其運費。此外我們將提供下次購買可使用的九折優惠券。

造成不便深感抱歉。希望本次錯誤不會影響我們長久以來的合作關係。

謹

Jason

解析 ▌▌▌▌▌▌▌▌▌▌▌▌▌▌▌▌▌▌▌▌▌▌▌▌▌▌▌▌▌▌▌▌▌▌▌▌▌▌▌

　　一般來說，為了有效解決投訴人所提出的要求，客訴回覆信通常會包括以下幾個部分：

❶ 感謝對方通知：

此一段落的作用主要在於向投訴人表示我方已經知道並開始處理問題。以本範例為例，我方感謝 James 寫信告知寄錯產品。

❷ 為錯誤道歉：

錯誤一定會對投訴人某種程度上的不便，故應誠心向客戶致歉。常見的句型有 Here we apologize for... 或 we feel regretful about...。本範例便是採用前者：Here we apologize for our mistake.

❸ 解釋並提出修正方法：

除了道歉外，更重要的就是解決問題，因此在信件應針對問題的癥結點提出適合的處置方式。以本範例為例，處理寄錯零件的方式是再補寄正確的零件，並負擔買方寄回錯誤零件的運費。

❹ 給予適度補償：

由於錯誤可能造成客戶其他的金錢或時間損失，為彌補這樣的損失，一般而言，都會提供相當程度的賠償。賠償的方式可能有退款、打折或是贈送禮券等。以本範例為例，我方提供的是下次購買可享九折優惠。

❺ 應酬語：

信末應酬語的主軸在信末通常會放在再次向客戶道歉，顯示我方非常重視其權益上。以本範例為例，除對錯誤再次致歉外，更壓低姿態表示希望這樣錯誤對彼此合作不會造成影響。

Unit
12

Unit
13

Unit
14

Unit
15

Unit
16

Unit
17

Unit
18

Unit
19

Unit
20

Unit
21

Unit
22

會說也會寫二：回覆客訴(服務)部份 ||||||||||||

範例

Dear Sam,

❶Thank you for telling us that our service has some space to improve.

❷As you described in the complaint form, our staff offered you poor service when you asked to experience our latest product. ❸We have talked to that staff. He told us that he had an argument with his parents few hours before the service, so he was impatient. And he is sorry for his improper behavior. ❹We are sorry for not providing good service to you, so we provide you with a 10 % discount coupon as compensation

❺Hope you will still buy our products in the future.

Yours,
Jason

翻譯

親愛的Sam：

感謝您告訴我們的服務尚有改善空間。

如你在抱怨表中所提到，當你想要體驗最新產品時，我們的服務人員態度不佳。我們已與該員工詳談，他表示在服務你的數小時之前，他與家人有爭吵，以至於表現出不耐煩的態度。他也為其不恰當的行為感到抱歉。對於無法提供你良好服務我們深感抱歉，於此特提供九折券做為補償。

希望你未來仍願意購買本公司產品。

謹
Jason

解析

　　在回覆服務部分的客訴時，由於不像產品那樣具體，在情況的描述上應多加著墨，方可確保能夠清楚回應客戶的不滿。一封完整的回覆大至會包含以下這個五個部分：

❶感謝對方通知：

　　雖然服務屬於無形商品，可能存有主客觀的疑慮，但仍須感謝對方告知。以本範例為例，我方對於告知服務需改善表示感謝。

❷為錯誤道歉：

　　在本範例中，投訴人表示我們的工作人員服務態度不好，對此我方應向投訴人致歉。

❸解釋並提出修正方法：

　　為了解當時情況，處理方式之一便是直接與當時的服務人員對談。在本範例中，該工作人員表示是因為之前與家人有爭吵，並將這樣的負面情緒帶至工作，以至於讓顧客覺得他表現出不耐煩。事後對此也深覺自己的行為不恰當。

❹給予適度補償：

　　雖然在本範例中的服務態度並未造成投訴人的金錢損失，但在心情上肯定有受到影響，基於補償顧客的心態，本範例所提供的是九折券。

❺應酬語：

　　由於客戶尚未購買產品，回覆此信目的就是希望他不要受到本次的不愉快經驗，而不再支持公司產品。

　　針對服務的客訴，由於服務本身就具有抽象與主觀認定的部分，因此在處理時應當多加查證，若確實有所疏漏或是態度不佳，則理所當然應向客戶致歉，若是顧客有心刁難或是同業間的惡性栽贓，則應想辦法安撫與澄清，以免這些抱怨影響到公司的商譽或是營運。

Unit
12

Unit
13

Unit
14

Unit
15

Unit
16

Unit
17

Unit
18

Unit
19

Unit
20

Unit
21

Unit
22

 **現在你會說** |||||||||||||||||||||||||||||||||||||||||||||||

請依句意填入 **A-E**。

A. ABC Company does value customers' rights.

B. We will send two new rechargers to you within 2 days

C. We're sorry for brining inconvenience to you

D. Hope you will still buy our product in the future

E. This is Jason from ABC Company, how may I help you

Jason just received a phone call.

Jason： _____1_____?

Caller： I buy ten rechargers from your online shop, but found two of them don't function well when I received the products.

Jason： _____2_____. May I have your order number please?

Caller： aaa-123.

Jason： Thank you. Let me check our system, so please wait for few seconds.

Caller： OK

Jason： According to our record, all of them passed the quality testing before shipment. As a result, the damage happened during the shipment. _____3_____. Besides, we will provide you a 15 US dollar coupon for the next purchase as compensation. _____4_____.

Caller： I am satisfied with your reply. _____5_____.

答案

1. (E)　2. (C)　3. (B)　4. (D)　5. (A)

現在你會寫 ||||||||||||||||||||||||||||||||||||||||||||

1. 讓我解釋為何無法給你優惠價。

_____

_____

中式英文出沒 ▶ Let me explain why can't give you a favorable price.

錯在哪 ▶ 中文可以省略受詞，此處的受詞為我們，位置在為何之後，因此翻譯時應將其補上，方可使句意完整。

正解 ▶ Let me explain why we can't give you a favorable price.

2. 我們提供的解決方法是更換新品。

_____

_____

中式英文出沒 ▶ The solution we provide is to replace the new product to you.

錯在哪 ▶ 在此例句中，若緊貼中文將更換翻譯為 replace，句意就變成把新品換掉。把 replace 換成 send 才是恰當的用法。

正解 ▶ The solution we provide is to send a new product to you.

Part 4

面對客戶

做簡報

挑戰難度 ★★★☆☆

真的你學過

　　做簡報是商場上重要的技能之一，一次好的簡報能讓客戶印象深刻，讓同事長官刮目相看。但畢竟英文不是我們的母語，一旦要以英文做簡報，很多人就會焦慮不已，覺得自己無法成功抓住聽眾的注意力。但事實上，只要利用片語讓簡報先具有層次性，再善用強調句型表示重點，人人都可以是英文簡報高手。

單元重點及學習方向

❶ 運用 I would like to talk about... 句型來說明要向何種對象說明何種主題。

❷ 運用 I will begin with/move on to... 句型來為簡報開頭與論述內容。

❸ 運用 To sum up/In conclusion, ... 句型來表達結論。

❹ 運用本單元的單字、片語與句型來練習做簡報。

 **必 check 句型** ||||||||||||||||||||||||||||||||||||

1. **I would like to** talk about the marketing strategy of our new product.

   我想跟各位談論關於新商品的行銷策略。

2. **I will begin with** the purpose of this campaign.

   我先從活動的目地開始說起。

3. **I will move on** to the difficulties we are facing with.

   現在我接著要談目前我們所遭遇的困難。

4. **To sum up,** this activity is feasible.

   總結來說，本活動是可行的。

 **你有學過的單字** ||||||||||||||||||||||||||||||||||

1. **distinction** [dɪ`stɪŋkʃən] *n.* 區別

2. **highlight** [`haɪ,laɪt] *v.* 強調

3. **theme** [θim] *n.* 主題

4. **outstand** [aʊt`stænd] *v.* 突出

5. **outline** [`aʊt,laɪn] *v.* 概述

6. **overview** [`ovɚ,vju] *n.* 總論

7. **pad** [pæd] *n.* 平板電腦

8. **projector** [prə`dʒɛktɚ] *n.* 投影機

9. **pointer** [`pɔɪntɚ] *n.* 指示物

10. **tablet** [`tæblɪt] *n.* 平板電腦

小試身手

1. I will show the _____ between latest model and old model.
   我會展示新舊型號的差異。

2. This report will _____ the importance of adjustment.
   這份報告將會強調調整的重要性。

3. Let me _____ the program we would like to carry out next year.
   讓我大致描述出明年要執行的計畫內容給你。

4. The _____ of this project will be submitted to you next Monday.
   本專案的總論會於下週一提交給您。

5. Please make sure the _____ is ready before the briefing.
   進行簡報前請確認投影機是否已準備就緒。

解答

1. distinction
2. highlight
3. outline
4. overview
5. projector

句型喚醒你的記憶

1. **I would like to talk to** all colleagues in my department **about** our annual marketing direction this year.
   我想跟部門的所有同事談論本年度的行銷方向。

   I would like to talk to... about... 意思為「我想與…談論…」，可用於說明談論的主題與目標對象為何。

   例 I would like to talk to you about the function of our product.
   我想跟您談論本公司產品的功能。

2. **I will begin with** the background of this project.
   我將從本專案的背景說起。

   I will begin with... 意思為「我將從…開始說起」，可用於說明簡報的起頭為何。

   例 I will begin with the purpose of this change in our design. 我將從設計變更的目地說起。

3. **I will move on to** core of this presentation—the new privacy policy.
   接著我要談論本次簡報的核心一新的隱私條款。

   I will move on to... 意思為「接著我要談論…」，可用於說明接下來所欲談論之內容。

   例 I will move on to the solution we have found. 接著我要談論我們目前已找出的解決方法。

4. **To sum up**, this project should be stopped temporarily.
   總結來說，此專案須暫時停止。

   To sum up... 意思為「總結來說，…」，可用於簡報的結論部分。

   例 To sum up, this promotion strategy is not feasible. 總結來說，這個促銷策略不可行。

Unit
12

Unit
13

Unit
14

Unit
15

Unit
16

Unit
17

Unit
18

Unit
19

Unit
20

Unit
21

Unit
22

知多少？多知道一點總是好

　　在商場上，大家都知道簡報的重要性，好的簡報可以讓產品的推銷更加順利，不好的簡報可能讓業績大大下滑，以下針對英文簡報所需注意的要點與應避免的禁忌做進一步說明：

不可不知的要點

1.因人而異：

根據聽眾群的不同，簡報的主軸與呈現方式也應隨之調整。當向上司做簡報時，由於主管職責在於彙整，因此我們的簡報應當簡單扼要。但當向客戶做簡報，則要盡可能文情並茂，讓對方留下深刻印象。

2.因時而異：

時間限制是左右簡報內容的另一個重要因素。五分鐘與三十分鐘的簡報需使用不同的策略，才能可能達到預期的效果。若報告時間很短，鋪陳不宜太多，開門見山為佳。相反地，若時間充足則可旁徵博引。

3.因地而異：

不同的場地也會影響簡報的進行，舉例來說，在會議室跟在咖啡廳向客戶簡報時，所採用的輔助工具就不同。在會議時我們可以使用投影機，但在咖啡廳使用平板或是筆電較為可行。

不可不知的禁忌

1. 停頓遲疑：
   簡報時若話語斷斷續續或是猶豫，會讓對方覺得我們準備不足，連帶對我們要介紹的產品或是服務抱持懷疑態度，因此實際上場務必先充分練習。

2. 組織鬆散：
   簡報的目的就是在有限的時間與內容內充分介紹產品服務或是表達概念想法，因此若內容太過空泛雜亂，容易讓人不知道簡報重點為何而分心。

3. 枯燥乏味。

Unit **12**

Unit **13**

Unit **14**

Unit **15**

Unit **16**

Unit **17**

Unit **18**

Unit **19**

Unit **20**

Unit **21**

Unit **22**

腦部暖身 一點都不難對話 ||||||||||||||||||||||||||

請將以下六個單字填入空格內。

(a) board   (b) specific   (c) background
(d) series   (e) casual   (f) news

Jason：Good morning, Sandy. Today I would like to talk to you about the overview of the new project.

Sandy：OK, please start the briefing.

Jason：I will begin with the ___1___. This new project is scheduled to be launched next March. The region we choose is USA, especially in the West Coast. Before I move on to the ___2___ content, let me ask one question. What is your impression of the West Coast?

Sandy：___3___ and relaxed are the ones come into my mind.

Jason：To reinforce this image, we are ready to cooperate with a famous local brand named B&F to release a ___4___ of new clothing collection. This project is expected to increase our brand visibility in USA. How do you feel about this project?

Sandy：It is a good idea. I will submit your report to the ___5___ , and you can wait for good ___6___ .

Jason：Thank you.

翻譯

Jason：Sandy 早安，今天我要跟你談的是新專案的總論。
Sandy：好的，請開始簡報吧。
Jason：我先從專案的背景說起。這個新專案預計明年三月開始執行。

我們所選擇的區域是美國，尤其是西岸。在我說明確切內容前，讓我問你一個問題，你對西岸的印象是？

Sandy： 隨興而放鬆是第一個我最先所想到的。

Jason： 為了要強化這樣的印象，我們準備要與一個當地的知名品牌 B & F 合作推出一系列的新款服飾。這個專案預期能夠提高我們品牌在美國的能見度。你對此專案有什麼看法嗎？

Sandy： 概念很好，我會把你的報告提交給董事會，請期待好消息。

Jason： 謝謝

單字 ....

- **launch** [lɔntʃ] *n.* 開始
- **region** [`ridʒən] *n.* 地區
- **coast** [kost] *n.* 海岸
- **visibility** [ˌvɪzə`bɪlətɪ] *n.* 能見度

Unit 12
Unit 13
Unit 14
Unit 15
Unit 16
Unit 17
Unit 18
Unit 19
Unit 20
Unit 21
Unit 22

答案 ....

1. (c)　2. (b)　3. (e)　4. (d)　5. (a)　6. (f)

會說也會寫一：專案簡報講稿 ||||||||||||||||||||||||||||

範例

❶Good afternoon, I would like to talk about the new project we want to cooperate with you.

❷I will begin with the background. The duration of this project is six months. It aims to stimulate the sales in UK.

❸We are going to run the campaign by holding special sales and releasing limited editions. The exclusive product is only available in our flagship shop in London.

❹This strategy is expected to attract our brand supporters to collect these special products.

❺How do you feel about this project?

翻譯

午安，我今天要跟您談的是與您合作的新專案。

我先從背景開始說起，這個專案為期六個月，目標刺激在英國的銷售。

專案中所採用的活動為特賣與販售限量商品，限量商品只在我們倫敦的旗艦店販售。

此策略預期能夠吸引品牌支持者收集這些特殊商品。

你覺得這專案如何？

解析 ||||||||||||||||||||||||||||||||||||||||||||||||

在撰寫專案簡報的講稿時，為了要在有限時間內讓聽眾可以了解大方向，講稿內容通常會包含以下五個部分：

❶報告主題：

在向客戶或是主管同事簡報時，先行說明本次主題為何，可讓對方馬上

進入狀況，對我們後續的內容說明有正面效用。以本範例為例，要談的是雙方的合作案。

❷説明主軸：

説明主題後，接下來就是講述整個計畫的大方向或是背景，讓對方可以了解計畫大致會怎樣進行，以及到底為何要執行。以本範例為例，近期會有一個為期六個月的專案，目標為刺激英國的銷售。

❸具體內容：

確切的計畫內容是此份講稿的核心，因此當中務必要提及重要的執行項目，讓對方在聽完這些資訊後，稍作吸收與思考，於整個簡報結束後給予回饋與看法。以本範例為例，這個專案所要執行的活動有特賣與發受限量商品。限量商品進行限點販售，消費者需至倫敦的旗艦店才能購得本次活動所推出的限定版商品。

❹預期結果：

在簡報進行結尾之前，很重要的一點就是説明計畫所可能帶來的預期效果，聽眾可以藉此思考此一結果的可能性，最後給予意見。以本範例為例，此計畫預期能夠吸引品牌支持者的蒐集熱潮。

❺要求回饋：

整個敘述部分結束後，最後就是詢問觀眾的看法。以本範例為例，就是請教對於專案的想法為何。

Unit 12

Unit 13

Unit 14

Unit 15

Unit 16

Unit 17

Unit 18

Unit 19

Unit 20

Unit 21

Unit 22

會說也會寫二：介紹產品 ||||||||||||||||||||||||||||||

範例

❶Good afternoon. Today, I want to talk to you about the features of our latest smart phone NC 1.

❷NC 1 is our first 4G phone. It is thin but robust, so users don't need to worry about the deformation problem that happened on the other brands' cellphones.

❸You may think high-end phones are all expensive, but the price of NC 1 will surprise you. It only costs you $399.

❹NC 1 is definitely the best choice for the consumers who want a high-end phone but with a limited budget.

❺How do you feel about NC1? If you are interested in it, please visit our official website for more details.

翻譯

午安，今天要與您談的是我們最新款智慧型手機 NC 1。

NC 1 是我們首支 4G 手機，它雖薄但卻堅固，所以使用者無須擔心會發生它牌手機所遇到變形問題。

你或許會認為高階手機都很貴，但 NC 1 的價格會令你驚訝，它只要 399 美金。

NC 1 無疑是想要高階手機，但預算有限的消費者的最佳選擇。

你覺得 NC 1 如何呢? 如果對這支手機有興趣，請上官網了解更多資訊。

解析 ||||||||||||||||||||||||||||||||||||||||||||||||||

在撰寫產品介紹簡報的講稿時，為了能夠有效吸引聽眾或是潛在消費者的注意，其內容通常會包括以下五個部分：

❶報告主題：

產品簡報多針對新產品，因此消費者對其可能感到陌生。在簡報一開始馬上講述名稱，再透過圖像或實體的輔佐，可快速建立初步印象。以本範例為例，要介紹的是最新型的智慧型手機 NC 1。

❷提出差異：

除非是極度複雜或是擁有多項專利的產品，否則在市面上難免有相似產品，提出我方產品的差異性，才有可能提高消費者的購買意願。以本範例為例，強調 NC 1 是本公司第一台 4G 手機，輕薄但卻不會產生他牌所遭遇的變形問題。

❸補充優點：

一兩個優點可能還不足以讓消費者願意花錢購買，因此在提出差異性時，要再說明本產品的其他特色，增加消費者對於產品的好感，從而提高購買的可能性。以本範例為例，提出的是價格上的優勢，打破一般人認為高階手機就一定貴的迷思，NC 1 價格的價格為 399 美金。

❹做出結論：

提出數個產品優點之後，重要的是讓消費者對於這些優點有印象，下結論時可以產生強化效果。以本範例為例，由於 NC 1 價格親民，因此這邊提出本手機為預算有限的消費者的最佳選擇做為結論，希望能夠打動消費者，真的進行消費。

❺請求回饋：

簡報過後，最後一定會與聽眾互動來尋求回饋。但由於簡報時間有限，通常還會在附帶說明哪邊可以獲得進一步資訊。以本範例為例，就是請有興趣了解更多資訊的潛在消費者造訪我們的官網。

Unit 12

Unit 13

Unit 14

Unit 15

Unit 16

Unit 17

Unit 18

Unit 19

Unit 20

Unit 21

Unit 22

 現在你會說

請依句意填入 A-E。

A. How do you feel about this logo at your first glance
B. I think this logo can give consumers a brand new feeling
C. Please pay attention to the letter J on the left and right
D. It shows our ambition in this industry
E. What you just said is our goal that we set

Jason：Morning, I would like to talk to you about our new logo. Please take a look of my first PowerPoint slide. ___1___?

Amy：It has something to do cool things.

Jason：___2___. We hope this new logo can re-built our brand image and create the trendy atmosphere. Now I will begin with the three elements. ___3___. It indicates our two founders' name. Then, please move the focus to the wings in the middle. ___4___. And finally we take a look of the hand on the bottom. It symbolizes our brand clearly and let others know what we want to do.

Alice：Good design. Simple but meaningful. ___5___.

答案

1. (A)   2. (E)   3. (C)   4. (D)   5. (B)

 現在你會寫 ||||||||||||||||||||||||||||||||||||||||||||||

1. 讓我從本產品與他牌的不同處說起。

_____

_____

中式英文出沒 ▶ I will begin with the distinction between our product and the other brand.

錯在哪 ▶ 英文在做比較時，雙邊的比較基礎一定要相同。中文雖然也是相同邏輯，在用字上確比較有彈性。以練習來說，應是「本產品」與「他牌產品」，因此在 and 之後加上 that 做為代名詞，即形成對等比較。

正解 ▶ I will begin with the distinction between our product and that of the other brand.

2. 總結來說，本產品的市場競爭力相對不足。

_____

_____

中式英文出沒 ▶ To sum up, the market competitiveness of this product is relative not enough.

錯在哪 ▶ 「相對不足」一詞很容易讓人忽略它其實是由「相對地」與「不充足的」兩個部分所組成，因此此處的 relative 應修正為 relatively。

正解 ▶ To sum up, the market competitiveness of this product is relatively not enough.

Unit 12
Unit 13
Unit 14
Unit 15
Unit 16
Unit 17
Unit 18
Unit 19
Unit 20
Unit 21
Unit 22

16 Unit 會議主持

挑戰難度 ★★★☆☆

真的你學過

　　不論是剛踏入職場的菜鳥，或是經驗豐富的老手都有機會主持會議。稱職的會議主持人可以讓意見交換順暢，但因為主持要比其他與會者更加了解討論主題，很多人一聽到要以英文主持會議時，都會焦慮不已。但事實上，只要懂得按主題討論事項，並善用重述與總結的技巧，就可讓會議順利進行。

單元重點及學習方向

❶ 運用 It seems... 句型來說明可開始會議或是進入下一個議程。

❷ 運用 I am afraid we will have to... 句型來控制會議的進行速度。

❸ 運用 I am glad we have reached consensus on/All agree upon... 句型來表示達成共識或決議。

❹ 運用本單元的單字、片語與句型來練習主持會議。

 **必 check 句型**

1. **It seems** all the representatives are ready.
   看來所有的代表都已經準備好了。
2. **I am afraid** we will have to move on to the next topic soon.
   我們恐怕得快點進入下一個主題了。
3. **I am glad we have reached a consensus on** the direction of the marketing campaign next year.
   我很高興我們已在明年度的行銷活動方向上達成共識。
4. **I am glad we all agree to** carry out the project.
   我很高興大家都同意執行此專案。

 **你有學過的單字**

1. **absent** [`æbsnt] *adj.* 缺席的
2. **announce** [ə`naʊns] *v.* 宣布
3. **attendee** [ə`tɛndi] *n.* 參與者
4. **exchange** [ɪks`tʃendʒ] *v.* 交換
5. **interrupt** [ˌɪntə`rʌpt] *v.* 打岔
6. **minute** [`mɪnɪt] *n.* 會議紀錄
7. **pardon** [`pɑrdn] *v.* 原諒
8. **perspective** [pə`spɛktɪv] *n.* 面向
9. **restate** [ri`stet] *v.* 重述
10. **variable** [`vɛrɪəbl̩] *n.* 變數

Unit 12
Unit 13
Unit 14
Unit 15
Unit **16**
Unit 17
Unit 18
Unit 19
Unit 20
Unit 21
Unit 22

小試身手

1. Here I _____ that this adjustment will come into effect next week.

    於此我宣布本調整於下週起生效。

2. We can have many opinion _____ in this meeting.

    我們於本次會議中可以有許多意見交流。

3. Sorry for the _____, but I have something I want to say here.

    抱歉打岔，但我這邊有點意見想發表。

4. This topic can be discussed from several _____.

    這個主題可以從多個面向進行探討。

5. We have to make sure those _____ won't affect our consensus today.

    我們要確保這些變數不會影響我們今天所達成的共識。

解答

1. announce
2. exchanges
3. interruption
4. perspectives
5. variables

句型喚醒你的記憶 ||||||||||||||||||||||||||||||

1. **It seems** the projector is ready.

看來投影機已準備就緒了。

It seems... 意思為「看來…」，可在會議時說明的開始與議程的進行。

例 It seems all the attendees have arrived. 看來所有的與會者都以抵達。

2. **I am afraid we will have to** move on to the panel discussion today.

我想我們恐怕得趕快進行本日的座談會。

I am afraid we will have to... 意思為「我想我們恐怕…」，可用於表示須加快或是減緩會議中的討論速度。

例 I am afraid we will have to leave some time for the last topic. 我想我們得替最後一個主題預留些時間。

3. **I am glad we have reached a consensus on** the budget of next year.

我很高興我們已在明年的預算上達成共識。

I am glad we have reached consensus on... 意思為「我們已在…達成共識」，可用於說明達成共識的具體事項。

例 I am glad we have reached consensus on the design of the product. 我很高興我們已在新產品的設計上達成共識。

4. **I am glad we all agree upon** the investment in the new market.

我很高興我們都同意在新市場的投資。

I am glad we all agree upon... 意思為「我很高興我們都同意…」，可用於說明所有與會者所同意的事項。

例 I am glad we all agree to continue the project. 我很高興我都同意延續這個專案。

知多少？多知道一點總是好 ‖‖‖‖‖‖‖‖‖‖‖‖‖‖‖‖‖‖‖‖‖‖‖‖‖‖

在商場上需要開會的場合很多，每個人都有機會以中文或是英文來主持會議，一位好的會議主持人能讓意見有效交流，提升開會效率，盡快達成共識或做出結論。但若要扮演好這樣的角色，其實有許多要點需留意，與避免觸及的禁忌。以下對此做更進一步說明：

不可不知的要點 ‖‖‖‖‖‖‖‖‖‖‖‖‖‖‖‖‖‖‖‖‖‖‖‖‖‖‖‖‖‖‖‖

1. 掌握人數：

在許多會議中其實只要出席人數達一定比例即可開始進行，因此主席須掌握與會人數，以便隨時宣布會議開始。另外有些與會者可能無法全程參與，主席也應對此有所掌握。

2. 留意進度：

開會前都會設定本日會議的預期目標，因此在會議進行中，主席應視情況加快或是減慢討論速度，舉例來說，當討論太過熱烈而延誤到下個議程時，主席應盡快針對當前主題做出結論，讓會議進度不致大幅落後。

3. 處理干擾：

在會議中，有些人會在別人發言時不停插嘴，或是不斷談論與本次會議無關之內容。針對這樣的干擾行為，首次發生時主席可以好言相勸，若屢勸不聽，則可運用會議主席職權要求其離席。

不可不知的禁忌

1. 缺乏意見交換：

開會的目的就是透過意見交換與協調達成共識，因此在會議過程中主席不讓與會者發表意見，就違背開會的根本精神。

2. 沒有明確目標：

開會就是有目的性的集合相關人士，因此若沒有設定本次會議所要達成之決議，整個開會過程就會流於意見的各自表述，無法產生具體結果。

3. 獨斷／少數決：

當進行意見交換後，若最後的決定權仍落在主席或是少數人身上時，會讓無決定權的與會者感到不滿。因此多數的會議會以多數決定全數決來達成最終決議。

Unit
12

Unit
13

Unit
14

Unit
15

Unit
16

Unit
17

Unit
18

Unit
19

Unit
20

Unit
21

Unit
22

腦部暖身 一點都不難對話 ||||||||||||||||||||||

請將以下六個單字填入空格內。

(a) model   (b) no   (c) certain

(d) modifies   (e) specifically   (f) coming

Jason：Frist of all, thank you for ＿＿1＿＿ today. It seems no one is absent, so we can kick the meeting off. Please take a look at the agenda on the table. We will begin with briefing of a prototype, so now let's welcome Sam to have the presentation.

Sam：Good afternoon, everyone. Please pay attention to the slide first. The picture you see is the ＿＿2＿＿ our R&D department just developed. Its design ＿＿3＿＿ the defect of our previous model. In that model, we found some of them have coloring fading problems due to long usage.

Leo：Sorry for interrupting you, but can you restate the fading problem more ＿＿4＿＿.

Sam：The fading problem means the color will get less bright after ＿＿5＿＿ usage.

Leo：I got it, thank you.

Jason：Is anyone not clear about the problem? If ＿＿6＿＿, let's move on to the next topic of this agenda.

翻譯

Jason：首先感謝各位與會。看來沒有人缺席，我們就開始開會了。請先看到放在桌上的議程。我們先從產品原型的簡報開始。讓我們歡迎 Sam。

Sam：各位午安，請先注意這張投影片，當中你所看到圖片就是我們研
　　　發部門剛剛完成的產品原型。其設計修正了前一代產品的缺點。
　　　在上一代產品中，有部分產品在長期使用後會有褪色問題產生。

Leo：抱歉打岔，但可能再更仔細說明褪色的問題嗎？

Sam：褪色問題指的是歷經一定程度的使用之後，產品顏色會變不夠鮮
　　　豔。

Leo：了解，謝謝您的回答。

Jason：還有人有問題嗎？沒有的話，我們就進入本議程的下一個討論主
　　　　題。

單字

- **kick off** [kɪk,ɔf] *ph.* 開始
- **prototype** [`protə,taɪp] *n.* 原型
- **defect** [`protə,taɪp] *n.* 缺點
- **fading** [`fedɪŋ] *n.* 褪色

答案

1. (f)　2. (a)　3. (d)　4. (e)　5. (c)　6. (b)

Unit 12　Unit 13　Unit 14　Unit 15　Unit 16　Unit 17　Unit 18　Unit 19　Unit 20　Unit 21　Unit 22

會說也會寫一：會議開始詞講稿 ||||||||||||||||||

範例

❶Good Morning, James and all my colleagues. Thank you for coming. I am Jason, the meeting chairman today.

❷It seems no one is absent, so I think we can start the meeting now. Please note all are presented in the minutes.

❸Today we have a lot of ground to cover, so please take a look at the agenda that is placed in front of you. The theme we will discuss first today is the feasibility of the new marketing campaign.

❹Let's welcome Andy on behalf of the International Sales Department to have the briefing about the evaluation report.

翻譯

James 經理、各位同事早安。感謝各位與會，我是 Jason，今日的會議主席。

看來沒有人缺席，我想我們可以開始開會了。請記錄人員在會議紀錄上註明全員到齊。

今天有很多事項要討論，所以先請各位看一下放在各位位置前方的議程。本日最先進行討論的主題是新行銷活動的可行性。

接下來讓我們歡迎 Andy 代表國貿部進行評估報告的簡報。

解析 ||||||||||||||||||||||||||||||

做為以英文為溝通語言的會議之主席，為了能讓整個議程順利進行，在準備會議開始詞時，其內容通常會包含以下四個部分：

❶問好與自我介紹：

雖然你是會議的主席，但需考量到與會人員可能有我們首次碰面的人

士，基於禮儀，應向所有與會者問好，並自我介紹。讓所有人認識我們，也間接強化做為會議主席的權威。以本範例為例，Jason 先向長官 James 經理與同事們問好，然後再介紹自己是本次會議主席。

❷確認人數/宣布開會：

開會前的重要事項之一就是確認開會人數。針對尚未抵達的與會者，應再次與其聯絡。確認不會出席後，統計實際參與人數，若達會議規章所訂立之最低人數，即可宣布會議開始。以本範例為例，由於無人缺席，主席便宣布會議開始，並要求記錄人員註記全員到齊。

❸說明本日會議主題：

做完上述的前置作業後，接下來就是簡述本日會議的主軸以及預計討論的項目有哪些。以本範例為例，主席首先告知與會人員本日會議有多個討論事項，請各位先看過桌上紙本的議程。第一個項目是探討新行銷活動的可行性。

❹開始第一個討論事項：

簡述議程過後，接下來就根據當中的順序，開始討論第一個項目。以本範例為例，第一個項目是由 Andy 代表國貿部進行可行性評估的報告，因此會議主席 Jason 向各位介紹接下來將由他開始做簡報。

Unit 12
Unit 13
Unit 14
Unit 15
Unit 16
Unit 17
Unit 18
Unit 19
Unit 20
Unit 21
Unit 22

會說也會寫二：宣達會議之決議講稿

範例

❶After the three-hour meeting, we have reached a consensus on several issues.

❷Now is 4:00 PM, March 15, 2014. As the chairman of this meeting, here I announce the agreements as follow:

1. The duration of the special sale is three months
2. The estimated budget of advertisement is $1500.
3. Bob is the person in charge of the program

❸Since all the attendees expressed their opinion actively, and we can't cover all the topics we scheduled to finish today. To go through the rest ones, we all agree upon that the next meeting will be held on March 20 in the same meeting room. ❹Once again, thank you for coming. This meeting is closed

翻譯

歷經三小時的會議後，我們已在許多議題上達成共識。

現在時間是 2014 年 3 月 15 日下午 4 點，做為本次會議主席，於此宣布以下幾點決議：

1. 特賣為期三個月。
2. 廣告預算 1500 美金
3. Bob 為計畫負責人。

由於所有與會者皆熱烈發表意見，今天我們無法完成所有的討論。為完成討論，大家都同意於 3 月 20 日於同一會議室再次開會。於此再次感謝大家與會，本日會議到此結束。

解析

　　經過會議中的意見交換之後，接下來就是針對這些議題進行表決或是投票，以便做出決議。當其結果出爐後，會議主席即可依其職權，向所有與會人士宣達其內容。雖然我們無法事先得知決議，但其內容架構有其共通性，因此完整的會議結果宣答詞都會包含以下三個部分：

❶ 表示達成決議：

　　當與會人員針對議題達成決議後，會議也將進入尾聲，此時主席會依其職權表示會議即將結束。以本範例為例，主席表示歷經三小時的會議之後，現在我們已在一些議題上達成共識。

❷ 宣達決議內容：

　　為了方便記錄人員記錄，以及會議主席之職權，在會議末段主席會向所有與會人重述會議日期，並宣布本次會議所達成共識的內容。以本範例為例，主席表示現在時間為現在時間是 2014 年 3 月 15 日下午 4 點，於此運用職權宣布以下之決議：

1. 特賣為期三個月。
2. 廣告預算 1500 美金
3. Bob 為計畫負責人。

❸ 會議未決部分：

　　開會經常會遭遇進度落後的問題，因此若無法在一次會議中完成所有議題的討論，在會末時應討論出下次會議的時間與地點，以利後續的討論。以本範例為例，主席表示由於意見發表熱烈，無法在本會中討論所有議題，因此大家同意於 3 月 20 日於相同地點繼續開會討論。

❹ 宣布會議結束

　　宣達完所有事項後，主席的最後一項任務就是感謝大家的參與並宣布會議結束。以本範例為例，主席對所有與會人表示感謝後，宣布本次會議結束。

 現在你會說 ||||||||||||||||||||||||||||||||||||||||

請依句意填入 A-E。

A. It is scheduled to be carried out for six month at least if the performance is good

B. My briefing today will be divided into two parts

C. Lance I know you want to clarify this part, but Bob has the floor now

D. Now let's welcome Mark to have the briefing

E. We are waiting for the approval from the Accounting Department.

Jason：According to the consensus we have reached in the previous meeting on April 12, today we will begin with the implementation of the project. ____1____.

Mark：Morning Manager Jason and my colleagues. ____2____.The first one is about the budget. The estimated expense is about $10000 which covers the promotion campaign and parts replacement. ____3____.

Lance：The old machine still work well. I don't think we need a new one. Can you…

Jason：____4____, so please hold your question. We can discuss it later. Bob please go on.

Bob：The second part is the duration of this project. ____5____.

Jason：Thank you Bob.

答案

1. (D)　2. (B)　3. (E)　4. (C)　5. (A)

 **現在你會寫** ||||||||||||||||||||||||||||||||||||||||||||||||||

Unit
12

Unit
13

Unit
14

Unit
15

Unit
16

Unit
17

Unit
18

Unit
19

Unit
20

Unit
21

Unit
22

1. 我想我們恐怕必須加緊完成討論。

_____

_____

中式英文出沒 ▶ I am afraid we will have to tighten and finish the discussion.

錯在哪 ▶ 若沒有仔細思考「加緊完成」中的「加緊」一詞的意涵，可能就會其理解為緊縮，而以 tighten 翻譯之。事實上，以 soon 翻譯之即相當貼切。

正解 ▶ I am afraid we will have to finish the discussion soon.

2. 我很高興我們已在專案執行面上達成共識。

_____

_____

中式英文出沒 ▶ I am glad we have reached consensus on the project implementation perspective.

錯在哪 ▶ 若將字面的「…面向」按照語序翻譯出來，表面上看起來句意完整，但事實上卻是句子產生錯誤。因此在翻譯應將 perspective 省略。若一定要使用，則須修正為 the perspective of project implementation。

正解 ▶ I am glad we have reached a consensus on the project implementation./I am glad we have reached a consensus on the perspective of project implementation.

17 Unit 部門會議

挑戰難度 ★★★☆☆

真的你學過

　　在進行年終檢討前，部門會先針對自己的表現做檢討，檢討的方式可能是透過圖表或是數據的分析。由於內容牽涉數學或是統計，許多人會擔心自己的英文可能無法清楚表達當中的意涵。但事實上，只要善用指示性的動詞或連接詞（例如 as）與子句敘述現象，以英文解釋報表並非難事。

單元重點及學習方向

❶ 運用 As you can see from... 句型來說明圖表或是文件的內容。

❷ 運用 The fact that... 句型來說明事情的確切情況為何。

❸ 運用 The...in... indicates that.../The... speak itself（themselves）來敘述現象或變化的意涵。

❹ 運用本單元的單字、片語與句型練習部門會議的應對。

 必 check 句型

1. **As you can see from** this line graph, the sales figure has reached the historical high in April.
   如曲線圖所示，銷售數字於四月時達到歷史新高。

2. **The fact that** our performance is much better than we expected.
   事實上我們的績效比預期的好。

3. **The trend** in the sales figure **indicates** that the product has a great potential.
   銷售數字的趨勢顯示本產品深具潛力。

4. **The sales figures speak themselves,** so we can say this product is not attractive to consumers.
   銷售數字會說話，我們可以說本產品無法吸引消費者。

 你有學過的單字

1. **bottom** [`batəm] *v.* 降至低點

2. **common** [`kamən] *adj.* 常見的

3. **deficit** [`dɛfɪsɪt] *n.* 赤字

4. **diagram** [`daɪəˌgræm] *n.* 圖表

5. **drop** [drɑp] *v.* 下降

6. **profit** [`prɑfɪt] *n.* 利潤

7. **peak** [pik] *n.* 頂峰

8. **revenue** [`rɛvəˌnju] *n.* 收入

9. **share** [ʃɛr] *n.* 部分

10. **steady** [`stɛdɪ] *adj.* 穩定的

Unit 12
Unit 13
Unit 14
Unit 15
Unit 16
Unit **17**
Unit 18
Unit 19
Unit 20
Unit 21
Unit 22

小試身手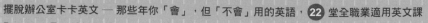

1. The sales figure _____ out in March.

   銷售數字於三月時探底。

2. As you can see from this _____, the price of the raw material gets higher and higher in the past one year.

   如本圖表所示，原物料價格在過去一年節節升高。

3. The _____ has reached the historical high in November this year.

   今年十一月獲利達歷史新高。

4. Our market _____ has great improvement this year.

   我們的市佔率今年大幅提升。

5. The cost remains _____ in the past six months.

   成本在過去六個月維持穩定。

解答

1. bottomed
2. diagram
3. profit
4. share
5. steady

句型喚醒你的記憶 |||||||||||||||||||||||||||||||||

Unit
12

Unit
13

Unit
14

Unit
15

Unit
16

Unit
17

Unit
18

Unit
19

Unit
20

Unit
21

Unit
22

1. **As you can see from** the bar graph, the sales in portable toolkits have reached the goal we set in June.

如圖表所示，可攜式工具組的銷售數字在六月時達我們的預設目標。

As you can see from... 意思為「如⋯所示」，可用於說明圖表或資料的內容。

㊀ As you can see from the pie chart, the sales of smart phones have accounted for more than 60 percent. 如圓餅圖所示，智慧型手機的銷售佔了百分之六十以上。

2. **The fact that** the overall performance is worse than we thought.

事實上我們的整體績效比預期的更差。

The fact that 意思為事實上⋯，可用於說明或是更正事情的真實情況。

㊀ The fact that the growth in the market share is greater than we thought. 事實上，市佔率的成長超過我們預期。

3. **The** deficit **in** the business in Italy **indicates** that we may need to find a new market.

在義大利的虧損代表我們可能需要另尋新市場。

The... in... indicate that... 意思為⋯指出⋯，可用於說明現象所代表意義。

㊀ The drop in the sales of our product indicates the preference of consumers may change. 商品的銷售數字滑落代表消費者喜好可能改變。

4. **The** profit **speaks itself**, so we can say that the new business in Japan has a good performance.

利潤會說話，我們可以說在日本的新事業績效良好。

The... speak itself/themselves 意思為「⋯不言自明」，可用於說明某種數據的代表性。

㊀ The deficit speaks itself, so we should review the project to find the problem. 虧損會說話，我們要檢視專案內容來找出問題。

知多少？多知道一點總是好

　　在進行全公司的年度檢討會議前，各部門會先針對本身的績效做分析，其目的為是在找出問題與提出因應對策。若能善用手邊資料，並搭配適合的報告技巧，將可是提高會議的效率。以下針對進行部門會議時，與會者應注意之要點與需避免之禁忌做進一步說明：

不可不知的要點

1. 善用圖表：

   在評估整體表現時，各式的圖表會是非常好的輔助工具，因為圖表能夠補足文字或口語所無法呈現的畫面感。當所討論的資料越複雜，這樣的補充效果就越明顯。

2. 指出變化：

   開部門會議的目的之一就是找出過去一段時間內，各項表現是變好、變壞還是持平，因此在進行報告時，務必要在此部分多加著墨，好讓同事能夠從中發現問題或是提出建議。

3. 說明意涵：

   雖然我們有時會說數字或圖表會說話，但畢竟有些資訊的呈現是間接的，因此在簡報時應將這些資訊文字或口語化，以方便其他與會者消化這些新資訊。

不可不知的禁忌 ||||||||||||||||||||||||||||||||||||||||||||||

Unit
12

Unit
13

Unit
14

Unit
15

Unit
16

Unit
17

Unit
18

Unit
19

Unit
20

Unit
21

Unit
22

1. 缺乏數據

   由於量化的資料較容易進行客觀的討論,因此報告內容中若沒有數據能夠支撐論點,相對就會需要大量文字與口語敘述,這樣的報告方式對於簡報者與聽眾都是一種負擔。

2. 內容空泛

   績效分析是在敘述客觀表現後,再對其當中的資訊做解析,因此當內容空有詞藻但卻無法清楚陳述情況時,這樣的簡報就彷彿是對觀眾說了很多內容,但實際傳達的資訊卻是寥寥無幾,對於後續的檢討幫助其實相當有限。

腦部暖身 一點都不難對話

請將以下六個單字填入空格內。

(a) explain   (b) latest   (c) theme

(d) graph   (e) interpret   (f) choice

Jason：Morning everyone, the ___1___ today is the performance review of 2014. The three teams in our department will have the presentation respectively. Now let's welcome Susan, who's on behalf of the European team to have the briefing.

Susan：Hello, everyone. Please take a look at the line ___2___. As you can see from this diagram, the sales figure of the ___3___ smart phone NC 930 grows month after month. The trend indicates that consumers have regarded this phone is a mustbuy. If we ___4___ this chart in detail, we can find that the figure has reached the annual high in December. This fact shows that our phone may also be a good ___5___ as the Christmas gift in this region.

Jason：I also found the other peak in February. Can you ___6___ it to me?

Susan：Sure. Since we have special sales for couples, so that's why we have the peak in February.

Jason：I get it.

翻譯

Jason：各位早安，本日的主題是 2014 績效檢討。本部門的三個團隊會各自進行簡報。現在讓我們歡迎 Susan 代表歐洲團隊進行簡

報。

Susan： 各位好，請先看到這張曲線圖，如此圖表所示，我們最新的智慧型手機 NC930 的銷售數字每月成長。這樣的趨勢顯示出消費者認為此款手機為必買商品。如果我們在更仔細解讀這張表，我們會發現銷售數字在十月時達到年度的最高峰。這個情況代表了我們的手機也被該區的消費者視為聖誕禮物的好選擇。

Jason： 我發現在二月也出現高峰，可以跟解釋一下為什麼嗎？

Susan： 二月的高峰是因為推出屬於情侶夫妻的特賣活動。

Jason： 我了解了。

單字

- **respectively** [rɪˋspɛktɪvlɪ] *adv.* 各自地
- **regard** [rɪˋgɑrd] *v.* 把…認為
- **mustbuy** [mʌstbaɪ] *n.* 必買品
- **couple** [ˋkʌp!] *n.* 夫妻情侶

答案

1. (c)　2. (d)　3. (b)　4. (e)　5. (f)　6. (a)

Unit 12
Unit 13
Unit 14
Unit 15
Unit 16
Unit 17
Unit 18
Unit 19
Unit 20
Unit 21
Unit 22

會說也會寫一：解讀曲線圖

範例

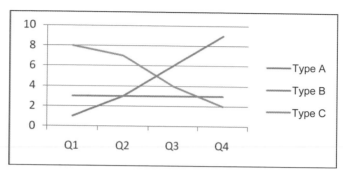

Unit: 1000 piece

1. The sales figure of type A reaches its annual peak to 10000 pieces in Q4.

2. The trend of type C's sales figure is declining.

3. Type A has the highest sales figure among the three types.

翻譯

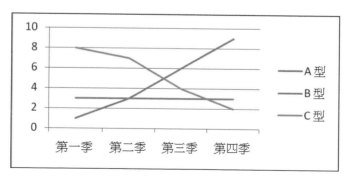

單位：1000 顆

1. A 型的銷售於第四季達到年度高峰。

2. C 型的銷售趨勢是逐漸下降。

3. A 型的最高銷售數字勝過其他兩者。

解析 ||||||||||||||||||||||||||||||||||||||||||||||||||||||||||||

　　曲線圖所能夠呈現的資訊非常多，本練習列舉出常見的三種。以下針對每一部分做進一步說明：

1. 區段高峰：

　　曲線圖的特性之一是可看出最大值落在何處，從而討論其相關產生原因。以本範例為例，A 型的銷售最大值出現在第四季，總數來到 10000 件。以此模式去解讀 B 型與 C 型，會發現前者的最大值是 8000 件，後者由於全年持平，數量為 3000 件。

2. 趨勢變化：

　　曲線圖可以表現出數值的高低變化，因此趨勢是另一項分析重點。趨勢的變化可能是上升、下降、持平或是不規則。以本範例為例，C 型的走勢一路下降，第一季有 8000 件，但到了年終的第四季只剩 2000 件。以此模式解讀 A 型，其走勢為上升，從 1000 件一路提升至 10000 件。B 型則為持平，從第一季到第四季都維持 3000 件的銷售量。

3. 數值比較：

　　除針對單一項目之內容進行比較外，曲線圖也可讓閱讀者比較多個項目之間的差異。以本範例為例，若比較三者的最大銷售量，以 A 型的 1000 件為最大。B 型的最大銷售量為 3000 件；C 型則為 8000 件。

　　上述的三種比較主要針對數值，僅屬分析的某一面向，若改從季銷售量為切入點，可從每季變化的幅度做更細部的分析。而第一季與第四季的銷售量也可單獨做為分析重點。換言之，一張圖表所含的資訊很多，從不同角度切入，就能看出不同的意涵。

　　另外，圖表所使用的單位大小與間隔也會影響內容的觀察與判讀。舉例來說，若數值的最大值為 10，最小值為 0，0 到 10 就適宜的單位，間隔部分則可以 1 或是 2 為單位，以便看出數值的變化。承上例，若將間隔放大至 5，整個圖表就只會出現 0、5、10 這三個分隔點，會使趨勢變化的明顯度降低。

Unit 12
Unit 13
Unit 14
Unit 15
Unit 16
Unit 17
Unit 18
Unit 19
Unit 20
Unit 21
Unit 22

會說也會寫二：解讀圓餅圖 ||||||||||||||||||||||||||

範例

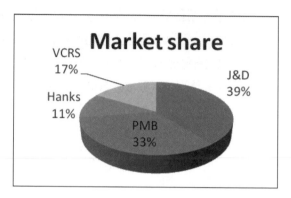

1. J&D owns the greatest market share which has accounted for 39%.
2. PMB is the main competitor of J&D.
3. There are four main brands in this market.
4. The difference between J&D and PMB is 6%.

翻譯

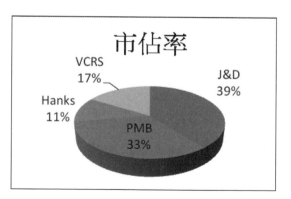

1. J&D 的市佔率最高，來到 39%。
2. PMB 是 J&D 的主要競爭對手。
3. 這個市場有四大主要品牌。
4. J&D 和 PMB 的差距是 6%。

Unit
12

Unit
13

Unit
14

Unit
15

Unit
16

Unit
17

Unit
18

Unit
19

Unit
20

Unit
21

Unit
22

解析

　　圓餅圖的優點在於呈現各數值在比例上的差異，本練習提出常見的四種，以下針對每一部分做進一步說明：

1. 最大值：

　　由於圓餅圖是將一個總量先視為圓，然後按照當中數值所佔的比例來分割此圓，因此哪部分佔最大比例屬於最容易判讀的部分。以本範例為例，J&D 佔 39%，為四個品牌中的最大者。

2. 競爭對手：

　　分析圓餅圖時，另外一個常見的切入點就比較最高與次高的數值，這樣的對照可以看出誰對於領先者最具威脅性。以本範例為例，領先者是 J&D 的 39%，次高的是 PMB 的 33%，因此 J&D 會視 PMB 為最大競爭對手，PMB 也會將 J&D 視為要迎頭趕上的目標。

3. 市場總資訊：

　　由於圓餅圖是將一個總量區分為數個部分，因此每一項目的比率也常見的探討方向。以本範例為例，一共分為四部分。J&D 佔 39%，PMB 佔 33%，VCRS 佔 17%，Hanks 佔 11%。

4. 差距：

　　圓餅圖的每個部分都有一確切數值，因此比較各部分的數值差異就有其參考參考價值，其中常見的比較方式又有最高減次高。最高減最低可以讓領先者看出目前尚有多少優勢存在，也能讓追趕者了解需要努力的空間有多少。以本範例為例，領先者 J&D 佔的比率是 39%，追趕者 PMB 是 33%，兩者間的差距為 6%。

註

　　由於圓餅圖主要是呈現各種分項所佔的比率，因此若要看出趨勢變化，此種表格並不適合。改繪製長條圖或是折線圖，方可看出走勢，便於後續的分析。

現在你會說

請依句意填入 A-E。

A. Since we have special sales, our sales in March have reached the peak.

B. The trend shows that the consumers in this region have regarded this phone is a mustbuy

C. This fact shows that our phone may also be a good choice as the Christmas gift.

D. Please pay attention to this graph

E. The two teams in our department will have the presentation respectively

---

Jason：Morning everyone, the topic today is the overall performance review of 2013. ___1___ . Now let's welcome Mary who's on behalf of the American team to have the briefing.

Susan：Hello, everyone. ___2___ . As you can see from this diagram, the sales figure of latest smart phone NC 935 grows month after month. ___3___ . If we interpret this chart in detail, we can find that the figure has reached the annual high in December. ___4___ .

Jason：I also found the other peak in March. Can you explain why?

Susan：Sure. ___5___ .

Jason：I get it.

答案

1. (E)   2. (D)   3. (B)   4. (C)   5. (A)

 現在你會寫 ||||||||||||||||||||||||||||||||||||||

1.如折線圖所示，A 型的成長比 B 型明顯

_____

_____

Unit
12

Unit
13

Unit
14

Unit
15

Unit
16

Unit
17

Unit
18

Unit
19

Unit
20

Unit
21

Unit
22

中式英文出沒 ▶ As we can see from the line graph, the growth of type A is greater than type B.

錯在哪 ▶ 與中文不同的是，英文在進行比較時詞性一定要對等。本練習中藥比較的是 A 型的成長與 B 型的成長，因此正確用法是在 type B 之前加上 that of 來做為成長的代名詞。

正解 ▶ As we can see from the line graph, the growth of type A is greater than that of type B.

2.在業績上的下滑顯示行銷策略需要三思。

_____

_____

中式英文出沒 ▶ The drop in sales figure indicate that we need to think three time in marketing strategy.

錯在哪 ▶ 中文的「三思」翻譯為英文時，並非真的翻成想三次，而是 think twice。

正解 ▶ The drop in the sales figure indicates that we need to think twice when developing the marketing strategy.

18 Unit 年度會議

挑戰難度 ★★★★☆

真的你學過

　　在經過一整年的努力後，公司會針對年度的表現進行檢討，對於績效良好部分，應繼續保持，不良的部分則須找出原因並提出改善方法。由於這樣的會議通常參與人員層級往往較高，許多人會擔心自己可能因為英文不夠好再加上緊張而出糗。但事實上，只要懂得運用敘述句型點出問題，再以比較法提出差異，最後說明解決方法，簡報時便能游刃有餘。

單元重點及學習方向

❶ 運用 To find..., I would like to bring together... 句型來說明彙整資訊的原因。

❷ 運用 ... increase/decrease by... compared to... 句型來比較兩者的差異性。

❸ 運用 To get the foothold in..., we... 句型來敘述支持想法的具體行動。

❹ 運用本單元的單字、片語與句型練習年度會議中所可能遭遇的應對進退。

⭐ 必 check 句型 ||||||||||||||||||||||||||||||||||||||||

1. **To find** the best solution of this problem, **I would like to bring together** the suggestions you provided.

   為了找出最佳解決方式，我想要彙整各位所提供的建議。

2. The market share has **increased** 5 percent compared to that of last year.

   本年度市占率較去年上升百分之五。

3. The complaint rate has **decreased by** 20 percent in Q3 comparesd to that of Q2.

   第三季的客訴率較第二季下降百分之二十。

4. **To get a stable foothold in** this market, **we** need to release new products periodically.

   為了要站穩這個市場，我們要定期推出新產品。

Ⓐ 你有學過的單字 ||||||||||||||||||||||||||||||||||||||||

1. **apparently** [əˋpærəntlɪ] *adv.* 顯然地

2. **correlate** [ˋkɔrəˌlet] *v.* 與…有關聯

3. **distribution** [ˌdɪstrəˋbjuʃən] *v.* 分配

4. **efficiency** [ɪˋfɪʃənsɪ] *n.* 效能

5. **negative** [ˋnɛgətɪv] *adj.* 負面的

6. **positive** [ˋpɑzətɪv] *adj.* 正面的

7. **promising** [ˋprɑmɪsɪŋ] *adj.* 有前途的

8. **overlap** [ˌovɚˋlæp] *v.* 重疊

9. **remarkable** [rɪˋmɑrkəbl̩] *adj.* 值得注意的

10. **wonder** [ˋwʌndɚ] *v.* 懷疑

 小試身手 |||||||||||||||||||||||||||||||||||||||||||||

1. The sales figure has highly _____ to the preference of consumers.

   銷售數字與消費者的偏好息息相關。

2. The _____ of production line has improved this year.

   今年生產線的效能獲得提升。

3. USA is a _____ market for our company.

   美國對我們公司來說是個有前景的市場。

4. The growth in the market share is _____ in 2014.

   市占率 2014 年的增幅相當可觀。

5. I _____ if the project is feasible.

   我對這個專案的可行性存疑。

解答 ....

1. correlated
2. efficiency
3. promising
4. remarkable
5. wonder

句型喚醒你的記憶 ||||||||||||||||||||||||||||||||||||

1. **To check** the feasibility, **I would like to bring together** the information I have gotten.

為了確認其可行性，我要彙整手邊已獲得資料。

To..., I would like to... 意思是「為了…，我要彙整…」，可用於說明整理資訊的原因。

例 To enhance the efficiency, I would like to bring together the data I have collected. 為提升效率，我要彙整目前已取得的數據。

2. The total sales of 2014 have **increased by** 30 percent **compared to** that of 2013.

2014 的總營業額較 2013 年增加百分之三十。

... increase by... compared to... 意思為「與…相比，…增加…」，可用於說明兩者間的提高幅度。

例 The satisfactory rate has increased by 10 percent this year compared to that of last year. 今年的滿意度較去年提升百分之十。

3. The defect rate has **decreased by** 10 percent in 2012 compard to that in 2011.

2012 年的不良率較 2011 年下降百分之十。

... decrease by... compare to... 意思為「與…相比，…增加…」，可用於說明兩者間的降低幅度。

例 The efficiency has decreased by 20 percent in March compared to that of the February. 三月的效能較二月下降百分之二十。

4. **To get a foothold in** European market, **we need to** find a partner.

為了站穩歐洲市場，我們需要找一個合作夥伴。

To get a foothold in..., we... 意思為「為了穩固…我們…」，可用於說明如何支持論點或想法。

例 To get a foothold in the meeting, we drafted an action plan. 為了要在會議中站得住腳，我們起草了一份行動計畫。

Unit 12
Unit 13
Unit 14
Unit 15
Unit 16
Unit 17
Unit 18
Unit 19
Unit 20
Unit 21
Unit 22

知多少？多知道一點總是好 ‖‖‖‖‖‖‖‖‖‖‖‖‖‖‖‖

　　年度會議是公司一年下來表現的總檢討，通常會由各部門主管帶著彙整過後的資料，向總經理或是更高層進行報告與討論。但有時主管也會讓職員代為報告，自己從旁補充。若有機會參加這樣的場合，應多加注意以下的要點與禁忌：

不可不知的要點 ‖‖‖‖‖‖‖‖‖‖‖‖‖‖‖‖‖‖‖‖‖‖

1. 重點提示：

　　在年度會議這樣的場合中，老闆或是長官們需要聽取許多人的報告，專注力與耐性都會隨著時間而遞減，因此先提出結論或重點可讓其理解報告的主軸為何，對資訊的傳達方與接受方皆有正面效益。

2. 比較差異：

　　年度檢討報告的重點之一，就是比較今年度與去年度在各項指標的變化，因此不論是變好或是變壞，都應在報告內容中加以呈現。以圖表輔以文字與口頭敘述可讓長官清楚理解我們所欲呈現之內容。

3. 提出方法：

　　年度會議的最大目的是在找出問題後，透過集思廣益的方式來找出解決之道，以避免來年仍受相同問題困擾。因此在報告時，務必提出自己部門所想出的方案，讓其他與會者看看是否有需要修正或補充之處。

不可不知的禁忌

1. 長篇大論：

   由於年度檢討會議需要討論的事項眾多，每位報告者所能分到的時間相對有限，因此若內容冗長而無重點，會使長官聽的不耐煩，徒增自己挨罵的風險。

2. 情緒字眼：

   會議中難免有人會與我們持相反意見或甚至刻意針鋒相對，在年度會議這種高層級的會議中，應更注意自己的情緒管理，以免因為一時口快而得罪其他主管或是在老闆心中留下壞印象。

Unit
12

Unit
13

Unit
14

Unit
15

Unit
16

Unit
17

**Unit
18**

Unit
19

Unit
20

Unit
21

Unit
22

腦部暖身 一點都不難對話

請將以下六個單字填入空格內。

(a) ground　　　　(b) mode　　　　(c) step

(d) edition　　　　(e) key　　　　(f) general

Jason：Good morning ___1___ Manager and all the directors, I am Jason, the Director of International Trade Department. Today, I will represent our department to have the briefing.

General Manager：Since we have many ___2___ to cover, so please keep your briefing precise and short.

Jason：OK. I will begin with the sales figure this year. As you can see from the pie chart, we can find that the figure has reached the annual high in June. To find out the ___3___ of this success, I have analyzed the details of the several diagrams and concluded that the release of limited ___4___ products is the reason. The event creates a fad and some products even sold out within few hours. To copy this successful ___5___, I suggest we can cooperate with some local brands to release jointed products.

General Manager：Good idea. What's your next ___6___?

Jason：I will find some suitable candidates.

翻譯

Jason：總經理與各位主管早安，我是國貿部的主管 Jason，今日代表

本部門進行簡報。

總經理： 由於本次會議議題眾多，報告請保持精簡。

Jason： 好，接下來就讓我從銷售數字說起。如圓餅圖所示，銷售額在六月達年度高峰。為找出其中的關鍵因素，在分析多份報表的細節後，得出的結論是因為有推出限量商品。這個活動在當時蔚為風潮，且有些商品甚在數小時內完售。為了複製此成功模式，我建議與當地知名品牌合作推出聯名商品。

總經理： 很棒的想法，你接下來打算怎麼做？

Jason： 我會先找出一些適合的候選人。

單字

- **precise** [prɪ`saɪs] *adj.* 精確的
- **copy** [`kɑpɪ] *v.* 複製
- **jointed** [`dʒɔɪntɪd] *adj.* 聯名的
- **candidate** [`kændədet] *n.* 候選人

答案

1. (f)　2. (a)　3. (e)　4. (d)　5. (b)　6. (c)

Unit 12　Unit 13　Unit 14　Unit 15　Unit 16　Unit 17　Unit 18　Unit 19　Unit 20　Unit 21　Unit 22

會說也會寫一：疊圖分析

範例

Unit: 1000 USD

1. The total sales have grown quarter after quarter.
2. The correlation between the total sales and the sales of product A is positive.
3. Product A and Product B have the same sales figure in Q2.

翻譯

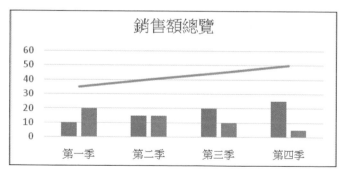

單位：1000 美金

1. 總銷售額季季上升。
2. 總銷售額與 A 產品銷售額呈現正相關。
3. A 產品與 B 產品在第二季的銷售額相同。

Unit
12

Unit
13

Unit
14

Unit
15

Unit
16

Unit
17

Unit
18

Unit
19

Unit
20

Unit
21

Unit
22

解析

做年度檢討時，單一圖表的作用在於研究變化程度，但若要細究各項變化之間是否存在關聯，則須使用疊圖分析，以下提出以長條圖疊合折線圖常見的三種研究方向做進一步說明：

1. 趨勢：

不論長條圖或是折線圖都可表現出整體的變化程度，因此趨勢就是常見的分析方式之一。以本範例為例，總銷售額呈現上升趨勢，A 產品的銷售額也是一路走高，但 B 產品卻是從年初的高峰一路下滑。以此趨勢為基礎，公司可在更進一步分析趨勢產生的原因，進而找出因應之道。

2. 關聯性：

疊圖分析與單圖分析的最大差異點在於前者可以更清楚比較關聯性。以本範例為例，總銷售額呈現上升，A 產品銷售額也是一路升高，兩者的變化就呈現正相關，也就是一者提高，另一者也提高。但此處特別要注意的是 B 產品與總銷售額的關聯性，因為 B 產品的銷售情況是一反總銷售額的走勢，呈現一路下滑，以關聯性來說，即呈現負相關。當分析圖表時出現這種相反於大趨勢（特別是呈現大幅獲利或成長）的情況時，應更加仔細探討產生的原因，以避免該因素影響公司整體表現。

3. 交叉點：

除觀察趨勢外，若兩個或者以上項目出現等值時，也是一個值得研究的重點。除非這些項目的起始值都相同，否則這樣的交叉能夠呈現出市場某些要素的改變。以本範例為例，A 產品第一季的銷售額為 10000 美金，B 產品為 20000 美金，兩個產品在第二季的銷售額同為 15000 美金，若再看第三季的表現，A 產品持續上升至 20000 美金，B 產品再下滑至 10000 美金。

綜合分析這樣的走勢，可以推測出以下幾個可能性，市場需求改變或是產品本身出現問題。此處的市場需求改變指的是市場可能突然大量需要 A 產品，導致 A 產品的銷售情況良好。產品出現問題指的是 B 產品可能在一二季之間就已出現問題，但一時間無法處理好，導致影響後續業績。

會說也會寫二：疊圖分析

範例

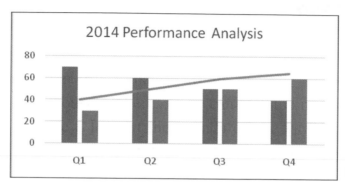

Unit: %

1. The total growth of market share in 2014 is 25 percent.
2. The growth in OBM is stable.
3. The correlation between market share and OEM is negative.

翻譯

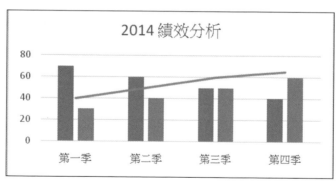

單位：%

1. 2014 市佔總成長率為 25%。
2. 自有品牌的成長率相當穩定。
3. 市佔率與代工比率呈現負相關。

解析

除以銷售數字做為分析指標外,各細項所佔的百分比也是值得探討的項目。觀察百分比的變化,可得出此要素的重要程度是否產生改變,以下利用折線圖疊合長條圖,説明以百分比為單位之圖表,常見的三個分析重點:

1. 總成長/下降率:

若以百分比為單位,其中的分析重點之一就是各項目的總變化程度。以本範例為例,第一季的市佔率是 40%,到了第四季來到 65%,因此總成長率為 25%。代工的比率則是逐季下降,從 70%一路下降至 30%,降幅為 40%。自有品牌則從 30%最終攀升至 70%,昇幅為 40%。

2. 單一項目的成長/下降率:

由單一項目的變化幅度可以看出其成長或下降率時否有軌跡可循。以本範例為例,代工的比率是以每季百分之十的速度逐季下降。自有品牌的則是以百分之十的速度逐季上升。另外在市佔率的部分,前三季是以百分之十的速度成長,到第四季略微趨緩,僅剩百分之五。

從這三個項目的變化率可看出,三者皆屬穩定成長。以資料分析的角度來看,其未來走勢較易預測。但倘若變化程度忽大忽小,若是一下正成長以下負成長,在研究上就比較不易找出邏輯。

3. 關聯性

找出個數值間的關聯性是疊圖分析的重點,正相關代表應讓兩相關相輔相成,負相關則應去探究原因,若會對公司造成危害,則須盡可能將其比率下降。以本範例為例,在市佔率提高的同時,自有品牌的比率也升高,這意味可能消費者對我們的品牌認同度提高,進而也支持我們自行生產的產品,是兩者產生正相關。

相對於自有品牌,代工產品的比率一路下降,與市佔率呈現負相關。但若據此就認定當代工比率為零時,市佔率會最大,這樣的看法可能需要再多加琢磨,因為市佔率在第四季的昇幅已出現縮小,代表可能已有其他因素對整體走勢產生影響。

 現在你會說 |||||||||||||||||||||||||||||||||||||||||||||||

請依句意填入 A-E。

A. The event did create a fad and some products even sold out within few hours

B. To find out the key of this success in sales

C. I will collect the related information and list some suitable candidates

D. Let me begin with the sales figure this year

E. Today, I will represent our department to have the briefing

Jason：Good morning Vice President and all the directors, I am Jason, the Director of International Trade Department. ___1___.

General Manager：Since we have many ground to cover, so please keep your briefing precise and short.

Jason：OK. ___2___. As you can see from the pie chart, we can find that the figure has reached the annual high in June. ___3___, I have analyzed the details of the several diagrams and concluded that the release of exclusive products is the reason. ___4___. To copy this successful mode, I suggest we can cooperate with some local brands to release jointed products.

General Manager：Good idea. What's your next step?

Jason：___5___.

答案

1. (E)　2. (D)　3. (B)　4. (A)　5. (C)

現在你會寫

1. 2014 年的銷售總額較 2013 年下降 10000 美金。

_____

_____

中式英文出沒　The total sales of 2013 decrease by $10,000 compares to 2013.

錯在哪　英文進行比較時一定要立基點相同，此練習所比較的是 2014 的銷售數字與 2013 年銷售數字，因此應於 2013 年之前加上 that of，方為正確用法

正解　The total sales of 2013 have decreased by $10,000 compared to that of 2013.

2. 為了要在新市場取得一席之地，我們分析了許多資料。

_____

_____

中式英文出沒　To get a land with a seat in the new market, we have analyzed many information.

錯在哪　若要以英文翻譯「取得一席之地」，並不是直譯為「取得一塊有椅子的土地」，而是以「取得立足點」解釋之，故英翻譯為 To get a foothold。

正解　To get a foothold in the new market, we have analyzed a lot of information

Unit 12
Unit 13
Unit 14
Unit 15
Unit 16
Unit 17
Unit 18
Unit 19
Unit 20
Unit 21
Unit 22

Part 5

職場應酬

挑戰難度 ★★☆☆☆

 真的你學過 ▌▌▌▌▌▌▌▌▌▌▌▌▌▌▌▌▌▌▌▌▌▌▌▌▌▌▌▌

　　商場上雖然充滿競爭，但對於同事乃至於競爭對手的成功或是晉升，仍應保有風度，給予祝福。由於英語畢竟不是我們的母語，許多人在以英文祝賀他人時，會覺得用字與分寸難以拿捏，但事實上，只要懂得抓出恭賀的重點，再加上些許的形容詞點綴，就能讓你的祝賀恰如其分。

🌐 單元重點及學習方向 ▌▌▌▌▌▌▌▌▌▌▌▌▌▌▌▌▌▌▌▌▌▌▌▌▌

❶ 運用 how is... /I heard that... 句型來詢問事情的進度或結果。

❷ 運用 I am/We are happy to... 句型來表達對事情的愉快感受。

❸ 運用 Wish（you）... 句型來表達祝福與鼓勵之意。

❹ 運用本單元的單字、片語與句型來練習祝賀他人。

 必 check 句型 ||||||||||||||||||||||||||||||||||||||

Unit
12

Unit
13

Unit
14

Unit
15

Unit
16

Unit
17

Unit
18

**Unit
19**

Unit
20

Unit
21

Unit
22

1. **How is** your project now?
　新專案進行得如何了？

2. **I am happy to** hear that you are promoted.
　很高興聽到你升官了。

3. **We are happy to** know that you have a new branch in Japan.
　很高興得知你在日本開了分公司。

4. **Wish** everything goes well in your job.
　祝你新工作一切順利。

 你有學過的單字 ||||||||||||||||||||||||||||||||||||||

1. **approve** [ə`pruv] *v.* 核准
2. **branch** [bræntʃ] *n.* 分公司
3. **breakthrough** [`brek͵θru] *n.* 突破
4. **congratulation** [kən͵grætʃə`leʃənz] *n.* 恭喜
5. **figure** [`fɪgjɚ] *n.* 數字
6. **performance** [pɚ`fɔrməns] *n.* 表現
7. **promotion** [prə`moʃən] *n.* 晉升
8. **raise** [rez] *v.* 提高
9. **open** [`opən] *v.* 開幕
10. **salary** [`sælərɪ] *n.* 薪水

小試身手

1. The new project is finally _____ .
   這個新專案終於通過審核。

2. We are happy to know that you have technology _____ in this field.
   很高興得知你在本領域有技術突破。

3. Wish your new business in New York has a great _____ .
   祝你在紐約的新事業能發展順遂。

4. I heard that your new shop in Japan just _____ few days ago.
   聽說你在日本的新分店幾天前剛剛開幕。

5. I am happy to hear that your salary has been _____ .
   很高興得知你加薪了。

解答

1. approved
2. breakthroughs
3. performance
4. opened
5. raised

句型喚醒你的記憶 ||||||||||||||||||||||||||||||||

1. **How is** your new project with ABC Company?
   與 **ABC** 公司合作的專案進行得如何了？
   How is... 意思為「…進行得如何？」，可用於詢問事情的進度或是結果。
   例 How is your business in Japan? 你在日本的事業狀況如何？

2. **I heard** that you have great a breakthrough in bio-technology.
   我得知你們在生技技術上有重大突破。
   I heard that... 意思為「我得知…」，可用於說明已經知道某些好消息。
   例 I have heard that you will develop a new brand in Taiwan. 我已得知你將在台灣創立一個新品牌。

3. **I am so happy to** hear that you are promoted as the Director of this Sales Department.
   很高興得知你升官擔任銷售部主管。
   I am happy to... 意思為「我很高興…」，可用於表示自己的祝賀之意。
   例 I am happy to hear that you get a raise in salary. 很高興得知你加薪了。

4. **Wish** your sales figure in USA grow year by year.
   祝你在美的銷售數字年年成長。
   Wish you (your)... 意思為「祝你（的）…」，可用於敘述自己所要祝福的內容。
   例 Wish your business successful in Spain. 祝你在西班牙的生意成功。

Unit
12

Unit
13

Unit
14

Unit
15

Unit
16

Unit
17

Unit
18

Unit
19

Unit
20

Unit
21

Unit
22

知多少？多知道一點總是好

　　在商場上，祝賀是門大學問。對於同事或合作夥伴，乃至於競爭對手的成功，皆應給予正面肯定。但這其中的分際需要拿捏得宜，才不會讓我們好意落人口實，以下針對祝賀時所需注意的要點與應避免的禁忌做進一步說明：

不可不知的要點

1. 選擇適當時機：

　　祝賀是為了表達我們對於別人的肯定之意，但對於時間點要特別注意。一些具有機密性的事件，例如人事調動（升官）或是合作案，可能會選定特定時間公布，提早恭賀反而會使其認為保密工作做不夠周延，讓你的好意打了折扣。

2. 適可而止：

　　中華文化常講說禮多人不怪，但對西方文化來說，過度的禮貌反而會讓覺得你的祝福不夠真誠，因此以英文進行恭賀時，選擇恰當的文字才不會使你的祝福適得其反。

3. 強調重要性／獨特性：

　　由於被祝賀人會接受來自各界的祝福，其內容可能也大同小異，若要讓對方留下印象，強調對方對自己的重要性是可行的方法。

不可不知的禁忌

1. 裝熟：商場上畢竟存在競爭與利益關係，對於剛剛合作或是不太熟悉的人或公司，太過熱情反而會讓對方覺得我們是有目的性的接近。

2. 過於官腔：雖然說祝賀是商場應酬話語的一環，但樣板化文字會給對方一種做表面功夫的感覺，因此送出祝福前，應稍加思考與調整用語，才會讓對方覺得我們誠意十足。

3. 道聽塗説：即便祝賀是件好事，在實際進行前應確定此消息是否為真。若不經查明究逕自道賀，萬一是誤傳，豈不尷尬萬分。

Unit
12

Unit
13

Unit
14

Unit
15

Unit
16

Unit
17

Unit
18

Unit
19

Unit
20

Unit
21

Unit
22

腦部暖身 一點都不難對話 ||||||||||||||||||||||||||||

請將以下六個單字填入空格內

(a) move   (b) partners   (c) Manager

(d) contact   (e) seasonal   (f) pity

Jason：Good morning, Martin. How have you been?

Martin：Fine, thank you.

Jason：I heard that you are promoted as the _____1_____ of R&D Department. Congratulations.

Martin：Thanks. Actually the board declares this promotion few days ago. I will _____2_____ my office to the new factory next week.

Jason：What a _____3_____ , we can't work together in the same building.

Martin：Don't worry. I will attend the _____4_____ meeting held in the conference room of the headquarters, so we can meet at least once every three months.

Jason：Indeed. We Sales Department have many opportunities to check the feasibility of marketing strategies with R&D Department, so maybe we will _____5_____ each other as usual.

Martin：Though we will work in different places from next week, we are still good _____6_____.

Jason：Right. How about having dinner together to celebrate your promotion after work?

Martin：Good idea.

翻譯

Jason： 早安 Martin，最近好嗎？

Martin： 還不錯，謝謝。

Jason： 聽說你升官擔任研發部主管了。恭喜！

Martin： 謝謝，事實上董事會幾天前才宣布這項人事令。我下週將移至新工廠辦公。

Jason： 真可惜，我沒辦法在同棟樓一起工作了。

Martin： 別擔心。我會參加在總部會議室所舉行的季會，所以我們至少每三個月會碰面一次。

Jason： 的確是。我們銷售部也常需要與研發部確認行銷策略的可行性，所以也許我們還是會跟往常一樣有業務上的聯繫。

Martin： 雖然從下週起就在不同地方工作，但我們仍是好夥伴。

Jason： 沒錯。下班後一起吃個晚餐慶祝你升官吧！

Martin： 好主意。

單字

- **board** [bord] *n.* 董事會
- **opportunity** [ˌɑpɚˈtjunətɪ] *n* 機會
- **feasibility** [ˌfizəˈbɪlətɪ] *n.* 可行性
- **celebrate** [ˈsɛləˌbret] *v.* 慶祝

答案

1. (c)　2. (a)　3. (f)　4. (e)　5. (d)　6. (b)

Unit 12
Unit 13
Unit 14
Unit 15
Unit 16
Unit 17
Unit 18
Unit 19
Unit 20
Unit 21
Unit 22

會說也會寫一：祝賀信：恭賀升官

範例

Dear Sam,

❶I know that you are promoted as the manager of your new factory in Thailand from the latest personnel announcement in your company's website.

❷Here I am on behalf of ABC Company to congratulate you. We have cooperated with each other for more than six years, and I think you are best business partner I have ever met. I am happy to see you to have the opportunity to pursue the greater achievement.

❸Wish everything goes well in your business in Thailand.

Sincerely yours,
Jason

翻譯

親愛的 Sam：

從你們公司最新的人事命令得知你升官為泰國新廠的主管。

於此謹代表 ABC 恭賀您。我們以合作長達六年，您是我所遇過最好的商業夥伴。很高興看到你有機會追求更大的成就。

祝您在泰國的事業一切順利。保持連絡。

謹
Jason

Unit
12

Unit
13

Unit
14

Unit
15

Unit
16

Unit
17

Unit
18

Unit
19

Unit
20

Unit
21

Unit
22

解析

　　一般來說，為了讓我們的祝福有效且即時的傳達給被祝福人，其信件內容大致會包含以下幾個部分：

❶消息來源：

在信件開頭應告訴對方我們是如何知道這個好消息的。告知的目的主要是讓對方檢驗我們的訊息來源是否正確。若發現誤傳，應盡快修正以免誤會持續擴大。以本範例為例，我方是從對方公司網站的人事令得知 Sam 升官的消息。

❷祝賀內容：

此部分的內容又可以再細分為：

・代表層級：

在祝賀信中，若不細究職位所對應的代表性。常見的説法是 here I on behalf of XXX Company 。由個人來代表公司，向某人道賀。以本範例為例，Jason 代表 ABC 公司向 Sam 祝賀升官。

・讚美：

此部分通常是在稱讚對方的能力或是表現，強調獲得晉升或加薪是實至名歸。可於其中添加詞藻，但不宜過量。以本範例為例，Jason 表示 Sam 是他合作過的夥伴中最棒的一位，也樂見他有機會追求更大的成就。

❸期許：

此部分其實與其他商用書信的應酬語格式相去不遠，只是此處將重點著重於祝對方發展順遂。以本範例為例，最後就是祝福 Sam 在泰國的新事業一切順利。

會說也會寫二：祝賀信：恭賀技術突破

範例

Dear Andrew,

❶I heard that you have a great breakthrough in the production of medicine from the headline of today's newspaper.

❷I'm writing in behalf of ABC Company to convey our congratulations. As your agent in Taiwan, we are so happy to be the business partner of the leading company in the world. We highly cherish the business relationship we have built.

❸Wish everything goes well in your business.

Sincerely yours
Jason

翻譯

親愛的 Andrew：

從今天的報紙頭條得知你們公司在製藥上有重大突破。

於此謹代表 ABC 公司恭賀您。做為您在台的代理商，我們很高興能成為世界頂尖的公司的商業合作夥伴。

祝您事業一切順利。

謹
Jason

 解析

一般來說，一封用於祝賀合作夥伴技術突破的信件，其內容通常會包含以下這三大部分：

❶消息來源：

　　不論是祝賀那種類型的事件，都應說明消息來源。在商場上有些好消息會選定特殊的場合與時間點再行公布，因此說明從何得知，可被祝賀人釐清是否為消息走漏。以本範例為例，我方是從報紙頭條得知技術突破，這樣的消息揭露方式應屬預期。

❷祝福內容：

　　不同於祝賀升官加薪，祝賀技術合作夥伴的技術突破，其重點通常放在我方很榮幸與之合作上（註）。以本範例為例，我方表示恨榮幸成為世界頂尖公司的在台代理商，並十分珍惜這樣的合作關係

❸期許：

　　由於是祝福合作夥伴，通常結尾都是希望對方發展順遂。以本範例為例，便是祝福對方事業一切順利。

註

　　商場上的合作關係是有層級性的，舉例來說，若是由供應商寫信祝賀被供應方，其情況就與本範例類似。雖然在企業規模上，供應商不見得比較小，但交易能否完成，被供應方的主導權還是較大，因此語氣上可更加禮貌些。但若今日角色互換，語氣維持一般即可。另外，若為雙方的合作在位階上是平行的，其文字彈性就更大，若我方很重視這個夥伴，語氣可以特別禮貌，若認為無此必要，維持一般禮數即可。

Unit

12

Unit

13

Unit

14

Unit

15

Unit

16

Unit

17

Unit

18

Unit

19

Unit

20

Unit

21

Unit

22

 現在你會說 ||||||||||||||||||||||||||||||||||||||||

請依句意填入 A-E。

A. Actually, the board declares this promotion few hours ago

B. We Sales Department have opportunities to check the feasibility of marketing strategies with the Designing Department

C. I will be the representative to attend the seasonal meeting held in the conference room of the headquarters

D. How about having dinner together to celebrate your promotion after work today

E. I heard that you are promoted as the Manager of Designing Department

Jason：Good morning, Martin. How are you today?

Martin：Fine, thank you.

Jason：＿＿＿1＿＿＿. Congratulations.

Martin：Thanks a lot. ＿＿＿2＿＿＿. I will move my office to the new factory in the other city next week.

Jason：What a pity! We can't work together in the same office.

Martin：Don't worry. ＿＿＿3＿＿＿, so we can meet at least once every three months.

Jason：Indeed. ＿＿＿4＿＿＿, so maybe we will contact each other as usual.

Martin：Though we will work in different places from next week, we are still good partners in business.

Jason：Right. ＿＿＿5＿＿＿?

Martin：Good idea.

答案

1. (E)　2. (A)　3. (C)　4. (B)　5. (D)

現在你會寫 ||||||||||||||||||||||||||||||||||||||||

Unit
12

Unit
13

Unit
14

Unit
15

Unit
16

Unit
17

Unit
18

Unit
19

Unit
20

Unit
21

Unit
22

1.目前公司在美國的營運狀況如何？

_____

_____

中式英文出沒 ▶ How is Company's business situation in USA now?

錯在哪 ▶ 此處的「公司」在翻譯時可翻也可省略，若要翻譯出來時，our company，若要省略，則以 the 代替為佳。另營運狀況一詞 business 即可，無須再加上 situation。

正解 ▶ How is the business in USA now?

2.祝你前程似錦。

_____

_____

中式英文出沒 ▶ Wish you future like brocade.

錯在哪 ▶ 若受到中文成語的影響，僅從字面來翻譯，整個句子就會被理解成「祝你的前途像錦帶一樣」，但事實上前程似錦是要表示未來很有發展性，因此應使用 a promising future 較為適宜。

正解 ▶ Wish you a promising future.

挑戰難度 ★★☆☆☆

 **真的你學過**

　　即便一個人的能力再好，在商場上不可能凡事都只靠自己，若遇到自己無法處理的狀況，就會需要別人的幫助。接受別人的協助後，理應表達感謝之意。當真的要以英文致謝時，很多人會擔心自己詞不達意。但事實上，只要說清楚事由，再加上適當的感謝辭，對方就能了解你的感激之意。

單元重點及學習方向

❶ 運用 We appreciate... /Thank you for Ving... 句型來表達感謝之意。

❷ 運用 Please accept our thanks for Ving 句型來表達感謝之意。

❸ 運用 Without your..., I... 句型來強調對方所給予協助之重要性。

❹ 運用本單元的單字、片語與句型來練習向客戶與同事致謝。

 **必 check 句型** ||||||||||||||||||||||||||||||||

1. We **appreciate** your help.
   很感謝您的協助。

2. **Thank you for** providing the detailed information.
   感謝您提供詳盡的資訊。

3. **Please accept our thanks for** your timely technical support.
   請接受我們對您提供及時技術支援的感謝之意。

4. **Without your** financial support, **the project** will be cancelled.
   沒有您的資金挹注，這個專案計畫將會被取消。

 你有學過的單字 ||||||||||||||||||||||||||||||

1. **bankrupt** [`bæŋkrʌpt] *adj.* 破產
2. **fail** [fel] *v.* 失敗
3. **gratitude** [`grætə͵tjud] *n.* 感激
4. **hospitality** [͵hɑspɪ`tælətɪ] *n.* 好客
5. **mention** [`mɛnʃən] *v.* 提及
6. **overcome** [͵ovɚ`kʌm] *v.* 克服
7. **prompt** [prɑmpt] *adj.* 快速的
8. **survive** [sɚ`vaɪv] *v.* 存活
9. **thankful** [`θæŋkfəl] *adj.* 感激的
10. **timely** [`taɪmlɪ] *adj.* 即時的

Unit 12
Unit 13
Unit 14
Unit 15
Unit 16
Unit 17
Unit 18
Unit 19
Unit 20
Unit 21
Unit 22

小試身手

1. Without your help, we will go _____.
   沒有你的協助，我們會破產。

2. Please accept our _____ for your assistance.
   請接受我們對您提供協助的感激之意。

3. Thank you for your _____.
   感謝您的熱情款待。

4. I am _____ for your technical support.
   我很感謝你的技術支援。

5. Without your help, we won't _____ from this crisis.
   沒有你的協助，我們無法度過危機。

解答

1. bankrupt
2. gratitude
3. hospitality
4. thankful
5. survive

句型喚醒你的記憶

1. **We appreciate** your support in the development of this new product.

   我們感激您在研發新產品過程中所提供的協助。

   We appreciate... 意思為「我們感激…」，可用於表達感謝之意。

   例 We appreciate your timely help. 我們感謝您及時給予協助。

2. **Thank you for** sparing your time.

   感謝撥空。

   Thank you for...，意思為「感謝…」，for 後面的動詞要加 ing，可於說明感謝對方的事由。

   例 Thank you for assisting us. 感謝協助。

3. **Please accept our** warmest **thanks** for your support.

   請接受我們對您提供協助的感謝之意。

   Please accept our thanks for Ving 意思為「請接受我們對…的感謝」之意，可用於表達我方之感謝。

   例 Please accept our thanks for sending the engineers to solve the problem. 請接受我們對您派出工程師解決問題的感謝之意。

4. **Without your** reminder, **we will** miss the deadline of shipment.

   沒有你的提醒，我們會錯過出貨的最後期限。

   Without your..., we will... 意思為「沒有你的…，我們將…」，可用於感謝對所做出的協助。

   例 Without your timely help, we will face the great financial loss.

   沒有你的即時協助，我們會面臨鉅額的財物損失。

Unit 12
Unit 13
Unit 14
Unit 15
Unit 16
Unit 17
Unit 18
Unit 19
Unit 20
Unit 21
Unit 22

知多少？多知道一點總是好 ||||||||||||||||||||||||||||||

　　雖然商場上充滿競爭，但也並非毫無人情味可言，當自己的同事或是夥伴有困難時，我們會伸出援手。反之，當我們遭遇危機時，他們也會給予協助。受人幫助後，應以口頭、書面甚至行動來表達感激之意，以下針對致謝時應注意的要點加以說明：

不可不知的要點 ||||||||||||||||||||||||||||||||||||

1. 說明事由：

致謝前要說明事由其目的大致有以下兩種：

(1) 協助回想：

對於熱心的人，可能把幫助別人視為小事，因此不會特別記住自己到底協助了那一些事。為避免我方滿懷感激，但對方卻一頭霧水的情況產生，道謝前應該先說明整件事情的原委，才能使你的感激有效傳達給被感謝人。

(2) 強化語氣：

在向對方道謝前，重述整個事情經過具有強調作用，表示我方對於協助的細節銘記在心。

2. 強調協助帶來之影響：

此處的影響指的是有無協助所帶來的差異。會需要別人的幫忙，就表示所遭遇的情況是無法獨立解決的。提及若沒有對方的及時幫助，會產生怎樣不好的結果，其實也是在表達感激。

3. 表達回報之意：

雖然對方幫助我們不見得是在期待回報，但基於受人恩惠，我方應表達出回饋之意。回饋的方式可以是：

(1) 口頭：親自拜訪或是以電話向對方致謝。

(2) 文字：寫電子郵件表達感激。

(3) 行動：請對方吃頓飯或是多加購買該公司產品。

Unit
12

Unit
13

Unit
14

Unit
15

Unit
16

Unit
17

Unit
18

Unit
19

Unit
20

Unit
21

Unit
22

腦部暖身 一點都不難對話 ||||||||||||||||||||||||

請將以下六個單字填入空格內。

(a) automatically   (b) mention   (c) figure out

(d) solve   (e) smoothly   (f) lucky

Jason：I should say I am so ____1____ to have such a good business partner like you.

Robert：Why do you say so?

Jason：You do me a big favor few days ago.

Robert：Oh! You mean the system problem, right?

Jason：Correct. On that day, our system ____2____ crashed several times, and our engineer can't find the specific reason. To ____3____ this problem, I ask you for help. And you sent one senior engineer to our company to ____4____ what happened to our system. After resetting some parameters, the system ran ____5____.

Robert：He is the best engineer in my team, so I send him to help you.

Jason：Thank you again. Without your timely help, the shipment will be delayed.

Robert：Don't ____6____ it! We are good partners, so just call me if you need help.

Jason：You are so nice.

翻譯

Jason： 我必須説我很幸運有你這樣的商業夥伴。

Robert： 為何這樣説呢？

Jason： 你幾天前幫了我一個大忙。

Robert：噢！你是説系統問題那件事對吧！

Jason：沒錯。那天我們的系統自動關機好幾次，但工程師無法找出確切原因。為了要解決問題，我向你求救。你派出資深工程師到我們公司來了解情況。在重新設定過一些參數後，系統就運作順暢了。

Robert：他是我團隊裡最優秀的工程師，所以我派他協助你。

Jason：真的很感謝。如果沒有你的即時協助，出貨就會延遲了

Robert：別這樣説。我們是好夥伴，如果需要幫忙就連絡我。

Jason：你人真好。

單字 ⋯⋯⋯⋯⋯⋯⋯⋯⋯⋯⋯⋯⋯⋯⋯⋯⋯⋯⋯⋯⋯⋯⋯⋯⋯

- **favor** [`fevɚ] *n.* 善意的行為
- **crash** [kræʃ] *v.* 當機
- **senior** [`sinjɚ] *adj.* 資深的
- **parameter** [pə`ræmətɚ] *n.* 參數

Unit
12

Unit
13

Unit
14

Unit
15

Unit
16

Unit
17

Unit
18

Unit
19

Unit
20

Unit
21

Unit
22

答案 ⋯⋯⋯⋯⋯⋯⋯⋯⋯⋯⋯⋯⋯⋯⋯⋯⋯⋯⋯⋯⋯⋯⋯⋯⋯

1. (f)　2. (a)　3. (d)　4. (c)　5. (e)　6. (b)

會說也會寫一：感謝提供技術協助 |||||||||||||

範例

Dear Mark,

❶Thank you for sending two senior engineers to Taiwan to help solve the problem that bothers us for long. Without your timely help, the shipment will be delayed.

❷To show our deepest appreciation, please do accept the invitation to have dinner together in ABC Restaurant after our seasonal meeting on March 1.

❸Once again, thank you for your assistance. We are so lucky to have a good business partner like you

Yours sincerely,
Jason

翻譯

親愛的 Mark：

　　感謝您派出兩名資深工程師來台解決長久以來困擾我們的問題。若沒有您的即時協助，出貨恐怕會延遲。

　　為了表達我們的感激，請接受我們的邀請，於三月一日的季會之後，一同前往 ABC 餐廳享用晚餐。

　　於此再次感謝您的協助，非常慶幸能有你這樣的商業夥伴。

謹
Jason

解析

在寫信感謝對方提供技術協助時，為了要清楚傳達我方的感激，其內容通常會包括以下三大部分：

❶感謝事由：

為了讓對方清楚我方道謝的原因，通常在感謝信件的開頭簡述事情經過，以本範例為例，寫信事由是要感謝對方派了兩位工程師來台協助解決問題。並補充說明，若這樣的問題未能及時獲得解決，會導致後續的出貨產生延遲，茲事體大。

❷致謝方式：

表達感激的方式有很多種，可是口頭、文字或是行動。在本範例中就採用了口頭加上行動這兩種方式。這封感謝信本身代表了口頭感謝，另外在信中我方又在邀請對方於雙方例行性會議後共進晚餐，做到了行動上的感謝。至於選在會議後請對方吃飯，由於雙方有個碰面的事由，對方會比較不好意思婉拒，如此一來我方的禮數也能做足。

❸應酬語：

此段落重點在於再次表達感激，為此封感謝信做個完美收尾。以本範例為例，採用的是再次感謝對方的協助，並提及我方很慶幸能有這樣好的商業夥伴，來彰顯對方的重要性。

註

以行動表達感激時，在方式與時間的選擇上可多用一些巧思。舉例來說，找一個雙方原本就會碰面的時間邀請對方吃飯，或是本來就要進行的交易額外增加購買量，都可以讓對不好推辭，讓我們的感激可以成功傳達。

Unit 12

Unit 13

Unit 14

Unit 15

Unit 16

Unit 17

Unit 18

Unit 19

Unit 20

Unit 21

Unit 22

會說也會寫二：感謝提供金援

範例

Dear Leo,

❶I'm writing in behalf of ABC Company to show our deepest gratitude to your financial support during our hardest time. Without you help, we will face huge indemnity and go bankrupt.

❷To show our appreciation, we decide to order ten thousand more parts from your company this year. Later we will send you the specification we need. We are so lucky to have a good business partner like you.

❸Wish everything goes well in your business

Sincerely yours
Jason

翻譯

親愛的 Leo：

　　於此謹代表 ABC 公司表達在我方最艱困時期你所提供金援之謝意。沒有您的協助，我們將會面臨巨額賠償而破產。

　　為表達感謝之意，我們決定今年向貴公司額外訂購一萬顆零件。稍後會附上我們所需的規格。我們非常慶幸能有你這樣的商業夥伴。

　　祝您事業一切順利。

謹
Jason

解析

　　在商場上資金難免有周轉困難的情況產生，此時若有夥伴願意提供資金協助解決燃眉之急，對我方來說是莫大的恩惠，因此在對方給予金援後，應寫信表達感激：

❶感謝事由：

由於資金挹注通常不會是個人對個人，多為公司對公司，因此在表達感謝時，宜表示是由本人代表公司向其致謝，在形式上較為莊重。並補充說明若沒有對方的幫助，所產生怎樣的財務缺口，再次強調我方的感激。以本範例為例，我方表示若無對方的金援，會面對巨額賠償款，最終走向破產一途。

❷致謝方式：

以行動致謝的另外一種方就是在既定的採購中提高購買量。在商場上，此種方式也是最實質的回報方式之一，因為此舉直接提高對方公司的業績。以本範例為例，我方要在既有的購買數量上，額外再購買一萬顆零件，做為感激對方的實質行動。

❸應酬語：

表達將以實際行動來感激對方後，最後通常以預祝對方事業順遂做結語。本範例便採用此思維，祝對方一切順利。

註

　　針對感謝對金援，由於往往層級較高，建議由職等較高的人員代表公司寫信感謝，禮數上較為周到。

Unit 12
Unit 13
Unit 14
Unit 15
Unit 16
Unit 17
Unit 18
Unit 19
Unit 20
Unit 21
Unit 22

 現在你會說 ||||||||||||||||||||||||||||||||||||||||

請依句意填入 A-E。

A. Is it possible for you to stay longer

B. Your hospitality really impresses me

C. In such case, I don't want to keep you

D. When is your flight tomorrow

E. I feel you just got here not long ago

Jason：Good Morning Mike, how are you?

Mike：Quite good, and you?

Jason：Very well. Actually, I come to say goodbye to you because I will go home tomorrow morning.

Mike：Don't be so soon. _____1_____.

Jason：I think so too.

Mike：_____2_____?

Jason：I wish I could, but I have a meeting with my boss tomorrow afternoon.

Mike：What a pity. _____3_____. Next time when you visit Singapore, please inform me first. Let me be your tour guide again.

Jason：Thanks a lot. _____4_____.

Mike：_____5_____?

Jason：9:30 AM.

Mike：I am free tomorrow morning, so let me pick you up to the airport.

Jason：Thank you.

答案

1. (E)   2. (A)   3. (C)   4. (B)   5. (D)

 現在你會寫 ||||||||||||||||||||||||||||||||||||||

1. 感謝你撥空協助我們。

_____

_____

中式英文出沒 ▶ Thank you spare time to assist us.

　　錯在哪 ▶ 感謝某人為我們做了某事，應使用 Thank you for
Ving，故於 you 之後加上 for，並將 spare 修正為
sparing，即為正解。

　　正解 ▶ Thank you for sparing time to assist us.

2. 沒有你的及時提醒，我們會損失大額資金。

_____

_____

中式英文出沒 ▶ Without your timely remind, we will lose great
capital.

　　錯在哪 ▶ timely 雖然字尾有 ly，但此處是做為形容詞用，形容
詞是用來修飾名詞，因此要將 remind 修正為
reminder 才是正確用法。

　　正解 ▶ Without your timely reminder, we will lose great
capital.

Unit 12
Unit 13
Unit 14
Unit 15
Unit 16
Unit 17
Unit 18
Unit 19
Unit 20
Unit 21
Unit 22

提醒

挑戰難度 ★★☆☆☆

 真的你學過 ||||||||||||||||||||||||||||||||||||||||

　　商場上的競爭無限，但人的記憶力卻是有限的。因此不論是準備會議、執行專案乃至進行交易，相互提醒會比一個人獨力確認更不容易產生遺漏。但為何些人寧可選擇沉默而不願提醒，原因在於怕使用了不適當的英文句型，會使原本的好意被對方解讀為對其能力或細心程度的不信任。但事實上，只要善用簡單的完成式與疑問句，搭配合緩語氣，就能使對方接受我們的提醒。

 **單元重點及學習方向** ||||||||||||||||||||||||||||||||||||

❶ 運用 Have you checked/listed... 句型來提示對方是否已進行事前檢查。

❷ 運用 Is everything ready for... 句型來提醒對方是否留意細節。

❸ 運用 Is there anything needed to... 句型來提醒對方是否需要重複某些動作或程序。

❹ 應用本單元之字彙、片語與句型練習如何提醒對方。

 必 check 句型 ||||||||||||||||||||||||||||||||||||||

1. **Have you checked** the details of the contract?
   你確認合約細節了沒？

2. **Have you listed** the item we have to purchase?
   你列出我們必須購買的品項了沒？

3. **Is everything** ready for the meeting tomorrow?
   明天的會議都準備好了嗎？

4. **Is there anything** needed to double check before we send the package?
   在寄出包裹前還有什麼要再重複確認的嗎？

 你有學過的單字 ||||||||||||||||||||||||||||||||||||||

1. **agenda** [ə`dʒɛndə] *n.* 議程

2. **approach** [ə`protʃ] *v.* 接近

3. **deadline** [`dɛd͵laın] *n.* 最後期限

4. **execute** [`ɛksɪ͵kjut] *v.* 執行

5. **finalize** [`faınḷ͵aız] *v.* 完成

6. **implmentation** [͵ımpləmɛn`teʃən] *n.* 執行

7. **purpose** [`pɝpəs] *n.* 目的

8. **particpant** [pɑr`tısəpənt] *n.* 參與者

9. **term** [tɝm] *n.* 條件

10. **upcoming** [`ʌp͵kʌmıŋ] *adj.* 即將到來的

Unit 12
Unit 13
Unit 14
Unit 15
Unit 16
Unit 17
Unit 18
Unit 19
Unit 20
Unit 21
Unit 22

小試身手

1. Have you checked the _____ of the meeting tomorrow?
   你確認明天會議的議程了沒？

2. Is there anything needed to be done if we want to _____ this deal soon?
   如果要快點完成交易，我們該怎樣做？

3. Is there anything needed to be modified before the _____?
   在執行前還有什麼地方要修正的嗎？

4. Have you checked the _____ of this project?
   你確認過本專案的最後期限了沒？

5. Is everything ready for the _____ event?
   對即將到來的活動我們一切準備就緒了嗎？

解答

1. agenda
2. finalize
3. implementation
4. deadline
5. upcoming

句型喚醒你的記憶 ||||||||||||||||||||||||||||||||

1. **Have you checked** the payment term of this deal?

你確認過本次交易的付款條件了沒？

Have you checked... 意思為「你檢查…了沒？」，可用於提醒對方要進行確認。

例 Have you checked the detail of the shipment? 你確認過出貨細節了沒？

2. **Have you listed** the parts we should buy next year?

你列出我們明年應該購買的零件清單了沒？

Have you listed... 意思為「你列出…的清單了沒？」，可用於提醒對方是否將注意的事項逐一列出。

例 Have you listed the types of machines we need to purchase? 你列出我們需要購買的機器型號了沒？

3. **Is everything ready for** the seasonal meeting next week?

下週的季會都準備好了嗎？

Is everything ready for... 意思為「…都準備好了嗎？」，可用於提醒對方是否一切已就緒。

例 Is everything ready for the presentation tomorrow? 明天的報告都準備好了嗎？

4. **Is there anything needed to** be modified before submitting this report?

在提交報告前還有什麼修正的嗎？

Is there anything needed to... 意思為「還有…需要…的嗎？」，可用於提醒對方是否有需要重複程序或動作。

例 Is there anything needed to be submitted before the application? 申請之前有什麼資料需要繳交的嗎？

Unit 12
Unit 13
Unit 14
Unit 15
Unit 16
Unit 17
Unit 18
Unit 19
Unit 20
Unit 21
Unit 22

知多少？多知道一點總是好

　　由於一個人的記憶力有限，工作繁忙時難免因為疏忽而遺漏或弄錯某些事項。若要避免這樣的情況發生，相互提醒是個好方法。但在以英文提醒同事或是合作夥伴時，對於語氣的斟酌跟句型的使用應多加注意，以免出於善意的提醒被對方解讀為對其能力的質疑。以下針對提醒對方時應注意的要點以及應避免的禁忌做進一步的說明：

不可不知的要點

1. 懂得變通：

　　一般來說，多數人對於別人的善意提醒，會選擇接受並表示感激，但有些人因為自尊心較強，當旁人（特別是長官）善意提醒時，容易將其解讀成對其能力與細心程度的不信任，若遭遇上述情況，可改採用問問題的方式，讓對方替你解答，從而逐一確認內容是否正確。

2. 以目的為導向：

　　提醒的目的在於不要產生遺漏或錯誤，因此內容應當緊扣重要項目。舉例來說，若希望會議順利，提醒內容通常會與會時間、地點與參加人員等要素有關。

不可不知的禁忌

1. 語帶質疑：

  提醒不是在責怪對方，表現質疑語氣容易會讓對方把你的好意解釋為你不相信他，而使場面有些尷尬。

2. 資訊不分類：

  會出言提醒就表示需要確認的項目可能不少，此時若不分類或是籠統地詢問，偵錯與檢查的效果肯定會打折扣，因此建議依主題來提示，讓對方可以逐一審視是否有遺漏或需要改正之處。

Unit
12

Unit
13

Unit
14

Unit
15

Unit
16

Unit
17

Unit
18

Unit
19

Unit
20

Unit
21

Unit
22

腦部暖身 一點都不難對話 ||||||||||||||||||||||||||

請將以下六個單字填入空格內。

(a) international   (b) exit   (c) twice

(d) settled   (e) sequence   (f) attendees

Jason：**Is anything ready for** the meeting tomorrow?

David：Yeah. I have checked all the details ____1____.

Jason：May I know when will the meeting begin?

David：7:00 PM

Jason：And location?

David：In the ____2____ conference room on the 10th floor of ABC Hotel.

Jason：**Have you listed** the participants of this meeting in an alphabetical order?

David：I haven't. I typed their names by the ____3____ of their reply time. Your suggestion is great, and I will re-arrange the information I just typed.

Jason：Do we provide the shuttle bus to pick up all the ____4____ from the airport?

David：Yes, the bus will arrive at the ____5____ thirty minutes before the flight lands.

Jason：Last question. Do we provide refreshments?

David：Yes, we do. I have requested the hotel to prepare some finger food.

Jason：It seems everything are ____6____, wish the meeting go smoothly tomorrow.

Unit
12

Unit
13

Unit
14

Unit
15

Unit
16

Unit
17

Unit
18

Unit
19

Unit
20

Unit
21

Unit
22

翻譯

Jason：明天的會議一切都準備就緒了嗎？

David：是的，我檢查所有細節兩遍了。

Jason：那請問會議幾點開始？

David：晚上七點。

Jason：開會地點呢？

David：在 ABC 飯店十樓的國際會議廳。

Jason：那你有按照字母排序來列出參加人員名單嗎？

David：沒有，我是按照他們回信的時間來排序。你的建議很棒，我會重新調整我剛繕打的清單。

Jason：我們有提供接駁車從機場接送與會者嗎？

David：有提供。接駁車會在班機降落前三十分鐘抵達機場出口。

Jason：最後一個問題。我們有提供茶點嗎？

David：有，我有要求飯店準備一些手拿食物。

Jason：看來一切都準備就緒了，祝明天會議進行順利。

單字

- **shuttle bus** [ˋʃʌt!bʌs] *n.* 接駁車
- **refreshment** [rɪˋfrɛʃmənt] *n.* 茶點
- **finger food** [ˋfɪŋɡɚ͵fud] *n.* 如手指般大小的，可一口塞入嘴裡的食物

答案

1. (c)　　2. (a)　　3. (e)　　4. (f)　　5. (b)　　6. (d)

會說也會寫一：提醒出貨事宜 ||||||||||||||||

範例

Dear Andrew,

❶Since the shipment is about to be made in one week, here let me remind few things.

❷Firstly, please check the customs document. Since we will need two more hard copies in this purchase, please make sure the customs have issued the documents we need to you. Secondly, please check the estimated arrival time. The products should arrive in Taiwan no later than May 15.

❸Hope everything goes well in this shipment

Yours,

Jason

 翻譯

親愛的 Andrew：

再過一週即將出貨，於此提醒幾件事情。

首先是關於海關文件。因為本次採購需要多兩份紙本文件，請確認海關是否已把文件開立給你。第二點是請確認預計到貨時間。貨品抵台日不得晚於五月十五日。

祝出貨一切順利

謹

Jason

解析

當寫信提醒同事或是合作夥伴出貨相關注意事項時，其內容通常會包含以下三大部分：

❶事由：

提醒的時機通常會落在預計執行的日期的數天之前，因此撰寫信件時常會以此為事由，提醒對方應去確認出貨的細節。以本範例為例，再過一週即將出貨，因此 Jason 發信提醒 Andrew。

❷具體內容：

此部分即為提醒事項。一般而言，會以分項敘述的方式進行。一次提醒一個項目。以本範例為例，提醒項目有二：

• 海關文件：

由於我方要求要多兩份紙本，因此特別提醒對方是否已從海關那邊取得文件。

• 預計到貨時間：

下訂單或是簽合約通常列出貨品預計的抵達時間。超過這個期限可能要賠償對方的損失。以本範例為例，雙方約定貨品不得晚於五月十五日前抵達台灣，故 Jason 提醒 Andrew 要確認預計到貨日是否晚於這個日期。

❸應酬語：

寫信提醒的目的就是希望不要有細節出錯，因此本範例所使用的應酬語是祝出貨一切順利。

Unit 12
Unit 13
Unit 14
Unit 15
Unit 16
Unit 17
Unit 18
Unit 19
Unit 20
Unit 21
Unit 22

會說也會寫二：提醒付款期限已過 |||||||||||||||||

範例

Dear Sam,

❶On March 12, you placed an order of 100 machines. The payment is scheduled to be made within seven days from the purchase date. Today is March 20, but we haven't received the payment, so here I send this mail as the reminder.

❷We think you are just busy and forgot to issue the check. Please finalize this payment within three bank business days. Here let me provide our account to you again. It is 4036-8888-6666-6455.

❸Thank you for your cooperation.

Yours,
Jason

 翻譯

親愛的 Sam：

你於三月十二日向我們下訂一百台機器，並預計於購買日起的七天內完成付款。今日已是二十日，但我們尚未收到款項，故發此信作為提醒。

我們相信你只是太忙而忘記開立支票，故請於銀行的三個工作天內完成付款。於此再次附上本公司之帳號：4036-8888-6666-6455。

感謝您的合作。

謹
Jason

解析 ||||||||||||||||||||||||||||||||||||||||||||||||||||||

在提醒信中，寫信提醒對方尚未付款是屬於需要斟酌語氣與用語的類型之一，其信件架構大致如下：

❶寫信事由：

由於付款延遲可能會導致後續的違約或是賠償問題，因此當此情況產生時，應說明對方是於何時購買產品，付款的最後期限在哪時候，目前已超過期限，故發信提醒。以本範例為例，**Sam** 所任職的公司於三月十二日向我方訂購了一百台機器，並預計在自購買日起的七日內完成付款。但今日已經三月二十日（付款最後期限為三月十九日），我方仍未收到款項，故提特別醒之。

❷具體內容：

面對剛剛或是首次發生逾期的客戶，在實務上通常不會馬上強硬催討，而是先提醒對方付款最後期限以至。並假設對方可能是過於忙碌而疏於注意付款期限，讓對方不致於覺得難堪。最後才提出希望對方於何時以何種方法完成付款。以本範例為例，**Jason** 就表示對方可能因位是太過忙碌而忘記開票，請他於銀行的三個營業日內完成相關事宜。

❸應酬語：

在說明完提醒內容後，最後肯定希望對方會趕快進行付款，故以感謝你的配合做為結尾應酬語。

註

針對經常性欠款或累犯之客戶，本範例之語氣可能就略顯不足。對於該類客戶應以訴諸法律做為主軸，告知對方若仍拖欠款項，將尋商業法或是按合約訂單內容進入司法程序。

 現在你會說 |||||||||||||||||||||||||||||||||||||||||

請依句意填入 A-E。

A. In the international conference room on the 12th floor of AC Hotel

B. The bus will arrive at the exit fifteen minutes before the flight lands

C. Do we provide refreshments for the participants between sessions

D. I have requested the hotel to prepare some finger food outside the metting room

E. Is anything ready for the meeting next Monday

Jason：_____1_____?

David：Yeah. I have checked all the details three times.

Jason：May I know when will the meeting begin?

David：6:30 PM.

Jason：And where are we going to have the meeting?

David：_____2_____.

Jason：Have you listed the participants of this meeting in an alphabetical order?

David：I haven't. I type their name in the sequence of their reply time. Your suggestion is good, and I will re-arrange the information I just typed.

Jason：Do we provide the shuttle bus to pick up all the attendees from the airport?

David：Yes. _____3_____.

Jason：Last question. _____4_____?

David：Yes we do. _____5_____.

Jason：It seems everything is settled, wish the meeting goes smoothly tomorrow.

Unit 12

Unit 13

Unit 14

Unit 15

Unit 16

Unit 17

Unit 18

Unit 19

Unit 20

Unit 21

Unit 22

答案

1. (E)　2. (A)　3. (B)　4. (C)　5. (D)

 現在你會寫

1.下週五的簽約事宜都準備好了嗎？

_____

_____

中式英文出沒 Is everything ready for the matter of the signing of the contract next Friday?

錯在哪 若仔細思考 everything 的意涵「所有事情」，就會發現其他 the matter of 其實是贅詞，因此去掉這個部分，即為正解。

正解 Is everything ready for the signing of the contract next Friday?

2.在出貨前有任何地方需要調整的嗎？

_____

_____

中式英文出沒 Is there anything needs to adjust before shipment?

錯在哪 由於此句沒有明顯的被動語氣，在翻譯時很容易忽略需要調整應該是 needed to be adjusted 而非 need to adjust。

正解 Is there anything needed to be adjusted before shipment?

22 Unit 道歉

挑戰難度 ★★☆☆☆

真的你學過 ||||||||||||||||||||||||||||||||||||||||

　　只要是人，就有出錯的可能性，因此在商場上出錯並非不可原諒，重點在於懂得認錯，並且盡快提出彌補與修正方案。若要以英文致歉時，很多人會擔心會因為自己的英文程度不足，而讓對方覺得沒有誠意，但事實上，只要能夠敘述自己的錯誤，並提出方法來解決錯誤所帶來的損害，對方肯定能感受到我們道歉的誠意。

單元重點及學習方向 ||||||||||||||||||||||||||||||||||

❶ 運用 Here I apologize for... 來表示我方願意為錯誤道歉。
❷ 運用 To compensate/settle..., I/we... 句型來表達我方願意彌補或是解決的誠意。
❸ 運用 I am sorry for... 句型來表達我方的歉意。
❹ 運用本單元的單字、片語與句型來練習向客戶或是同事致歉。

 必 **check** 句型 |||||||||||||||||||||||||||||||||||||||||

1. **Here I apologize for** my carelessness.
   於此針對我的粗心大意表示歉意。

2. **To compensate** your loss, **we** provide a free small gift to your and deduct the freight.
   為彌補你的損失，我們致贈一份免費小禮物給您並減免運費。

3. **To settle** the problem, **we** will send two technicians to your factory.
   解決此問題，我們將派出兩名技術人員至您的工廠。

4. **I am sorry for** bringing such inconvenience to you.
   對於造成您的不便我深感抱歉。

 你有學過的單字 |||||||||||||||||||||||||||||||||||||||||

1. **accounting** [ə`kaʊntɪŋ] *n.* 會計
2. **carelessness** [`kɛrlɪsnɪs] *n.* 粗心
3. **deduct** [dɪ`dʌkt] *v.* 減免
4. **examine** [ɪg`zæmɪn] *v.* 檢查
5. **face** [fes] *v.* 面臨
6. **forgive** [fə`gɪv] *v.* 原諒
7. **judgement** [`dʒʌdʒmənt] *n.* 判斷
8. **sincerity** [sɪn`sɛrətɪ] *n.* 誠意
9. **reassure** [ˌriə`ʃʊr] *v.* 再次保證
10. **waive** [wev] *v.* 免除

Unit
12

Unit
13

Unit
14

Unit
15

Unit
16

Unit
17

Unit
18

Unit
19

Unit
20

Unit
21

Unit
22

小試身手 ||||||||||||||||||||||||||||||||||||||

1. I have asked our _____ Department to revise the invoice.

我已經要求會計部門修正發票。

2. I am sorry for my _____ .

我為我的粗心大意致歉。

3. Here I show my apology for wrong _____ .

於此我為我的判斷錯誤致歉。

4. To show our _____ , we will provide you a 15 percent discount coupon.

為表示我們的誠意，我們贈送八五折優惠券給您。

5. To compensate your loss, we will _____ the freight.

為補償您的損失，我們將減免運費。

解答

1. Accounting
2. carelessness
3. judgement
4. sincerity
5. deduct

句型喚醒你的記憶 ||||||||||||||||||||||||||||||

Unit
12

Unit
13

Unit
14

Unit
15

Unit
16

Unit
17

Unit
18

Unit
19

Unit
20

Unit
21

Unit
22

1. **Here I apologize for** the improper behavior I have.
   於此我為我的不當行為道歉。
   Here I apologize for... 意思為「於此我為…道歉」，可用於說明欲道歉的事由。
   例 Here I apologize for postponing the meeting time. 於此針對延後開會時間表示歉意。

2. **To compensate** the time you are wasted, **we** provide a 10 percent discount in this purchase.
   為了要補償你所損失的時間，本次購買可享九折優惠。
   To compensate..., we... 意思是「為了補償…，我們…」，可用於說明補償對方的方式。
   例 To compensate your loss, we provide a 10 percent discount coupon to you. 為了補償你的損失，我們提供九折優惠券給您。

3. **To settle** the trouble I have made, **I** will visit your company tomorrow.
   為了處理好我所闖出的麻煩，我明日會拜訪貴公司。
   To settle..., we... 意思是「為了解決…，我們…」，可用於說明我方將如何解決問題。
   例 To settle the error in payment, we will cancel the previous invoice. 為了解決付款上的錯誤，我們將會取消原來的發票。

4. **I am sorry for** delaying the shipment.
   對於出貨延遲我深感抱歉。
   I am sorry for... 意思為「對於…我深感抱歉」，可用於說明致歉的事由。
   例 I am sorry for sending you the wrong product. 對於寄錯產品我深感抱歉。

知多少？多知道一點總是好 |||||||||||||||||||||||||||||||||

任何人都可能出錯，因此在商場上出錯其實是能被允許的。但除了道歉外，更重要的是如何去解決問題。以下針對以英文致歉時應注意的要點與應避免的禁忌做進一步說明：

不可不知的要點 |||||||||||||||||||||||||||||||||

1. 說明事由要避免對方不知我方為何道歉，而是讓對方了解我方已了解狀況，正在進行處理。不論是在道歉信的開頭，或是口頭的道歉，都宜先行說明整個事件的原委，並於其後進行第一次的致歉。
2. 提出具體解決方式：
   道歉若只徒具形式並無法解決問題，因此務必針對問題的癥結點提出因應之道，例如打折、賠償或是贈送禮物等，藉此表現出我方的誠意。
3. 請對方繼續支持：
   在致歉過程的最後，最大的重點在於向對方承諾未來不會再發生相同情況，希望對方仍對我方的產品或是服務有信心。

不可不知的禁忌

1. 基於禮儀道歉：

   由於西方思維主張有錯才道歉，這樣的思考邏輯碰上東方禮貌式的道歉時，就會產生文化衝擊。即便錯不在我，但因為此種思維而先行道歉，容易使我方平白造成損失。

2. 試圖卸責：

   雖然衝突或是錯誤的發生可能不全然是我方的責任，當決定向對方致歉時，就不宜再次提及責任歸屬問題，以免讓對方覺得我方沒有解決誠意，有推卸責任之嫌。

Unit
12

Unit
13

Unit
14

Unit
15

Unit
16

Unit
17

Unit
18

Unit
19

Unit
20

Unit
21

Unit
22

腦部暖身 一點都不難對話

請將以下六個單字填入空格內。

(a) favorable   (b) apology   (c) freight

(d) send   (e) purpose   (f) care

You are on the phone .

Jason： This is Jason from ABC Company, may I speak to Mr. Brown?

Operator： Please wait for few seconds, I will put you through.

Brown： This is Brown from DEF Company, how may I help you?

Jason： The ____1____ of this call is to show my ____2____ to the mistakes I have made. I sent the wrong product to you.

Brown： Wrong product, you mean?

Jason： Last Monday you ordered 100 VNS parts, but we sent you VSN type instead due to my typo in the document. I have asked our International Trade Department to send right ones within two days. Please ____3____ the wrong parts back to us, and we will cover the ____4____ .

Brown： I see.

Jason： To compensate your loss, we will provide you a 10 percent discount coupon for next purchase. You can enjoy the ____5____ price without the limitation of minimum purchase amount.

Brown： Thank you, ABC Company does ____1____ its customer.

翻譯

電話中。

　Jason：我是 ABC 公司的 Jason，請問 Brown 先生在嗎？

　接線生：請稍待片刻，我將為您轉接。

Brown：我是 DEF 公司的 Brown，有什麼能為您效勞的嗎？

　Jason：我打這通電話的目的是要為我的粗心行為道歉。我寄錯產品給您了。

Brown：寄錯產品？你指的是？

　Jason：上週一您訂購了一百顆 VNS 零件，但我們因為我的打字錯誤，寄成 VSN 型號給您。我已經要求我們的國際貿易部寄正確的零件給您。請將寄錯的零件寄回給我們，我們會負擔運費。

Brown：我了解了。

　Jason：為了補償你的損失，我們提供下次採購九折優惠券。你可以在沒有最低採購量的限制下享有此優惠價。

Brown：謝謝。ABC 公司真的很重視客戶。

單字

- **instead** [ɪn`stɛd] *adv.* 卻
- **typo** [`taɪpo] *n.* 打字錯誤
- **limitation** [ˌlɪmə`teʃən] *n.* 限制
- **minimum** [`mɪnəməm] *n.* 最小數量

答案

1. (e)　2. (b)　3. (d)　4. (c)　5. (a)　6. (f)

Unit

12

Unit

13

Unit

14

Unit

15

Unit

16

Unit

17

Unit

18

Unit

19

Unit

20

Unit

21

Unit

22

會說也會寫一：為不當行為道歉

範例

Dear Russell,

❶Here I on behalf of ABC Company to show our most sincere apology to you for the improper behavior of Robert, one of our employees last Mondy.

❷To compensate the inconvenience we have brought to you, here we provide a $50 gift card to you. You can redeem this card in any branch.

❸We will re-educate our staff and prevent such situation from happening in the future, so please accept my apology and be confident in our service as usual.

Sincerely yours
Jason

 翻譯

親愛的 Russell：

於此謹代表 ABC 公司針對本上週一公司員工 Robert 的不恰當行為向您致歉。

為彌補您的損失，於此致贈面額五十美金的禮物卡。本卡可於任何分店使用。

我們會再教育員工，並避免相同情事再次發生，故請接受我們的道歉並對我們服務仍保有信心。

謹
Jason

解析

　　當我方要寫信為自己或是公司員工不當行為道歉時，為了表示誠意，其內容通常會包含以下三大部分：

❶ 寫信事由：

當代表個人或是公司對不當行為時，為了表示我方以了解情況，通常會在信件開頭重述事件發生的人事時地物，之後再進行第一次的道歉。以本範例為例，Jason 代表 ABC 公司為旗下員工 Robert 上週一的不當行為向對方致歉。

❷ 具體作法：

雖然行為或是服務不像商品具有實體，但造成對方的不愉快是既成事實，因此在實務上會給予實質的補償，補償的方式可能是折價或是贈送禮物等。以本範例為例，ABC 公司選擇贈送面額五十美金的禮物卡，讓對方可以在旗下任何一間分店進行購物。

❸ 應酬語：

在商場上最怕客戶因為單一事件而失去對整個公司或是品牌的信心，因此在道歉信的結尾一定要強調已對員工或是自身進行檢討，本次事件絕對不會重演，好讓客戶願意繼續支持我方的產品或服務。以本範例為例，Jason 表示已再次教育員工，不會讓本次情況在未來重演，希望對方能夠接受我們的道歉並繼續給予支持。

註

　　即便是當客戶或是顧客刻意找麻煩所引發的事端，為避免事態擴大影響到其他人或是整體的服務，建議由我方先行放低姿態，以四兩撥千金的方式將讓對方不易找到借題發揮的空間，如此會使整個事件較容易解決。

Unit 12
Unit 13
Unit 14
Unit 15
Unit 16
Unit 17
Unit 18
Unit 19
Unit 20
Unit 21
Unit 22

 會說也會寫二：弄錯金額 ||||||||||||||||||||||||||

範例

Dear Paul,

❶Thank you for pointing out the error in the invoice No.1234 that we issued to you last Monday.

❷We are sorry for the error in billing and we have asked our Accounting Department to revise the amount from $960 to $930. Please find the revised invoice in the attachment

❸Once again, thank you for informing us this mistake we have made.

Sincerely,
Jason

翻譯

親愛的 Paul：

感謝您來信指出我們上週一所開立編號 1234 的發票內容有誤。

對於發票金額錯誤我們深感抱歉，並已要求會計部門將金額由美金 960 元更正為 930 元。隨信附上更正過後的發票。

於此再次感謝告知我方所造成之錯誤。

謹
Jason

解析

　　當我方要寫信要為發票金額錯誤或是總價計算錯誤道歉時，由於牽涉到最後所需支付的總額，為表示態度上的慎重與我方處理的誠意，其內容通常會包含以下三大部分：

❶寫信事由：

　　弄錯金額或發票金額錯誤的影響程度可大可小，若未及早發現，可能會讓對方或是我方蒙受損失，因此當對方來信告知此類型的錯誤時，我方應當表達感激之情。以本範例為例，Jason 對於 Paul 來信告知編號 1234 發票金額錯誤一事表達感激。

❷具體作法：

　　對於弄錯金額，除了道歉之外，最重要的就是透過公司的會計部門去檢查為何出錯，將發票更正為正確金額，然後隨信寄給對方。以本範例為例，Jason 透過公司會計部門的檢查，請會記部門將金額從錯誤的九百六十美金修正為正確的九百三十美金，並隨信附上修正過後的發票。

❸應酬語：

　　在弄錯金額的道歉信中，最後得應酬語通常是感謝對方告知錯誤，願意給我方改正機會，沒有馬上追究。以本範例為例，Jason 對於 Paul 來信告知發票金額錯誤表達謝意。

註

　　透過上述架構之道歉信，可讓弄錯金額的事件即早獲得處理，始對方不至於藉此向我方要求賠償，徒增更多事端，因此對公司而言，若發生相似情事，當以此模式進行處理。

 現在你會說 ||||||||||||||||||||||||||||||||||||||||||||

請依句意填入 A-E。

A. You can get the favorable price without the limitation of minimum purchase amount

B. Last Monday, you ordered 1000 VWS parts, but we sent you WVN instead due to my typo in the document

C. The purpose for the call is to show my apology to the mistakes I have made

D. This is Jason from DES Company, may I speak to Mr. Brown

E. Please send the wrong part back to us, and we will cover the freight

Jason： _____1_____ ?

Operator： Please wait for few seconds. I will put you through.

Brown： This is Brown from SDF Company, how may I help you?

Jason： _____2_____ . I sent the wrong product to you.

Brown： Wrong product, you mean?

Jason： _____3_____ . I have asked our International Trade Department to send right ones within three days. _____4_____ .

Brown： I see.

Jason： To compensate your loss, we will provide you a 15 percent discount coupon for next purchase. _____5_____ .

Brown： Thank you, ABC Company does care its customers rights.

答案 ···
1. (D)　2. (C)　3. (B)　4. (E)　5. (A)

 現在你會寫

1.於此僅代表 ABC 公司向您致上最深的歉意。

_____

_____

中式英文出沒 ▶ Here on behalf ABC Company to show our deepest apology to you.

錯在哪 ▶ 中文可省略主詞的習慣容易是我們在翻譯時忘記將其還原，而造成語焉不詳的情況產生，因此將本句中被省略的「我」還原，翻譯為 I，即為正解。

正解 ▶ Here I am on behalf of ABC Company to show our deepest apology to you.

2.為彌補你所損失的時間，本次購買是免運費的。

_____

_____

中式英文出沒 ▶ To compensate the time you waste, this purchase is no freight.

錯在哪 ▶ 我們說出此話時，客戶已經多等待一定的時間，因此要以完成式表示。另外若要表示「免…」或是「禁止…」應使用 n + free，因此免運費應為 freight free。

正解 ▶ To compensate the time you have wasted, this purchase is freight free.

Unit 12

Unit 13

Unit 14

Unit 15

Unit 16

Unit 17

Unit 18

Unit 19

Unit 20

Unit 21

好書報報

好書報報

Best Publishing

心理學研究顯示，一個習慣養成，至少必須重複21次!
全書規劃30天學習進度表，搭配學習，
不知不覺養成學習英語的好習慣!!

圖解學習英文文法，三效合一!
　　◎刺激大腦記憶 ◎快速掌握學習大綱 ◎複習迅速

英文文法學習元素一次到位!
　　◎20個必懂觀念 ◎30個必學句型 ◎40個必閃陷阱

流行有趣的英語!
◎「那裡有正妹!」
◎「今天我們去看變形金剛4吧!」

作者：朱懿婷
定價：新台幣399元
規格：368頁 / 18K / 雙色印刷 / 軟皮精裝

文法再弱也有救! 只要跟著解題邏輯分析句子，
釐清【文法重點】找出【判斷依據】並運用【關鍵知識】
《英文文法有一套》讓你一套走天下，三步驟有答案!

【一套邏輯】
　　文法重點＝ 常考、愛考、一直考的文法
　　判斷依據＝ 題目中足以判斷「文法重點」的依據
　　關鍵知識＝ 不受誘答選項影響，正確答案立即浮現的
　　　　　　　 「關鍵文法知識」
【十大主題】
　　10大考官最愛文法主題 建立考生精準文法觀念
【三步驟解題】
　　先10題範例: 3步驟 全面掌握解題邏輯
　　再10題練習: 3步驟 完全熟練必考重點

作者：黃亭瑋
定價：新台幣369元
規格：372頁 / 18K / 雙色印刷

Leader 015

擺脫辦公室卡卡英文：那些年你「會」，但「不會」用的英語，22堂全職業適用英文課

作　　者　邱佳翔
封面構成　高鍾琪
內頁構成　菩薩蠻數位文化有限公司

發 行 人　周瑞德
企劃編輯　徐瑞璞
執行編輯　饒美君
校　　對　陳欣慧、陳韋佑
印　　製　大亞彩色印刷製版股份有限公司
初　　版　2015 年 3 月
定　　價　新台幣 349 元
出　　版　力得文化
電　　話　(02) 2351-2007
傳　　真　(02) 2351-0887
地　　址　100 台北市中正區福州街 1 號 10 樓之 2
E - m a i l　best.books.service@gmail.com

港澳地區總經銷　泛華發行代理有限公司
地　　　　址　香港新界將軍澳工業邨駿昌街 7 號 2 樓
電　　　　話　(852) 2798-2323
傳　　　　真　(852) 2796-5471

國家圖書館出版品預行編目(CIP)資料

擺脫辦公室卡卡英文 : 那些年你「會」，但「不會」
用的英語, 22 堂全職業適用英文課 / 邱佳翔著.
-- 初版. -- 臺北市 : 力得文化, 2015.03
　面 ；　公分. --(Leader ; 15)
ISBN 978-986-91458-4-8(平裝)

1.商業英文 2.讀本

　805.18　　　　　　　　　104003253

力得文化
Leader Culture

Lead your way. Be your own leader!

力得文化
Leader Culture

Lead your way. Be your own leader!